T0127347

18%
Gray

18% Gray

Zachary Karabashliev

a novel

Translated from
the Bulgarian by
Angela Rodel

OPEN LETTER

LITERARY TRANSLATIONS FROM THE UNIVERSITY OF ROCHESTER

Copyright © 2008 by Zachary Karabashliev
Translation copyright © 2012 by Angela Rodel

First edition, 2013
All rights reserved

Library of Congress Cataloging-in-Publication Data: Available upon request.
ISBN-13: 978-1-934824-71-9 / ISBN-10: 1-934824-71-2

This book is published within the Elizabeth Kostova Foundation's
program for Support of Contemporary Bulgarian Writers and in
collaboration with the America for Bulgaria Foundation.

AMERICA FOR BULGARIA
F O U N D A T I O N
Фондация Америка за България

Elizabeth Kostova
FOUNDATION *for*
CREATIVE WRITING

Printed on acid-free paper in the United States of America.

Text set in Bodoni, a serif typeface first designed by Giambattista Bodoni
(1740–1813) in 1798.

Design by N. J. Furl

Open Letter is the University of Rochester's nonprofit, literary translation press:
Lattimore Hall 411, Box 270082, Rochester, NY 14627

www.openletterbooks.org

For man does not know his time. Like fish which are taken in an evil net, and like birds which are caught in a snare, so the sons of men are snared at an evil time, when it suddenly falls upon them.

—Ecclesiastes 9:12

She's been gone nine mornings.

The blinds in the bedroom are shut tight, but the day still finds a way in, and with a roar—the garbage truck. That means it's Wednesday. That means it's 8:15. Is there a noisier noise than the noise of a garbage truck at 8:15?

I crawl out of bed, stagger to the living room, and flop down on the couch. The cool leather doesn't help me fall back to sleep, the garbage truck rumbles closer. I get up, push aside one of the blinds, a bright ray burns my face. I focus my powers and attempt to dismember the roaring green monster with a gaze. The effort only succeeds in waking me up completely.

I look at the flowers in the vase on the coffee table. Dead freesias in murky water—she left them behind.

I open a kitchen drawer and pull a Toblerone out of the stash of candy. I pick yesterday's white shirt up off the floor and plug in the iron. I iron with one hand, while breaking off triangles and gobbling them down with the other. I put on the shirt and a blue tie, make instant coffee, slosh some on my sleeve while I

5

fumble for the car keys, throw on a gray suit coat, and slam the door behind me.

Another scorching Southern California day. I gun the Corolla. I make a right onto Jefferson and get on the highway. Five lanes of cars in one direction and five lanes in the other. Exhaust pipes roar, engines rattle, fenders gleam—as if preparing for battle.

At work, I think about her. I can't stop talking to Stella in my head—it won't stop simply because one of us is not here. Can I stop? I try.

OK—from this moment on, I will not think about her. I will *not* think about her. I *will* not think about her. *I* will not think about her. I will not. I will do yoga, I will open my chakras, I will repeat *OM* until I clear my mind, I will eat rice with my hands, I will grow a beard, I will do headstands. O-m-m-m-m. O-o-m-my God, I'm tired of thinking about her. O-o-o-m-m-my God, I'm tired of thinking about her. O-o-o-o-m-m-m-m-my God, I'm so tired of thinking about her.

At the morning meeting, Scott, the manager, announces the latest structural changes in the department and talks about the new clinical trial. There's a box of doughnuts on the table. There is orange juice and steaming coffee. *". . . to monitor the progress of this clinical investigation . . ."* Why is the AC so cold in here? *". . . and this new drug . . ."* O-m-m-m. *". . . since it is a Phase One . . ."* Why is the coffee sour? *". . . what you should monitor at each site and how much attention should be given to each activity . . ."* What is he talking about? *". . . strict adherence to the procedures by the treating physicians . . ."* Who are these people? Scott hands out personal agendas for the upcoming quarter to everyone, his eyes filled with that perkiness, that perkiness . . . He shakes our hands energetically—the way only short people do—but hangs on to mine a bit longer. Where am I?

Everyone heads to their cubicles while Scott gestures for me to follow him into his dark gray office down the hall. Office minimalism—a desk, a computer, a personal coffee maker, and a water cooler under a poster of a long boat (kayak? canoe?) powered by a squad of rowers. Below the photograph, a sign reads TEAMWORK. Scott is speaking to me in a concerned voice. He is looking at me with *that* look. I don't hear what he's saying; I just nod and want to puke. *That* look. I don't remember how the rest of the day goes. Horribly, I imagine.

On the way back from work, during rush hour at the traffic light on 11th and Broadway, the stream of cars slows down. Somewhere up ahead, I see fluorescent reflective vests holding stop signs and redirecting traffic. I notice the white corpse of a semi sprawled on its side in the middle of the road. It's hot. I try to change lanes at the last second and cleverly take Cedar Street, but don't make it—the schmuck on my right won't let me in. Fine, I'll sit in traffic like everyone else then. I look to my right: a guy around fifty, with crow's feet and a dry California tan, is picking his nose and watching a small plane in the sky trailing a giant red banner. I also look up to see what is written in the sky behind the plane and catch myself picking my nose, too. I look at the plane overhead, I look at the man. His left elbow—resting on the rolled-down window; his right index finger—up his nose; his hair—gray. That's how I'm going to look in about twenty years.

A honk from behind jolts me and I press the clutch to shift to first. It suddenly sinks. I press harder, I push and pull the stick to shift into gear, but it won't move. I watch the gray-haired man pull away. The light is still green, but it won't be this green forever. I start shoving the stick harder (damn—yellow), I hear the honking grow more impatient behind me. An intolerably hot day (it's red now) and longer than any other (scarlet red). I feel the rage of those accountants, lawyers, software engineers, waiters, and real estate agents focusing on my tiny tan car. Had there been someone to coordinate their thoughts, with a single conspiratorial glance they would have tossed me down by the docks where the bums hang out. Where I belong.

I start scouring the dashboard for the red triangular button; I have no idea where it is. Behind me, more and more of those jerks, safe in their anonymous vehicles, start honking. I see only their expressionless faces in the rearview mirror, but I know that a little bit lower, down where I can't see, they are laying on their horns. I'm sweating. Can't they see that I'm stuck, that I'm miserable? The more intelligent ones signal left and go around my immobile vehicle. The rest refuse to accept my misfortune.

Now I really start sweating and it smells like French onion soup. If they keep pissing me off, I'll get out of my car, fling open my arms like the statue over Rio, and blow them away with the stench. They'll be jumping out of their cars in a panic, hands clamped over mouths and noses, running frantically like in a Godzilla movie. Finally, at the corner of 11th and Broadway, there'll be only me and countless abandoned vehicles with open, beeping doors. They'll go peep-peep-peep-peep like chicks. Peep-peep-peep-peep. And I'll stride down the street like a conqueror and laugh a loud, ominous laugh.

I finally find the hazard light button. I push it and jump out, half-suffocated by my own smell. The air is hot and dry. I make apologetic gestures to those behind me, my shirt soaked with sweat. I loosen my tie, grin guiltily, and shrug (it could happen to anyone), while in my mind I mercilessly rape and murder every single loved one of those fucking slimeballs who now avoid making eye contact with me.

I use a payphone to call a towing company.

Half an hour later, a tow truck rumbles up and a Vietnamese guy jumps down. He'll be towing my car to the body shop. He wants eighty bucks. I ask him who to make the check out to.

He shakes his head, "Cass, cass!"

"*Cass?*" I say. "I don't have any *cass.*" I write a check for eighty dollars and hand it to him.

"No!" The Vietnamese guy insists. "Cass, cass!"

"*Cass,* my ass." I say.

"Huh?" He frowns, he doesn't get it. Well, I don't get why Stella's gone either.

"I don't have any cash." I say. "No credit card either." The Vietnamese guy sees he's got no other choice and decides to accept the check, but now he wants more money. I write a new check for ninety dollars. Whom should I make it out to?

"Howah." He says.

"Howah?"

"Howah."

"Oh, Howard? OK, Howard." Look at them Asians and the noble names they appropriate! I've yet to see one named Bill or Bob. I write *Howard Stern* and hand him the check.

"No! No!" He screams. "No Howard Stern!" and rips up the check. "Howah!"

"Howard what!?" I snap.

He grabs the checkbook and writes the name himself: *Hau Ua.*

"Oh!" I pat him on the shoulder. "I know lots of Vietnamese guys, Hau. Good people." Hau stares at me with no expression. "Good people!" I say, "the Vietnamese."

"I from Laos." Hau gives me a nasty look and turns his back on me. Now they'll skin me at the garage. Let them.

I take a cab home. Quiet and shady. I water the plants in the backyard. Nothing is their fault. The neighbors' orange cat shows up. He wants to play with somebody. "Do you miss Stella?" I ask. He meows, which means of course he does. Stella used to buy him canned food. She insisted that ocean whitefish was his favorite. I find some cans under the sink and open one. I take it out and set it under the easel where her last abandoned painting sits. A sheet spattered with blue paint covers it. I watch the cat eat for a couple minutes. I gave Stella this easel five years ago as a Christmas present. I lift one corner of the sheet and look at the canvas. I don't get it. This is the only painting of hers in the house—the rest are either in her studio or in storage—and it's unfinished. Why don't I throw it in the trash?

I'm hungry. I turn around and accidentally knock over one of the jars with watery paint and brushes sticking out. It rolls over, spilling an ugly trail of muddy, grayish paint. I angrily kick the jar and it shatters.

The only things in the fridge are some rotten vegetables from before she left, and some beer, which I stashed there afterwards. Lately, my life has been divided into *before* and *after* she left. The latter is made up of nine days of loneliness. Loneliness that I feel most acutely at dusk. The world sighs with relief after a workday, while I choke up with her absence. Alone like a Sasquatch, I wander through my thoughts, and there's no shelter, absolutely none.

"You need to be alone. To decide what to do with your life." I can hear her words in the room now. I didn't say anything then. I just watched CNN and didn't say a single thing. What was on the news then?

I find half a baguette in the breadbox. I take out a can with a colorful sombrero and an "El Cowboy" label and pour its contents into a small pan to heat it up, stirring it from time to time. The smell of spicy Mexican beans fills the room. She doesn't like beans. She doesn't like Mexican spices, either. I go pick something to listen to. While I sift through CDs and LPs, I hear a "pf-f-f-f"— the beans are boiling over and spilling onto the burner. I get up and start sponging away the mess before it's dried up. Suddenly, my wrist—where the skin is most tender—sticks to the hot pan. That sizzling sound, the smell of burned flesh, the pain . . . I don't even scream in pain. Why should I? Shit, my hand, shit, fuck my stupid hand! Fuck, fuck, fuck, fuck! Fuck? All of a sudden, the idea of porn doesn't seem as pathetic as it has for the last week and a half. I will reward myself with a serene hand job after my spicy bean dinner.

I put a tablecloth on the table. I lay out the silverware on a linen napkin. I take out a jar of hot chili peppers and arrange it on the table. I light a candle. I serve up the bowl of beans in the middle and set two beers next to it. I pick a record—*La Sonnambula* by Bellini, performed by Maria Callas at La Scalla 1955—and play the aria "Ah! non credea mirarti." I pump up the volume, like I never did when she was here. I drop pieces of dry baguette into the bowl, stir, and slurp up the hot chunks, rolling them around in my mouth. Beans are an experience. You have to devour them hot and spicy, otherwise there's no point.

The aria lasts five minutes and forty-three seconds. Two minutes in, I see the bottom of the bowl and spend the next three listening with my eyes closed. The telephone rings right at the last note. I don't pick up. I haven't picked up the phone since Stella left.

Leave a message!

"Zack, are you there?" It's the annoying voice of Tony, who's been calling me three times a day.

"I've been calling you three times a day. Where are you, Zack? We need to talk, man. Pick up the phone. Zack?!"

Thirty-three messages blink on the machine. Not one from her. I look around. Every single thing in this house is in its place because she put it there. Every square inch is covered with her fingerprints. I try to get used to the fact that she's gone.

The porn is lame, pink bodies lurch on the screen for a while, then everything ends in a napkin. I toss it into the trash along with a few old papers, bills, and junk mail. I get ready for bed. I brush my teeth meticulously and wash my face. I turn the lights off everywhere. I lie down on the right side of the bed. The left side—her side—feels like a wound. I'm suffocating on sadness. I stare at the dark ceiling for a long time, then roll over to where she slept until nine nights ago. I curl into a six-foot-long embryo and press my heart with the full weight of my body. The heart is like the neighbors' cat—it doesn't get it. It doesn't understand that she's gone. The heart is an animal.

•

1988, Varna, Bulgaria
Stella.

I saw her for the first time just before I was discharged from the army. I was on day leave and was wandering around the central part of the old Black Sea town where I was stationed. It was a warm afternoon in late May and the scent of blooming linden trees hung in the air. I had read in the newspaper that ancient ruins had been discovered during the construction of a mega-department store. The subsequent excavations unearthed the remains of a Roman arena, and a third of downtown had been turned into an archeological site. It was worth checking out, I thought.

It wasn't. It was a big hole in the middle of the city filled with bored students brushing stones. I crisscrossed the central promenade several times and started seriously thinking about having a bite to eat. Then I headed half-aimlessly toward the beaches, my ravenous stare making the local girls move to the opposite side of the street. Or was it my hideous buzz-cut?

I remember walking into a café and there she was. First her lips? No. First her eyes, then her lips. Then her breasts—her round breasts stretching her uniform. Then the curl of light brown hair hanging down to the dimple in her cheek. The feeling of destiny. And then the dread that whatever I would do was pointless. She was the most beautiful girl in town. There was no way she didn't belong to somebody.

There was no way some lucky bastard wasn't counting off the minutes until the end of her work day. Miracles don't happen, I decided, and walked out.

.

Something suddenly thrashes in my stomach and my insides knot up into a small, hard ball. I sit up in bed and stare into the silvery threads of darkness. I listen. Is there someone in the house? I hold my breath and try to figure out if there's someone in the living room. I swear I heard something. THERE IS someone. I can hear the blinds moving. I get up cautiously. I reach for the bedside lamp, unplug the cord, roll it up and grab it by its metal stand. Then I realize I'm naked. I can't just burst out of the bedroom nude and start chasing off criminals like in a Swedish film. In the dark, I manage to make out the three white lines of my running pants. I put them on carefully, without dropping the lamp stand, and move toward the door. I press my ear to it, struggling to catch a sound.

I hear the ticking of the clock. I hear the hum of the fridge. I hear the blood in my head like a distant freeway. I also hear another, barely perceptible noise.

I take a deep breath, burst through the door, and leap into the living room with a scream.

No one. Then something on the patio clatters, and I fly in that direction. A raccoon, paw stuck in the cat-food can, frantically tries to scramble over the fence outside. I lower my improvised weapon and start laughing.

You felt like eating some cat food, huh, fatso? I almost want to help him push his chubby butt up, but I know that I'll scare him even more. The can slips off his paw and rolls under a chair. The raccoon gets over the fence. He stops for a second and throws a final glance at me. "Hey," I yell. "You know you look like a bandit with that funny black mask on your eyes. You scared the shit out of me, Zorro! Now shoo! Go away!"

I doubt I'll be able to fall back to sleep after this. I stay on the patio for a while. The canyon beneath the house rustles. The palm tree in the backyard sways. The wind has picked up. One of those winds that slides down from the cold mountains in the fall, whooshing through the sizzling hot desert, drying up everything in its path to the Pacific within a matter of days. One of those sick, dry winds named after a saint.

I throw a jacket over my shoulders and go out. I take a left at the traffic light, then a right—I don't know where I'm going, so I don't care where I'll end up.

I come to my senses somewhere near the freeway, walking through one of those newly built neighborhoods with artificial lakes and cute miniature waterfalls, petite jet-powered streams and little bridges decorated with "Made in China" gas lamps. I walk along the winding trail past the houses, trying to peek into other people's windows when I can. In some, I see bluish light flickering through the blinds, framed family pictures on the walls, posters of movie stars in the kids' rooms, pianos with the lids down, unlit candles, a vintage calendar of Manhattan, a Thomas Kinkade print.

The normality of this night is insulting.

It's insulting that sooner or later they will all turn off their TVs, brush their teeth, and fall asleep. Then it will be dawn again and a new day will come as if nothing ever happened. It's insulting that tomorrow the sky over the neighborhood will be the same as it was when Stella was here. It's insulting that people will keep working at places like General Electric or AT&T; they will go on being truck drivers, florists, accountants, postal workers, and receptionists. It's insulting that there are words like "shingle," "nugget," "waffle," "halibut," "persnickety," "boodle," "dungarees" . . . It's insulting that the craters on the moon will be the same, the salinity of the ocean—the same; the octane number of gasoline—the same; the calories in a Pepsi—the same. Some things just stay the same.

•

—look at me
—i'm thirsty
—look at the camera
—i'm cold
—c'mon, please
—i need coffee . . .
—we're almost done
—i want to get dressed already . . .
—this is the last roll of film and i swear we're done
—the last one?
—the very last one

•

I walk back to the house, grab the keys to her sports car, the one *I* surprised her with for her last birthday, and turn on the lights in the garage. I unlock the car and get in. Before I turn the ignition, I close my eyes and lean my head back. The interior of the car, unaired since she's been gone, still smells like her. I exhale loudly and start the car. The garage door opens and I peel out, tires screeching in the night. I roll down all the windows to chase away her presence. The cold canyon chill seeps in. At the ramp for I-5, I stop at the light. West Hollywood is an hour north. I know someone there. Mexico is less than an hour south. I have no reason to go to Mexico. I will have to decide which way I'm going before the light turns green.

The light turns green and I hit the gas pedal.

·

Miracles don't happen, I repeated in my head as I crossed the street. She was a beautiful blue-eyed girl with big, round breasts and an intelligent face who would never pay attention to a guy with a uniform and a moronic haircut. I hadn't smelled a girl for two years. Before I got drafted, I was always the "life of the party" and had lots of friends and all, but I had no idea how to act around girls, and it seemed I would never learn. I would always try too hard to come up with something clever and hilarious to say, and would always end up going home alone while my boring buddies made out with girls under the lindens. I was a loser. A dumb, dorky loser.

I strode down toward the beaches, beating myself up, but I knew, mercilessly, clearly, I knew that I had seen and felt something different this time. Sure, I had the same major hard-on I always did when I fed a pretty girl to my inflamed imagination, but this time there was something more. My mind—as ridiculous as this might sound for a guy in an army uniform—my mind had a hard-on this time; my intellect was aroused.

I walked into the city park known as "The Sea Garden," wandered around the cool pathways for a while, until I reached a row of benches scattered with old people, overlooking the bay. I found an empty one and sat down. The view was nice—the sea, the sky, the horizon. North was to my left, the old Gala Lighthouse to my right, Varna Bay in front of me, and behind me, the love of my life.

I took a deep breath, got up, and walked back to her.

·

—will you always take pictures of me?
—always

—even if i get fat?

—yep, even then

—with a huge booty?

—all the more to photograph

—really?

—really

—don't worry, i'm not going to get fat

—we'll see

—i'm never gonna get fat

•

I park Stella's car in front of the still-open McDonald's on the US side. I have no business driving in Mexico. I cross the border into the Third World on foot. The Tijuana cab drivers chat in front of their cars, eat sunflower seeds, and look at the passersby just like cab drivers anywhere in the world.

"Hola," I say.

"Hola," says the one at the front of the line. I get in.

Where am I going? Avenida Revolución?

Avenida Revolución sounds good.

We take off. The radio is playing Mexican rap with accordion. A gilded Jesus glued to a plastic crucifix and a pine tree air-freshener swing from the rearview mirror.

The cab stops before the end of the song. I pay and get out. I inhale deeply.

The intersection of Avenida Revolución and Paseo de los Héroes blasts from the speakers of every nightclub, penetrates the air with the smells of the street grills, stares at me with the hungry eyes of every vendor of everything that's ever been for sale, and wants my money with every beggar's hand.

A mariachi family plays sloppily tuned guitars and sings their heads off. No one pays any attention to them.

Under a street lamp, a scrawny dog stretches a piece of gum off the pavement.

From the roof of a nightclub called Spiderman, a guy dressed as Spiderman swings from one side of the street to the other on a rope over the heads of the crowd. On the sidewalk across from me is a donkey painted with black and white stripes like a zebra. The zebra is hitched to a cart as colorful as a Christmas tree. *$5 photo, Viva Mexico.*

People, people, people . . . that's why I'm here. People, people, people, people, people, people. The energy of Tijuana pulsates through every aorta, thrives in every germ south of the border. This very energy sucked me out of our empty house on the canyon, away from go-to-work-in-the-morning suburbia.

I go into the first bar I see. The bartender, thank God, speaks English. I ask if he can make a vodka martini.

"Sí, señor."

"You got olives?"

"Sí, señor."

"Can you make a dirty martini?"

"Sí, señor."

"Now, the señor here wants a dirty martini with three olives."

"Sí, señor."

Three martinis later, *Señor* finally looks around. It hits me that if I had done so earlier, I surely would have left. What kind of a place is this? Dirty, dark, and it stinks something awful. A TV set on a wooden crate in the corner plays a never-ending soccer game. A few customers in cowboy hats watch the crate and drink beer from green bottles. During every commercial break, though, the hats turn to look at me. I pay and get out.

Outside, Tijuana enfolds me in its sweaty, open bosom. Noisy merchants pull me left and right, trying to lure me into their stuffy little shops.

I dive into another bar. This time I look at the crowd carefully. A TV set on a wooden crate in the corner plays the same soccer game. Men in cowboy hats are drinking beer and watching the game. The commercials begin, the hats turn toward me. I stay. On my way out, the stairs seem funnier.

The night now is hot and throbbing. I need *panocha* now. *Panocha*. A fat tattooed neck pulls me up fluorescent stairs. A whorehouse? No. A nightclub. The speakers slam Latin-Electro. The lights change with every beat, the girls under them, too. It's full of girls. A waitress shoves her huge tits under my drunken head. What do I want to drink?

"Martini," I yell.

She brings me a margarita. I'll drink margaritas, then.

The dance floor is packed. The crowd consists of American military men, Mexican pimps, bleached-blond hookers, drug dealers, and losers like me. While normal people north of the border rest before the workday, Tijuana is wide awake.

An hour later I realize that the margarita was a mistake. I get dizzy from the lights, bodies, mirrors, boobs, sweat, glasses, tables, chairs. In the bathroom a geezer with a bowtie and pencil mustache hands out toilet paper for pesos. I dig out crumpled bills, drop them in his bowl, stagger to the sink, and splash water on my face. In the spattered mirror, a gray man frowns at me. I frown back. His wife left him. *Boo-fucking-hoo. If I were her, I'd leave you, too.*

Outside the john, Tits greets me with a new margarita. I didn't order a new margarita.

"Sí," says Tits.

"No," I say.

"Sí, sí."

"No *sí sí,*" I say.

"Sí, sí, sí, señor!" Tits insists.

"I did not order a margarita!"

Tits is angry. She whirls around and heads over to the bouncer. I pull out money and chase her. Mexicans understand English when they want to. I pay before she makes a scene. I down the watery margarita and shove the glass in my pocket—a little payback, fucking extortionists. They treat me like a regular *gringo*. I might be *boracho*,[1] but I wasn't born yesterday. And, no, I am no *gringo*. The whole world spins fiercely before my eyes; I am going to die here. I stagger down the stairs, grabbing the railing with all my might, and end up next to the tattooed neck. I attempt to hug the bouncer as I stammer *panocha*. I've got to have a *panocha* before I die.

"I want *panocha*!"

"*Panocha, sí, sí.*" The fat neck grins and makes that gesture that all of us idiots make. "Fucky, fucky, huh, señor?"

"Fucky, fucky, yes."

"Fucky, fucky?"

"Yes, find me a *panocha* before I perish! I need *panocha*."

He points to a man on the other side of the street. I can't quite make him out. I set off in that direction, but the sidewalk has something else in mind—it suddenly ends. I trip and hop on the pavement, barely keeping my balance. Out of nowhere, a little hunchback midget in a white sombrero appears and pulls me aside. "Donkey show, donkey show, donkey show." I have no idea what's going on. To my right against a wall, a sailor kisses a whore while tugging on her g-string. She smirks at me over his shoulder.

To my left, leaning on a crumbling wall, a man with no legs stretches out a plastic cup—he wants *dolla*.

A scruffy five-year-old girl sucking snot from her upper lip stretches out a plastic cup—she wants *dolla*.

---

1 Drunk (Spanish).

An Indian with a baby on her breast reaches out a plastic cup, she wants *dolla.*

A one-eyed grandma holds a plastic cup, she wants *dolla,* too. *Dolla-dolla-dolla-dolla,* everyone wants *dolla.*

Something swings over my head, I duck at the last second and make out Spiderman.

"Donkey show, donkey show, donkey show . . ." the white sombrero wiggles his ass back and forth. ". . . fucky, fucky . . ." I don't understand. "Donkey fucky señorita." A-ha! A spectacle involving a donkey and a naked female suddenly seems appropriate. I follow him. "Donkey show, donkey show, donkey show . . ."

We cross Revolución and go down the steps of a side bazaar. The white sombrero stops in front of a beat-up door lit by a dirty naked bulb and rings the bell. The door cracks open and a shaved head peeks out. Sombrero turns to me—he wants *dolla.* I give him *dolla* and he slinks away up the stairs. I pay the shaved head an entrance fee and go a few steps further down.

Smoky bar, maroon booths, brown padding on the walls, columns painted in black enamel, Christmas lights, on the walls are faded posters for Corona, Dos Equis, and Tecate. Leather jackets, Hawaiian shirts, and navy uniforms are crowded around the tables. There's a stage at one end of the room. I enter when the music stops and go to the end of the line at the bar, behind a row of square backs, so I have to stand on my toes to see anything. Now all eyes are focused on the red velvet curtains, which draw open. A couple of Mexicans drag a gray donkey on stage and disappear. Whistles and claps. Dollar bills reach toward the bartender. He hands back beers.

The curtains open again and a naked brownish woman with short legs, a flabby stomach and floppy breasts comes out. I picture her, laundry pins in her mouth, hanging saggy bras on a clothesline. Her legs perch atop a pair of white glossy sandals and meet in a black bushy tuft on top. Her hair is the color of henna. The makeup is bad. Her eyebrows have been waxed off and drawn in with a brown pencil. Booing from the audience. Ungrateful bastards, what do you expect for five bucks—Shakira? After a little foreplay, the woman shoves herself under the animal. She grabs his thing and starts rubbing it energetically. The donkey shakes his head, showing two rows of yellow teeth. The woman keeps working it, but the donkey does not respond. The woman moves her hand faster and faster. Suddenly, the donkey snorts and reaches back to bite her, but only gets a bit of her hair. The woman manages to escape cursing and yelling at someone behind the curtain. Two Mexicans hop out; one of them grabs the donkey by the muzzle and the other hits him in the teeth.

A-a-a-a-h-h-h-h! The crowd groans in disapproval.

The animal snorts louder and rears back, but a pair of mustachioed mariachi show up and tackle him to the floor. One of them, guitar hanging from his back, traps the animal's head between his bow-legged *pantalones* and firmly grabs the front hooves, which are now pointing towards the ceiling. His buddy, accordion strapped to his back, grabs the hind legs.

The entertainer works the donkey's hard-on with both hands now. The audience, who thought they had gotten ripped off just a minute ago, now exclaims its approval.

The donkey reciprocates with size.

Silence. Then someone claps. A drunken female tourist starts laughing hysterically.

I turn my back on the spectacle. I weave my way through the crowd and climb up the steps so I can throw up the margarita and everything else I've ingested tonight. I make it out, wobbling. I'm dizzy and I need to lie down. I turn the corner and lean against a wall. Breathing heavily, I force myself to eject the poison.

Then I see them. I stagger toward them clinging to the wall.

The body is sprawled on the ground. The two men kick it

silently, indifferently. As if in a dream, I hear the dry thumping sounds and see the head jerk back and forth with each blow.

"Hey!" I yell. I can't stand violence. But this doesn't even look like violence. No one is screaming, no one is angry. Just two men kicking a third, as if knocking the mud off their boots. I get closer, still leaning against the wall.

One of them turns my way and looks at me, motionless. The other one keeps kicking, but soon he stops as well. They are big; short leather jackets and short black hair. They wait for me to get closer. The body on the ground stirs, thank God. I smile and wave.

"Hola, amigos," I say before the fist hits my forehead. The sidewalk meets my face. A kick to the ribs lifts me off the ground. I manage to half scramble up—only to receive another blow to the face. I spot a flight of stairs, a railing. I grab the railing, fly down, trip over, and keep going. They are a few feet behind me. I keep flying down more stairs. I try to catch the railing again, but no luck. I trip and start rolling down for a long time. I finally stop as my head collides with a metal door. The glass in my pocket shatters.

Their silhouettes thump down the stairs. Their shoes flash as they speed towards me. Then their kicks. They pull me up by the collar. One pulls out a lighter and studies my face. They drag me up the stairs. I'm on the sidewalk now. I stumble on a shoe. There was a body here a moment ago, nobody now. We reach a trailer with a few cars parked around it; barbed wire, gravel crunching underfoot, urine-colored light. They start pulling me toward a shabby van with California plates. One of them cracks the door open and it starts dinging. The other tries to push me inside. Hell no—they can beat the shit out of me, but I am not getting in their fucking van!

I spread my arms wide so they can't ram me inside like livestock. One of them kicks me in the stomach, and I double over, clutching my midriff. A pair of hands grabs me by the hair and pushes my head down. The anticipation of another blow to my belly—a strong blow, a blow that will leave me as breathless as a sack of potatoes. I tighten my abdominal muscles as much as I can. The kick doesn't come. The seconds stretch on endlessly. I gather my strength and, in a last, desperate effort, jerk my head away, and jab at the face of the guy holding me with the broken glass. He screams. The other one has been busy looking for the end of a thick roll of duct tape to tie me up with. I get his throat. Something dark spurts geyser-like several feet in the air. I turn to the first one, who keeps screaming while staring at his hands, now black with blood. I punch him in the forehead and hurt my wrist.

Somewhere in the dark a window slams shut.

The open van door is still dinging. I jump in and slam the door behind me, turn the key in the ignition, and stomp the gas pedal. In the rearview mirror, I see one of the men rolling in the dirt, the silhouette of the other one hovering over him.

I am in a narrow, unlit street. A dog starts barking.

I realize that I'm driving with no lights and slow down until I figure out how to turn them on.

Five or six turns later, I'm on Boulevar Constitución. I speed up. I reach a traffic light, turn right, and drive fast until I reach Avenida Revolución. Seeing the crowded well-lit place, somewhat familiar already, I relax a little and take a deep breath.

I start replaying the scenes from a few minutes earlier in my head. What have I gotten myself into?

Before I know it, I've reached the US border. I get in the line of cars. At this ungodly hour, there are only about ten other vehicles ahead of me, but the checks are somewhat slow. I take off my jacket and slip out of my bloodstained T-shirt, wipe my face with it as well as I can, then shove it under the seat. I put my jacket back on and try to fix my hair. I can hardly keep my head up. I'm still drunk and feel like throwing up and sleeping at the same time. I start dozing off behind the wheel.

I go back to the café. My heart is going to explode. But what does the heart know? I get in line in front of her register and wait. Just before my turn, I spin on my heel and leave. Why does my damn heart want to burst? Why does it give me away? I gather up my courage and go back in, but a few people are in line in front of me. I start doing some breathing exercises. I have to act normal, damn it! I can't. If I only knew then that so many years later I would still feel the same way every time I thought of her!

"What can I get you?" Her voice. Her lips. Then she glances at me. The blue of her eyes glows and spills out as in a watercolor. And then, a miracle: I manage to stutter a few words. For the first time I speak to a girl without forcing myself to come up with the most clever line ever. She doesn't answer. She keeps looking at me. I don't sense that annoyance or boredom that I get from most of the girls I try to strike up a conversation with. It's more like curiosity. While she's probably wondering how to get rid of me, I ask what time her shift ends. She answers calmly, and I take off immediately, before she regrets talking to me.

•

"Rough night, huh?" A voice wakes me.

"Uh-huh."

"Sir, are you in a condition to operate this vehicle?" Where is the voice coming from? Border patrol booth, US border, young officer, kind eyes.

"Yes, sir," I say, trying to sound chipper. I hand him my driver's license and passport. "Must have dozed off while waiting." He looks at the passport, then the license, then back at me, clearly checking to make sure the pictures match up.

"It's your birthday today, huh, Zachary?"

"Yes, sir."

"By yourself?"

I don't answer. I look straight ahead.

"Anything to declare?" He says, scanning the inside of the van.

"No, sir," I say, catching a glimpse of myself in the mirror.

"Why didn't you take a cab, Zachary?"

"I ran out of money, sir." I notice a smear of something on my right cheek.

"Where are you from, Zachary?"

"A small country far away." An ugly dark smear.

"No, Zachary, I meant . . ."

"Sorry, officer! Rancho Penasquitos." Could be blood.

"Where's that?"

"Just north of San Berna . . ." It could be mud. But then again, it could be blood. It's on my right cheek though. The officer is inches to my left.

"I know where Rancho Penasquitos is, Zachary," he cuts me off. "Where is the *small country far away?*"

"Oh, I'm sorry, sir. It's . . . just north of Greece, sir."

"I see. They don't drink and drive just north of Greece, do they?" His voice seems louder.

"No, sir, they don't."

"Well, we don't drink and drive just north of Mexico, either."

"We certainly don't, sir." I wait for him to ask me to *step out of the vehicle.* There's no point in trying to run. There's no point trying to hide my smeared right cheek.

The radio on his shoulder buzzes. He picks it up, lowers his chin to listen to the distorted voice. His eyes are still on me.

"Ten-four, sir," he barks at his shoulder. I slowly exhale my last moments of freedom.

"Happy birthday, Zachary," he says and hands me my license. "Go straight home now, you hear?" He says as he waves the next car over. "Straight home."

I press the gas and head back into civilization.

·

When I came back to meet her after work, she was wearing a pair of faded jeans and a tight, light-blue T-shirt. She had on high-heeled platform sandals and a bag slung across her shoulder. It's easy to fall in love with a girl who wears everything with such ease.

I had my hands shoved deep in my pockets, most likely.

The regular summertime crowd must have been swarming around us. We walked, I remember, toward the Sea Garden. Somewhere around the Museum of Art, I lose the thread of this memory. I can't remember what we did between six, when she finished work, and the time it got dark. Did we sit somewhere? Did we just walk? Later, we went into a bar on the corner of First and the street she lived on, a small, dark place called "Impulse." We sat at one of those little round tables with a black tablecloth pressed under a circle of glass. We drank gin and tonics and munched on peanuts. And started talking. We talked over each other. We talked as if we had been talking forever and someone had just interrupted us. We talked as if we were only pretending we didn't know each other. We finished each other's sentences, completed each other's thoughts, and reminded each other of where we stopped. We talked as if tomorrow we would have to go our separate ways forever.

·

California! I'm saved! There's the parking lot where I left Stella's car. I feel like stopping, jumping out, and kissing the pavement.

I stop, jump out, and kiss the pavement. Then I get back in and park the van. I jump into Stella's car and gun the engine. Then it hits me—I might have killed somebody an hour ago in Mexico. I've stolen a van and left a ton of fingerprints. One must think about these things. I get out, open the trunk of Stella's car and look for something—anything—to wipe down the inside of the van. Nothing. I walk back to the van and open the passenger door. Nothing on the front seats that I can use. I open the back door.

I stifle a yell when I see the prone body and slam the door shut. My heart bangs crazily. I open the door again slowly. I exhale. Not a body. I sigh with relief. A giant plastic bag, stuffed full, slightly bent in the middle. It *does* look like a corpse. It's soft to the touch, yet dense, as if packed with straw. I glance around the parking lot, then open the bag up. The pungent smell hits me. I know what it is. I know what I should do. Instead, I pull the bag out of the van, drag it across the parking lot, and spend several risky moments shoving it into the trunk of Stella's Mercedes.

I get behind the wheel, turn the ignition, buckle up, cross myself, and head north into the bluish daybreak with a trunk-load of marijuana.

•

". . . what to do with your life . . ."

My exit is just a few miles away. What I want to do more than anything right now is sleep, sleep, sleep. I roll down the window for some fresh air, to keep myself awake these last few minutes. The morning chill laps at my face. Along with it comes the unbearable thought that I am headed toward an empty house.

Who am I kidding? What am I going to do *at home* without her? Sleep? I already tried that a few hours ago and ended up almost dead in Mexico. No more sleep. I need to decide what to *do with my life* . . .

In the bag behind me, there are at least seventy pounds of marijuana. I haven't the slightest idea how many joints that makes and I suspect that if I start calculating right now, I'll get sick and throw up inside the car. That shitty margarita did me in, I know it. One joint is about five bucks. Ten joints are about fifty. A hundred joints are five hundred. One pound makes . . . there, shit, I'm getting fucking sick to my stomach. Here we go-o-o-o. I'm already in the emergency lane, slowing down, throwing up out the open window. I vomit for some time, painfully, while still driving. I finally stop, get out of the car, and bend over, clutching my stomach. Just when I feel I've purged everything, I throw up at the thought of throwing up. Excruciating, bitter, sour convulsions clench my stomach.

Jesus, what a night! What a night.

Back in the car. There, I see the exit to our street. There's the street sign I'm so sick of, beyond it, the traffic light I'm so sick of. What am I doing? What am I doing, what am I doing, what am I doing?

I pass the exit sign and press the gas pedal.

Farewell, street sign.

Farewell, traffic light.

Farewell, canyon.

Farewell to you, too, empty house.

·

I thought about her constantly my last few weeks in the military. We saw each other a couple more times before my discharge. When I got off the train with a green army surplus bag slung over my shoulder, instead of going straight home to see Mom and my little sister, I grabbed a cab and gave the driver her address. In the rickety elevator, I pressed number seven and rehearsed my opening lines. I rang the doorbell. She opened the door and smiled. I wondered whether I should hug her or shake hands. I forgot what I was planning to say. She kissed me on the cheek and invited me in. Her room was white, clean, minimalistic. Stereo on the floor, bookshelves with lots of books, some paintings on the walls, low bed, little glass table, a vase with freesias. We sat on the floor

sipping gin and tonics. We listened to music all night long. We did it
for the first time at dawn, on the carpet in her room. We did nothing,
actually. I was so excited, tired, and crazy about her that I lasted only
a few seconds. She understood. She understood everything. She passed
me the T-shirt she had just taken off to wipe myself, and told me to lay
down for a while. Then I saw her open the window and, like a cat,
jump up on the windowsill. I leaned back on my elbows, amazed at
this sight. She turned to me and calmly sat on the ledge as if there were
something beautiful and safe on the other side. It was chilly out. Late
September. The last thing I saw before falling asleep was her silhouette
against the light-bluish dawn. Hard nipples, the flash of a lighter, a
cigarette. Why was this beautiful girl here with me? Wasn't she afraid
of heights?

•

I stop in a surfer town between San Clementino and Los Angeles.
I find a shabby beach hotel, check in, and lie down.

The sound of a vacuum next door wakes me up. I look at my
watch; I've slept for four whole hours. My head is throbbing. I
take a shower. I wash off the Tijuana filth, but the hangover clings
to me. I look at myself in the mirror. Indigo bruises have started
darkening under my eyes. My scalp hurts. I'm missing some hair,
but that's all right—better bald than dead.

I decide to go out, get some fresh air, and do some thinking. I
haven't thought straight for ten days. I go down to the lobby and
ask the girl at the front desk about the closest coffee shop. There's
a Starbucks three blocks away. I find it and get in line behind several other customers. Now it's my turn. At the register, a redhead
with a tongue piercing asks me what I'd like. What? I turn around
and look toward the door. Why doesn't Stella just appear right
here, right now? Why doesn't she just come to this little town and
have coffee with me like we used to, and we'd talk until . . .

"You waiting for someone?" The redhead with the tongue piercing asks calmly.

"Pardon?"

"Would you like anything, sir?" I don't respond. Behind my back, an orderly line of men and women has formed. I look at the girl with red-streaked hair but no words form in my throat.

"Sir?"

Stella, Stella, Stella, if you show up at the door right now, I promise:

I will take the garbage out without you reminding me, I will give you massages anytime you want, I will learn not to slam the doors, I will buy you flowers, fields of flowers, I will be quiet when I get up in the middle of the night, I will make the bed on Sundays, I will water the plants, I will vacuum, I will lift the toilet seat before I pee (and put it back down afterward), I will stop being a jerk to your mom, I will take you on a paddleboat ride, I will teach you three guitar cords, I will explain what the F-stops mean on my Nikon without yelling, I will give up drinking two beers at dinner, I will quit being a small fish, I will leave my terrible job and we'll still have money, money, money, lots of fucking money, we will finally sell this house, we will go to . . . India?

Stella. I also promise:

I will not correct you when you're telling jokes, I will not interrupt you when you're excited about something, I will not sing over your favorite songs, I will not be a smartass when we watch sentimental movies, I will not share my opinion about every single thing, we will not have Josh and Katya over for dinner ever again, we will never ever go to Vegas again, ever, I will not rent Hitchcock films, I will not order Chinese, I will not leave the room when we fight (what am I saying? we won't ever fight!), you will never see me picking my nose, I will not burp loudly (or strain to fart on purpose), I will never be silent with you for so long, never,

I will never watch CNN, I will never promise you the moon—you are a star, Stella.

"Long night?" The redhead tries one last time to get an order from me before turning to the next person in line. I rub my temples, shrug, take a deep breath, and try smiling.

"Triple espresso, please. Actually," I reconsider, "two triples." I sit outside and gulp them down. The caffeine kicks me in the heart. Good. I sum things up—I am an hour and a half away from home. It's still Thursday. It's still before noon. If I get on the San Diego freeway immediately and drive south, I can show up at work just after lunch and make up some excuse. Because I've never done this before, Scott, the manager, will understand and won't give me a hard time. I'll wait until nighttime and get rid of the dangerous load in my trunk. Then I'll go home. I'll return all my phone calls, I'll read a book until I fall asleep. The next day I'll go to work earlier, then go home again, pull the blinds open at last, and try to go on without her.

I leave the coffee shop in a better mood, get in the car, and head north.

•

From the beginning of our relationship, we realized that we could either talk or be quiet for hours without ever getting bored. Our interests were absurdly similar, the same music, the same books, the same films. We were both fascinated to see how our paths gradually converged, overlapped, and eventually became one. The old magic of love was brand new for us. Our unconsummated high school crushes had nothing to do with what we were experiencing: a passionate, beautiful, intelligent, restless, dazzling sensation. During our first months together, I didn't miss a single chance to make love to her, no matter where we were—at some of the many parties we went to, in dark, cold bedrooms while everyone else was screaming and dancing in the other rooms, at her parents' house, in hotels, on trains, in a car, in the park, in the sea. I'm not sure she experienced any pleasure whatsoever then. I was so insistent and wild in my hunger for her. There must've been a way for her to tame me. Or maybe there wasn't. Maybe she wasn't looking for one.

I remember the first time she came—tight, tasty, firm. I remember the way she began pulsating, then her accelerated breathing, her confused look (what's happening? is this it?), her moaning, the short scream, the silence afterwards. It was late afternoon. I remember the smell of roasted red peppers coming from somewhere in the neighborhood.

·

At the last second, I notice the Venice Beach sign and take the exit west. On a weekday in November, parking is not such a hassle. I buy orange swimming trunks and a towel from one of the boardwalk vendors. I step onto the warm sand. The strong wind makes long, tall waves, their crests are scattered with surfboards. OK, now I'll rush in and thrust all my sorrows into the salty bosom of the Pacific, thrus-s-s-s-s-s-s-s-s-s-s-s-s-s-s-t! I run, water splashing around me. I wade in chest-high, but the waves push me back to the beach. I take a deep breath and dive in. I stay underwater for a long time. I hop out. From my low vantage point, I see the ocean swallowing and spitting up surfers. One of them manages to take off, catching a wave in my direction. He passes close by, young, long-haired, calm, with the inspired expression of someone who walks on water. Our eyes meet for a second and he disappears. I keep on battering the waves until exhaustion empties my head. At some point I stop, float on my back, close my eyes, try to free my body of fatigue for a while, but can't. I turn around and start swimming toward the distant shore. Getting out of the ocean proves to be harder than I expected. The same waves that wanted to toss me onto dry land earlier now won't let me reach the shore. I battle them for a long time before realizing that I am the only one out here acting like an idiot. I understand that resistance is pointless. I relax my muscles, watch the surfers, and try to understand how the ocean operates. A few futile attempts to take advantage of the breaking waves follow; the undertow thrusts me deep into the water and spins me around, leaving me without any sense of up and down, of bottom and surface. At last, almost breathless, I manage to come up and see *my wave*. I catch it, seconds before it breaks. I relax on its crest, stretch my arms forward, I become one with it as countless, small, invisible turbines beneath my body drive me joyfully toward land.

I dry off and head back to the tourist-scattered boardwalk. A group of Japanese sightseers come toward me. They politely ask if I can take a picture of them by the ocean. They hand me the first camera. Before I snap the shot, I arrange them so all of their smiling little heads are in focus. I lift my left hand up, *one, two, three, cheese*, click—there you go. At once, several more hands pass their cameras to me. I pose them a little more carefully this time—four squatting down, six standing behind them and again, *one, two, three, cheese*. In no time, I'm holding a Canon, two digital Sonys, a small Yashica, a Panasonic, and something else. While I am clicking the shutters, I wonder what would happen if I suddenly took off with all this loot. Would they chase me? What would happen if they caught me? Is there a kung fu master among them? I hand back the gear and accept their compliments with a slight bow. The last camera someone hands over is a Nikon F3. Grasping the familiar body, I feel chills run down my spine. I love this model. After a few shots, I return it hesitantly. Its weight, its reliability, its grace . . .

Again, Stella storms my thoughts.

•

—don't take pictures of my legs, please
—they're part of your topography. now please lift up this knee
a little
—topography in blue. anytime i bump into something, bam—
another bruise . . . see . . .
—you have delicate skin
—am i delicate?
—the most delicate thing ever . . .
—m-m-m-m-m . . .
—the most, most, most delicatest thing ever . . .
—hey, dog-eyes . . . stay focused

•

I was a freshman majoring in English literature. Stella was in her senior year at the High School of Fine Arts. Yet the idea of going to the Art Academy had somehow never crossed her mind. Her classmates took private lessons in painting. She took English instead. Next year she was accepted into my college and moved in with me. She never stopped painting. She just said that she was tired to death of painting what other people told her to. Because I was a year ahead of her, I told her which classes were important, which were a waste of time. I gave her my notes and pointed her to the "right" books. I introduced her to interesting people, to her future professors and instructors, some of whom I had become friends with. I filtered her education—I realize now—with the noble desire to make things easier for her. We spent countless dark mornings in our warm bed because I wouldn't let her go to an early-morning lecture or a boring seminar. Half-awake, she would let herself be conquered, we would sleep in, roll in bed until late, then we would have coffee, listen to music, read novels, laze around, waste our time—we had time, God, we had so much time.

•

I park in front of a liquor store a few blocks from where Elijah lives. I know Elijah from a screenwriting class we took together a few years back. We got to be friends and kept in touch after the class was over. I go to a pay phone, pick up the greasy receiver, and dial his number. Elijah Ellison is large, redheaded, and freckled. He's twenty-nine and rents a shed by the pool at Steve and Tara's place. He doesn't drink, doesn't smoke, and doesn't eat meat. The remarkable thing is, despite a complete lack of any success whatsoever, he continues to write screenplays 24/7. Elijah is obsessed by the idea of writing a romantic comedy—something along the lines of *When Harry Met Sally*, *Pretty Woman*, or *Sleepless in Seattle* . . . Whether he has talent or not is hard to say. What he definitely has is perseverance. If I were an envious person, I would envy him.

The last time we saw each other was two years ago. I was jobless and desperate. I had slipped into one of those moments of madness (or enlightenment), in which you feel that nothing is impossible. I was writing a script then. We met to discuss it.

"The idea is great," he said, "but it's hard to figure out whether it's a comedy or a drama. What is it? You've got to clear that up."

"Well, Elijah," I countered, "is it really so important whether it's a comedy or a tragedy or . . . ?"

"It's important."

"Elijah, it's easy for you to say this is comic, that's dramatic, and this . . . well, this is a tragedy. To me, man, everything I write is a giant jar of salsa: salty, sweet, sour, with a hot aftertaste!"

"So what I'm hearing is that you're only interested in doing Great Things." Well, it's hard for me to say no to *that*. "Now me, I don't have a single *great* idea, nothing even close, but I've finished seven romantic comedies and a dozen more short scripts. I have short stories and a complete novel. It's better to have an *average* but completed idea than a *great* unstarted one!" Sometimes I want to strangle the guy. But now I call him from a pay phone.

I park on the street, under the blooming magnolia. Pacino, the dog, starts barking and Tara answers the door.

"Zack, how are ya?" She immediately notices my black eye but says nothing. I say "Hi" and hand her the bag with the bottle of wine. She and Steve like good wine. The other dog, I forget his name, licks my shoe. I go inside.

"Where's Steve? Where's Elijah?" I say.

Tara talks very fast and a lot. In fact, Tara talks fast precisely *because* she talks a lot. "Elijah is here, and Steve should be home any minute now. Where's Stella? Why didn't she come with you?" Without waiting for an answer, she goes on: "She's probably busy. How are you guys anyway? You know what? Her painting, the one with the scorched trees that I saw at her show last year . . . I just can't forget it. What with all these wild fires now . . ." On the TV screen there is a forest burning somewhere in Southern California. "I want to buy it. Can I buy it? How much would it be? But where can I put it here? No, no, no . . . it belongs in a gallery. It's huge! How big is that painting, Zack? Seven, eight, nine feet? And black. It's not black, actually. It's dark, very dark, but not black. But it's huge!" She whistles and waves her hands. "Big, it's gigantic. Yes, Stella is amazing, amazing! Last year she painted burned forests, now we have wild fires all over the place. Hmm. How does that work, huh? It's like she knew, it's like she knew in advance. You'll sleep here tonight, right?"

Here's the story—Tara and Steve were theater actors in Boston, where they met Elijah. Ten years ago, they moved to Los Angeles to get into the film industry. They founded a theater company, started staging new plays, and did all kinds of things to survive. Now, Steve is a producer and Tara owns a casting agency and directs plays from time to time in small theaters, just for the heck of it. When Elijah later decided to storm Hollywood with his *average* screenplays, they offered him a place to crash until he found a job. He accepted the offer and four years later he's still there. He occupies a tool shed crammed with mowers, junk, and boxes of books. At least it's by the pool.

"Hey, Zack Attack!" I see his big orange head peek through the door. "Who gave you that black eye?" He grins.

"I fell down the stairs," I say as I collapse on the couch. A Hummer parks outside, the dogs bark, and Steve opens the front door. He's been shooting a commercial all day and is glad to see me. He grabs a bottle of scotch and offers ice. I say, "No, thanks, no ice." He smiles and we lift our glasses for a toast.

Hours later, the four of us are standing around the bar in the kitchen, sipping wine and munching on cheese, ham, and grapes arranged on a pig-shaped cutting board. We talk about movies, theater, Hollywood, Europe . . . Steve tells a funny story about something that happened to him in South Africa while producing a stupid movie. Tara laughs loudly, throwing her head back. Her cheeks are already flushed. Elijah is gloomy. Elijah is always gloomy. Maybe because he doesn't eat meat, drink, or smoke. I've never seen him with a girl, either. Elijah is not gloomy only when we talk about romantic comedies. Pacino, the dog, is sleeping at my feet. The other one, I still don't remember his name, follows the fish in the tank with his amber eyes.

"Hey, guys," I begin nonchalantly. "I want to meet with that Jamaican dude you introduced me to last year at Jeff's party. Remember? What's his name? The guy . . . with the turban?"

"Oh, you mean Chris?" Steve says.

"Yeah, that's the guy."

"You need some pot? We've got some here if you want." He looks at Tara with that *it's ok to light a joint, right?* glance.

"Pot," I say, "is the last thing I need right now. I just wanted to talk with him about something."

"He's a little . . . you know," Tara begins, "discrete. I'm not sure whether he'd like to . . ."

Steve jumps in. "A discrete guy."

Chris is an enormous, muscular black man with a handsome, inspired face that radiates peace and wisdom. He wears white, free-flowing clothes and, sometimes, a colorful turban on his head. Last year I spent half an hour with him at a party and, while we were drinking (I—wine, he—orange juice) by the pool, we talked about inner peace, freedom of choice, inspiration, happiness, and all sorts of nonsense. The next few days I was in a cheerful mood. I was later told that he provided Steve and Tara with marijuana; they liked to smoke from time to time.

"I'm writing a novel," I start lying through my teeth, detecting how Elijah instantly perks up, "in which the main character stumbles upon a bag of marijuana." Elijah relaxes; a lame idea, nothing new. "So, I guess, my question is . . . what can my hero do with a bag of weed? Could he sell it, how much would it cost, stuff like that?"

"Don't you know?" Steve asks.

"Well, if I did, why would I be looking for Chris?"

"And how does the story end?" Elijah says.

"I'm not sure."

"Well, how can you start writing something without knowing how it ends?" He almost snaps.

"Goddammit, Elijah, if I knew how it ended, why would I start writing it in the first place? That would be totally boring for me."

"How can you reach the *end* when you don't know where you're going? The end is the most important part."

"It's no more important than the way there."

"You have to know the end. Start at the end. Start there and go backwards, to the beginning."

"Go *backwards?*"

"Sure! What does your hero want? That's the question. What does he want? What drives him? What drives the story chapter after chapter after chapter?"

"A bag of weed."

"A bag of weed can't do that. What does your hero want to do with this bag of weed? Can he possibly achieve it? Or not? From there, you know whether you've got a tragedy or a comedy. But there's another problem." Elijah pauses. "Pot is too . . ." he gesticulates, "harmless. It doesn't have that aura of . . . evil, so to speak. It doesn't push people to do terrible things. On the contrary, it brings joy, relaxation, peace. Nobody kills somebody for a joint." Pause. "Plus, it's not expensive either. So the stakes are low. You should think of a different drug: heroin, cocaine, methamphetamines, something like that. You should raise the stakes to the max—money or *death!*"

"Listen, my friend. This isn't a script for a thriller. This is a story about . . ." I try to calm down and sound convincing. "Actually, this is not a story about drugs. This is a story about a guy who loses his talent . . ."

"His . . . what?" Elijah's eyes narrow, puzzled.

". . . loses his faith," I keep going.

"Ay, ay, ay." He shakes his head mockingly.

". . . loses his appetite for life . . ."

"Existentialism?" Pure disgust.

". . . loses his love . . ."

"So you're writing a love story?" Sarcasm, plain sarcasm.

". . . himself . . ."

"And he finds a bag of ganja? Genius!" Elijah slams the table with his fist.

"But one night, one crazy night, as if in a dream, he stumbles upon a bag of marijuana." I sigh and stop. I won't bother telling the skeptical bastard what my story is about. He doesn't ever leave his shit-hole because he's too busy reading countless how-to handbooks on screenwriting written by losers who haven't made a single film. I know Elijah is searching for the formula behind the romantic comedy. He talks like a character from a romantic comedy, yet he's neither romantic, nor comic. Elijah is just a benign tumor on my life story, and Lord only knows why I like him.

Silence.

Tara nods at Steve. He goes to the post-it spotted fridge and starts looking for something. Somewhere among the numbers for insurance agents, dentists, auto mechanics, producers, actors, lawyers, bankers, handymen, and the like, is the link to Chris. Then Steve dials a number and makes an appointment for me for the next day. We drink more wine and go to bed very late. I fall asleep the second my head meets the pillow.

I dream about Stella.

•

I can't remember myself ever doing less than three things at the same time, which has made me confusing—I suppose—for people who neatly catalog their acquaintances. In college, I wrote short stories and articles for the local paper, I loved photography, and played the guitar. While I did the former two less frequently and only for pleasure, I took my music very seriously. I had a cheap electric guitar, which I plugged into an old Russian radio, turned the volume up to the max, and wailed on the strings. I played with the volume cranked up because it was the only way to distort it enough to make the sound unidentifiable. I was looking for my *sound then. Later, I added several more people to this mayhem and created something like a punk-rock band. We would play three-chord tunes all night long. Gradually, grandiose plans for worldwide success started taking shape in my head, and for some odd reason, they seemed realistic. I managed to inspire the poor souls around me with some kind of wild enthusiasm and belief, absolute belief, that we were destined for glory.*

The lead vocalist was a metalworking machinery operator with thick glasses, the drummer was a cousin of mine who worked in his father's beekeeping business, and the bass player was an overweight, acne-stricken kid from a small town nearby who was about to graduate in accounting. However, the three of them were good musicians, so the rest just didn't matter. My own musical education consisted of a hand-ful of classical guitar lessons and countless hours of heavy metal on the old Kashtan *eight-track. I didn't really know the guitar technically, which is why I tried to compensate with high volume, distortion effects, and insane onstage behavior. And because I was on familiar terms with only a few guitar chords, my songs were simple and exploded with the fury I felt precisely because I couldn't write music. I secretly hated my inability to master the guitar musically, but, on the outside, I was all confidence and authority in front of the boys. It was my energy, I believe, that kept people coming to our small gigs. Stella spent hours with the band in basements and garages, a silent witness to the chaotic rehearsals and quarrels. She just sat off to the side and drew in those countless notebooks of hers, submerged in her own world whose soundtrack, I suppose now, was a compilation of my angry songs.*

·

Chris and I meet at the Aladdin Café on the beach. It's still over-cast, but the skies seem promising. I tell him my made-up story, trying to sound like an inspired writer. This marijuana thing is just one of the story lines in the novel, but I want to sound authen-tic. I tell him I want to know what the odds are of my character being caught. I've heard that every other surfer around here is an undercover cop and, although everyone smokes, if my character tries selling pot just like that, they'll get him sooner or later and the novel will have to end. That's why I want to learn more, how it works, how he gets rid of a bag of pot, retail or wholesale, and, of course, everything will stay just between us. He knows who hooked me up with him so there's no danger of . . .

"What's your question, man?" The low velveteen Jamaican voice interrupts my stream of bullshit. I take a breath and shoot:

"How can the hero in my story sell a bag of marijuana?"

"He can't," the big black man answers calmly.

"What do you mean, he can't?!"

"He can't."

"Well . . . how about half a bag?" I decide to take what I can get.

"He can't."

"Why?"

"He don't know how."

"That's why I'm here with you, my friend. Tell me how." Chris studies me carefully, sizing up the bruises on my face.

"Listen, man. Your *hero* has a problem. First, he loses, then he finds, yes? What he finds, though, he doesn't need. And what he needs, he already has."

"Well . . ." I clear my throat. "What can my hero do?"

"Let him move on now. OK, man?" The big black figure with a white turban leans back in his chair and sips his orange juice.

"Chris, you don't think I'm . . . ?" I make small circles around my temple with my pointer finger.

"No." He smiles for the first time and the big golden hoop in his ear trembles.

"You don't think I'm a cop or . . ."

"No."

"Then why?"

Chris turns his head. After a pause, staring at the ocean: "See the waves, man. Each one is born, it grows, it fights, it foams, and then comes ashore, bsh-sh-sh-sh, and it dies and becomes ocean again. Beautiful, yes? And again, and again, and so on . . . and so on . . ."

"You're not helping me, man," I say.

"I help, man. I help."

•

We put together eight songs and found a studio where we recorded them on a primitive four-track recorder. The album was entitled The Winds of Hell. *We produced a cardboard box of TDK cassette tapes, and now the only thing we needed was an album cover. I asked Stella to draw something. The next day, she gave me a picture. It was an expressionistic, somewhat naive silhouette of a girl, arms stretched out as if ready to fly out of the frame of a dark-blue window. It was beautiful, but the boys from the band didn't like it. I didn't think it fit, either. So we went to Angel the Artist. He listened to Judas Priest, wore ironed jeans, and lived with his mom in a gloomy apartment that always smelled like sauerkraut.*

Our album came out illustrated by Angel the Artist, with a picture of a snarling monster clutching a guitar in its tentacles.

God, was I really that blind?

•

It's clear that I'll have to deal with this on my own. I need to improvise. There's a bookstore across from the coffee shop. I go in and buy a roadmap of the United States, a college-ruled notebook, and two 99-cent pens. Then I stop at the photography section. I open a book of portraits by Henri Cartier-Bresson. I sit down between the aisles *tête-à-tête* with the faces captured by the great master's little camera. I turn the pages one by one. There's Matisse with a pigeon in his hand; William Faulkner in the company of two stretching dogs; Jung with a pipe looking straight at me; one very innocent Capote; Ezra Pound, who here reminds me of my late grandfather, Stefan Nichts; a smiling Che Guevara; Samuel Beckett staring at the bottom left corner of the photograph; Albert Camus with a short cigarette butt in his smile and a turned-up jacket collar; a suspicious Sartre on a winter bridge over the Seine; Stravinsky with two large hands and a walking stick; a tired Marilyn Monroe . . . All dead, dead, dead.

Half an hour later, I put the book back on the shelf. I feel like crying. I wish I could cry. I leave the bookstore and wander down the sidewalk aimlessly. I stop in front of a bridal store. It's still Friday. It's still not too late to call Scott the manager and come up with an excuse for my absence today. I can see his grimace. *Ok, I'll let it slide this time, things happen, but from now on* . . . I can show up earlier than usual on Monday. I can stay late. I'll work on my attitude. I'll be more blasé in my inspections. I'll forget about my Tijuana adventure and about the bag in my trunk. Everything will be fine. I'll bandage my heart and get back into the traffic on my way to work.

•

–i don't want you to be quiet like . . .
–like what?
–like . . . that
–i'm taking your picture
–OK, but I want to talk to you
–all right. you talk, i'll listen
–well then, this session is over. i'm getting dressed
–wait, wait, wait, wait. just a few more shots and it's over
–but we'll talk
–we'll talk
–and you won't be quiet like that
–i won't
–ever?
–never

•

Then came those several years I don't remember clearly. The government changed overnight, the Berlin Wall came down, protesters were killed in the streets of Romania, and evil things were happening in Yugoslavia. I wished something profound would come about at home, too, something earth-shattering. Something that would make me put on my black leather jacket dramatically and leave Stella at our door crying, not knowing whether she'd see me again.

I remember the night was cold. I put on my black leather jacket, zipped it up, took a blanket and a pillow under my arm, a thermos full of hot tea, kissed her as we made plans about where to have coffee in the morning, since the college was going to wake up to an occupied campus and the cafeteria would be closed.

The occupation. In our Alma Mater that night, we watched TV, listened to the radio, cursed the communists, and waited for instructions to come from somewhere. I was elected to be part of the occupation committee. Now I can't actually remember what we were protesting about. I think it was because of ". . . better get the tanks rolling."[1] I think we demanded changes to the Communist Constitution, and free and democratic elections. Really, I can't remember why we were protesting.

The second night. Stella came to spend the night in the occupied building. Student activists had already turned the dean's office into their headquarters and had put on new worried faces, which they wore as they paced up and down the corridors. They started using the copy machines, faxes, and telephones with such businesslike efficiency—as if they had practiced for this occupation their whole lives. The rest of us lay around on the floors, read books, watched American soldiers in Arabian deserts on CNN. The next day Stella decided that there was no point in her spending any more time there; nobody needed her, the floor was too hard, it was boring, and most of all she wanted to paint, but she couldn't there. I walked her home and went back to

---

1 A phrase that the communist president of Bulgaria allegedly mumbled after seeing hundreds of thousands of protesters on the street in 1989. This was caught on camcorder and replayed on TV over and over again. He was forced to step down after student protests, strikes, and general unrest.

the campus, cutting through an old graveyard so I could keep up the anti-communism. I remember that night there was a power outage, and with nothing else to do, some friends and I gathered around the piano in one of the auditoriums. We lit candles and lanterns, and a guitar appeared from somewhere, and a real party broke out. We sang The Beatles, The Crickets,[2] and Pink Floyd, we took breaks with Gershwin, and then with renewed strength we screamed "Bohemian Rhapsody" in our broken English.

After midnight, the activists *sent a freshman to tell us to stop the commotion—we were not making a good impression. What if somebody passed by the university campus? What would they think? We were taking part in a serious endeavor; the occupation was no joke; we had to be responsible and accountable for these events, which were oh-so-important for our future; after all, we had not come here to party and sing.*

I slammed the piano shut and we all fell silent. I folded up my blanket, said goodbye and took off, walking down the candle-lit corridor toward the exit. On my way, I kicked the upholstered door of the dean's office and walked back to our cozy apartment. Stella was my velvet revolution. I decided never again to miss a night next to her warm body. I swore that I'd never ever waste my time with made-up coups and fabricated riots. After all, the real changes are invisible and the rest simply are not worth the pain.

·

I find a pay phone and dial the familiar office number. Scott picks up. His voice starts buzzing in the receiver and I hang up in disgust. I pull my thoughts together and call Danny in New York.

"Hello?" He sounds as if I have just woken him up.

"Hello."

---

2   A Bulgarian group formed in the late 1960s as a local "answer" to the Beatles.

"Hello-o-o?" Drowsy.

"Danny boy!"

"Zack, is that you?"

"It's me. What's happening in the Big Apple?"

"Nothing."

"We'll have to do something about that, then."

"Well, let's do something about that, then."

"I'm coming to New York."

"You're coming."

"I'm coming."

"How about Stella?" Here we go again.

"I'm coming on business."

"Are you being transferred, or what?"

"I'm transferring myself."

"And what are you going to do here, if it's not a secret?"

"No secrets from you, friendo. I'm going to sell marijuana."

He laughs. "Marijuana?"

"Pot. Grass. Cannabis."

"Nice! You'll make it big!" Danny keeps laughing. Then he stops. "Come on, man, tell me!" I guess I didn't sound serious enough.

"I told you. I'm gonna sell marijuana."

"Well . . . no problem then. You'll have tons of customers. Half of them undercover cops, too!"

"I know."

"So what's with the bullshit then?"

"No bullshit. Just fresh marijuana."

"Are you crazy?"

"I might be. But I have a bag of weed in my trunk." This paralyzes him for sure. For one long minute I listen to his breathing. I can hear a car honking in the background. The building next to his is a bar that closes at 2 A.M. It's never too quiet around Danny. It's never too dark, either. I remember how the orange light from the street lamp in front of the bar cast stripes through the broken blinds as Stella and I tried to make love silently on his hard mattress.

"Where did you get it?"

"What?"

"The bag."

"I found it."

"You found it?"

"Yeah!"

"No one finds bags of marijuana on the street!"

"I never said I found it on the street."

"Where did you find it?"

"In a van."

"And how about the van?"

"Two guys wanted to shove me inside it and do something awful to me, I'm sure, and I . . ."

"And you?"

"I somehow managed to . . . Come on, man. Something happened and maybe it wasn't supposed to happen. Now, I have a bag of grass. About fifty-sixty pounds . . . maybe more. I don't know anybody here who could help me get rid of it all at once. If I start selling it ounce by ounce, I'll stumble across some asshole and end up in jail. I have no idea how to reach a serious player. And, I suspect some local douche is in trouble because of this bag. There's no way they wouldn't be looking for it, right? What I'm saying is, if I try to sell it locally, I'll either bump into a cop or someone who knows someone who has heard of someone else who is missing a bag of weed. You get the picture. So, I want to get rid of the whole thing and I want to do it safely! I expect you to help me resolve this situation. I think thirty percent will convince you to cooperate." Long pause. "So what do you think? Can we do something about this?"

"Look here . . ."

"Danny?"

"Yeah?"

"Can you do me a favor and don't start with *look here*? Just don't *look here* me, OK?"

"OK."

"OK. If it were easy, I wouldn't have called you in the first place!"

"Give me some time to think. I'll ask around. I need to talk to some people. I'll call you as soon as I know more. You said about fifty pounds?"

"Something like that."

"Fresh?"

"Aromatic, pungent, strong . . ."

"Yeah, yeah, I got it! How can I reach you?"

"I'll call you, Danny," I say matter-of-factly. I hang up the receiver and slowly walk across the sun-scorched parking lot.

•

We were poor. Although I never stopped inventing ways to earn the next buck, we were poor, always on the edge, and sometimes beyond it. In between midterms and finals I bought and resold jeans with the Gypsies at flea markets; I smuggled duty-free coffee from Romania; boom-boxes from Macedonia; beach towels from Greece; and leather jackets from Turkey. One summer we were in such dire straits that I had to steal corn from some fields, boil it in a barrel over a fire made from stolen pallets, and sell it to the tourists on the beaches of Varna. Humiliation.

How was I so arrogant as to ask her to marry me? How was she so foolish as to accept? Stella, I know now, often prefers saying "yes" instead of inconveniencing herself with explaining why no means no. She has a natural talent for minimizing situations in which she has to say either one. Perhaps back then I was one of those few cases in which she needed to give an answer. Maybe she had said yes. I think I remember where it happened. It was winter. A smoke-filled tavern at a train station in Pleven (what train were we waiting for there?). It was a white, cold night outside, warm and dim inside. I held her soft hand in mine, touched it to my cheek and I knew, I so ruthlessly and clearly knew that I did not want any other hand touching my cheek. I tenderly kissed her fingers where I was supposed to place an engagement ring and asked her to marry me. I did it instinctively. Tears streamed down my face (did I have any idea how this would end?). I promised her, I remember, "I'll always take care of you." What was I thinking then?

.

I decide to stay in the Los Angeles area one last night before I go. I find the closest Walmart and supply myself with a pair of shorts, blue jeans, socks, T-shirts, sandals, towels, toilet paper, bottled water, and air-fresheners for the car, as well as Toblerones. I get in line at the cash register along with the usual clientele—fat white women and their ice-cream-stained, pink-tank-top-wearing, snot-nosed kids hanging off the shopping carts, and fat black women with their oversized-shorts-and-shiny-basketball-jersey-sporting, buzz-cut, boogery kids hanging off the shopping carts. The cashier is unfriendly and slow. Next to her a kid with Down's Syndrome wearing an "Our People Make the Difference" pin bags the purchases. I wait in line for a long time to get to the register. Then the cashier screws up and the system crashes. My credit card is not working, and we all wait for the store manager to come and fix the mess.

Walmart: a leech sucking on the flabby back of democracy. I leave in the usual misanthropic mood the place inspires. I unload my purchases in the car, unwrap the coconut air freshener, and inhale its trashy scent. Stella loathes it. So do I.

I find an ATM and withdraw two hundred dollars from our

joint account. No more credit cards. No more complications. No more comfort. I want to go back to the beginning of things. I want to touch, feel, taste . . . I want to live again, God damn it.

•

Things were somehow going well with the rock band. The tapes of our first album sold before we were totally sick of the songs. Musically, we were supposedly reaching a new level. I needed a better guitar. Good instruments were not easy to find in those days. Needless to say, they were expensive. My grandpa stepped up and gave me his old Zhiguli[1] as a gift. I fixed it, painted it red, and sold it. With the money, I bought a stolen Fender Stratocaster. For the first time, I realized what it meant to have the right instrument. I kept on writing songs, which we played in front of ever more people. At one of the gigs in a neighborhood bar along with the band Lucifer, our speakers blew and we sat on the edge of the little stage, dejected, waiting for a new amplifier. A gray-haired, serious-looking man approached us. He dropped some compliments and offered to organize a concert for us the next Sunday in the center of a nearby industrial town called Devnya. The money was good, too. He said they had professional sound and lighting equipment—we just needed to show up. We accepted the offer, of course. This was our first paid gig.

This time, I took my camera, along with the Fender, to capture the memorable event. A beat-up Chavdar[2] bus drove us into a gray town, covered in what seemed to be ashes. The gray houses had gray roofs. On the gray streets we passed gray people bent over gray bicycles. It was as if I had ridden into a black-and-white dream.

We got off the bus, instruments in hand, and we found ourselves in the middle of a large crowd of old people waving red flags. Up on stage,

---

1   A Russian-made car.

2   Bulgarian-made buses from the socialist era.

under a giant red banner with the slogan of the newly reformed Communist party, a much decorated veteran from WWII was finishing his speech, thrusting a bony fist in the air. After him, schoolteachers got up, then nurses, then machinists, bakers, crane operators, factory workers, retirees, school girls, and even one local artist. Our promoter had conveniently forgotten to inform us about the nature of our audience. We, on the other hand, had never asked. He was nowhere to be seen, and we were forced to deal with his assistant—a round-faced, plain woman, with the well-intentioned and energetic radiance of a Girl Scout leader. She assured us that we could do anything we wanted and say whatever we wanted on stage—they were modern people. We put our heads together and decided that we would better serve democracy if we made ourselves heard instead of refusing the red party paycheck and going back to the bus stop and waiting for a bus (which would not come for another hour anyway).

After the communist rally was over, the crowd started thinning out, for it was almost time to drink some rakia.[3] The murky sun was setting behind the bellowing smokestacks of the largest cement factory in Eastern European, which had discolored this town. We plugged in our instruments and blasted away with our most ferocious songs. From time to time, we shouted anti-communist slogans. The communists left the town square one by one, angrily turning gray overcoated backs on us and shaking gray heads.

And, of course, we didn't get paid. Those were the times.

I didn't give up. I kept at it, living in my own world, where things would always happen one way or the other. I somehow managed to conceal my technical impotency on the guitar. To the band, I elaborated theories on how I was looking for new musical structure and new ways of expression. I spoke of punk rock and heavy metal, but secretly listened to Bach, Beethoven, Paco De Lucia, Al Di Meola, Pat Metheny,

---

3 Brandy, often homemade, the national drink of Bulgaria, usually imbibed before dinner with a salad.

Wes Montgomery, Miles Davis, The Beatles, Stravinsky, Pink Floyd, Tchaikovsky, Schoenberg . . . Eventually, I started digging deeper into jazz. I was reading more and more. I began having less and less time for rock and roll with the boys. We weren't rehearsing as often anymore. I wasn't satisfied with the conversations we had anymore. Often, I felt like I was sitting at a dinner table with some distant relatives. We didn't have much to say to each other. When all of us were hanging out together, Stella and I could not wait to ditch them, so we could switch back to our own frequency.

I read like a maniac then—Nietzsche, Kant, James Fraser, Berdyaev, Hegel, Levy-Strauss, Propp, Mircea Eliade, Freud, Jung, Barthes, Bachelard, and Schopenhauer, especially Schopenhauer's The World As Will and Idea *. . . whatever I came across, whatever was translated. I would spend hours drifting away with Castaneda's visions, listening to Mahavishnu Orchestra. How indelibly did I mess with my head then?*

•

I check into a shoddy motel a block away from Grand Ave. This neighborhood has a long-standing reputation for its nightclubs, pubs, striptease joints, hookers, and dope dealers. In the parking lot, there are old, beat-up Jeeps hung with surf boards and drying wetsuits. A bumper sticker showing a dog licking his thing reads: "Because they can." This almost makes me smile.

I take a shower and shave. I register that the bruise on my face is even more noticeable. While deciding what to wear, I realize that I have forgotten to buy underwear, damn it. I put on my blue jeans, run down the stairs, cursing in my head, cross the dim lobby, pass the dark reception desk, and step outside.

The sun bursts in my eyes and, for the first few seconds, the police cars and the pointed guns don't seem to have anything to do with me.

I freeze.

A very long moment passes until everything penetrates my mind and I understand that this is real.

Just then I reach down to zip up my still-open fly.

"Get down! Hands in the air! Let me see them! Get on the ground! Get down, get down, get down!" There are cops everywhere, leaning on the hoods of their vehicles, guns pointed at me.

I lift my hands in the air and fall face down on the hot asphalt. Here I am, you motherfuckers! Catch me! Cuff me and take me away from here. Shove me in the darkest prison, in its dankest cell. Rid the world of me. Take my health, my youth, my life, my time, take everything. I need nothing if she is not here.

And she's not here.

Someone grabs my neck, pushes me down. Two strong hands search me for weapons. Handcuffs tighten around my wrists. All this hurts. My right cheek and the burning asphalt. The black shoes of the police officer pushing me to the ground. He pulls my wallet out of my back pocket. Out of the corner of my eye I can see him flipping it open with one free hand, looking at my driver's license, and then dropping it on my back. He seems disappointed. They drag me behind the cars. I notice that none of the cops have changed positions. Then I realize that I might not be the only one with a problem in this motel. In the doorway I had just come out of a moment ago, a brown, muscular, tattooed body appears, throwing his hands in the air:

"OK, OK, OK, I'm here. Here I am, here I am." The man looks calm.

He's almost smiling, obviously resigned to his fate and the number of cops. Our eyes meet. The cops again start screaming for him to lie down. He breaks into a big grin as he's kneeling down. He bends forward and, just before his body hits the ground, his face twists. His right hand disappears behind his lower back, and reemerges quick as a snake, holding a pistol.

"Die, bitch, die!" He yells, shooting at me. Gunshots from everywhere blend into a single, long, deafening bang.

Seconds later, it's strangely quiet again and his body is lying in the parking lot. One of his legs is trembling. My ears are shrieking. Gravel chips are stuck in my cheek, the back of my head itches, my eyelid twitches. And I am handcuffed.

Blue uniforms swarm the body. I hear the wailing ambulance and police sirens. Onlookers appear out of nowhere. Somebody shoves me into the back seat of a squad car. As we take off, I see how trickles of blood begin creeping out from under the dead body.

The next hours pass in taking fingerprints, running a background check, and a long Q&A session. The detective interrogating me is more or less my age. He assures me that this is something he has to do, it's nothing personal. He offers coffee and I turn it down. He tells me about the shoot-out. The suspect who was shot and killed was a gang member wanted in several states for the possession and dealing of narcotics, gun trafficking, racketeering, rape, and the murder of a police officer, etc. . . . He most likely thought that I had ratted him out or that I was an undercover cop helping with his arrest. He most likely wanted to take me with him wherever he was going. Who knows what actually passed through his head along with the bullets.

"Well, that's about it, Zack." It seems like the conversation with the detective is almost over. "I'm sorry about the misunderstanding." The detective hands me his card. "If you remember something on your way home, I'd appreciate a call."

"No problem." I say. I'm still summing up the facts. While I was studying photography I'd spent hours adjusting the camera so that I could capture a bullet going through an apple. That was one of my exams. Now I can *visualize* the bullet entering my skull and what will happen when it exits. I can also *imagine* the less deadly scenario in which they throw my ass in jail. If you have a good imagination, you don't need life experience. "If I remember something, I'll call, sir." We shake hands and I am almost out the door when I hear:

"I forgot to ask you, you've got a car here, right?" I stop with my hand on the doorknob. My heart is about to burst. Why don't I just open the door and run? Why don't I fly out of here like a fireball and burn to ashes anyone who dares touch me? I take a deep breath before I answer. I furrow my brow in what is supposed to look like an astonished *wasn't-it-enough* expression and slowly turn to him.

"Which car is yours?" I hear his voice as if there is a thick, glass wall between us. I tell him the model. "Oh? Great," he says. "License plate?" He is writing something down. Plate, plate, plate . . . I can't remember the license plate number. It's my wife's car, for Christ's sake. It is Stella's car. And I realize that I am in deep, thick, slimy shit. I realize something else, too. Not only have I gotten myself into this shit, but I've also dragged Stella into it as well. Why did you have to go anywhere, baby? Why did you have to go *back to yourself*?

I hope my mom won't think her son is a drug dealer. I hope my sister will still believe in me. I hope that everybody one day will understand that what happened during these last few days was only an accident. I was at the wrong place at the wrong time.

But then again, every place is the wrong place, and every time is the wrong time, if you are not there, Stella.

"I can't remember the license plate number . . ." I stammer. The detective lifts his head from the paper he is writing on and puts the pen back in the jar. He gives a rather absent look and smiles. "OK, no problem. If the vehicle was damaged by bullets directly or by ricochets or whatever . . . call this number. Your insurance might need more information. This is the number to call. OK? Do you need a ride back to the motel?"

•

—have you seen those really old photographs where people look kind of stiff?
—yes
—cameras were very slow back then and they needed to pose for an hour or even more for just one shot. they had to stay still. they needed to put braces on people's necks so they wouldn't move
—what a nightmare
—now, what I want from you is to stay very still and not move at all . . . just for fifteen seconds
—like this?
—yep. i'm taking this picture at a very low speed
—why?
—because i believe that the longer i keep the shutter open the more life gets captured on the negative

•

I cannot stay in the motel, of course. FOX News and Channel 10 trucks are parked next to my car. Reporters, photographers and camera crews are walking around. A helicopter is hovering above, it's a total circus. I take my stuff from the room, stop at the reception desk, but, guess what, I don't need to pay anything.

I find another motel, throw myself across the bed, and fall asleep immediately. I have a dream that I'm in my grandparents' old house in their village. It's winter. I press my forehead to the frozen window and look at the snow-covered backyard. Suddenly, in the distance, I see an animal running toward me at great speed—as only happens in dreams or films. The next thing I see on the other side of the glass is the enormous, toothy head of a gruesome wolf. I pull away from the window, but I just can't stop looking at him. I wake up. I don't know where I am. Evening is nearing and I've slept through yet another sunset. I close my eyes and let my head fall back on the pillow.

·

As time passed, I became more and more depressed by my own inability to master the guitar. I found a teacher and started taking classical guitar lessons and spent countless hours practicing—technique, arpeggios, arpeggios, arpeggios. I wanted to play like Steve Vai, but everything I tried sounded like the Sex Pistols. Sometimes, at night, I dreamed that I could play like a virtuoso. My fingers obeyed me. They moved wonderfully, joyfully fast. In my dreams, I extracted each note with no effort whatsoever, as if I didn't play the instrument but rather thought with it. There were no secrets for me. I wanted to share all this with Stella and the world. I would be awakened in the middle of the night by difficult, gorgeous symphonies echoing down through the nothingness. I would desperately chase them, trying to grasp at least a few chords with which to put together a song. The results were murky reflections of the real music which flowed through me and which I was incapable of capturing.

We were still poor, but managed to keep our heads above water. We were together all the time—not just hugging, but clenched to one another. We were both excellent students, even though we never studied too hard. We received scholarships and lived in a cheap, small loft from which we could see the red roofs and beautiful sunsets. I started taking pictures and writing short articles for the local paper to make money. I had a Russian camera and a Bulgarian typewriter. The most expensive thing I owned, though, was the Stratocaster. My calling, my gift—I had fooled myself into believing then—was music. Stella never seemed to question her true calling—she just kept on painting. In the uninhabited space adjacent to our loft, she made an improvised studio under the eaves where she started experimenting. Since we didn't have any money for art supplies, she painted with anything she had at hand on anything she could find—oils on bed sheets, industrial paint on cardboard, house paint on sheet metal.

I wonder where all those paintings are now?

.

It's cool outside. I find a coffee shop. I order espresso. I sip it as I write some random thoughts in one of the notebooks. Why do I write them down? For whom? Another diary by someone who didn't need a diary until recently? Aren't there enough losers in the world already?

I ask the girl behind the register where the cool places are for Friday nights around here. I don't learn much besides that it's cool everywhere Friday night. Life begins Friday night. America lives for Friday night! TGIF, America!

It's still before eight. I leave the coffee shop. I find the closest movie theater. The movies playing this summer are mostly stupid sequels of stupid movies that were playing the summer before. I debate for a while before stopping on a flick starring Jack Nicholson. Stella finds him repulsive as both a man and an actor.

I get out of the movie theater around ten. The film wasn't bad, not at all. Only Jack Nicholson . . . Isn't there anybody to tell him that those days are long gone and acting with your eyebrows isn't funny anymore?

I decide to walk until I reach the ocean and, after that, I haven't really decided what to do.

The bars start filling up. The night gets cooler with every

block. Music sounds from the open restaurants and bars. The ocean is near. I can feel its chill. I can hear it. Here it is.

There are moments when you expect the answer to come precisely from there, from that endless dark mass they say we all crawled out of. I walk through the sand until I reach the water. That's it. This is where the west ends. And here I am at its very edge. Here I am—at the brink of Western civilization, whose sunset I slept through today.

So what's beyond this? The East?

I take off my shoes and let the ocean, calm as a cat, lick my bare feet. The foam wraps around them. I close my eyes and inhale—the ocean's scent now reminds me of blossoming linden and smashed watermelon.

Pacific Ocean, what am I doing here in your calm caress while the Black Sea thumps inside my head?

There is a lifeguard tower further down the beach, and I see a few figures dragging wood and trying to start a fire. From time to time one of them cups her hand around her mouth and yells toward the closest pub: "Bobby-y-y-y-y-y-y, you asshole! We're out here-e-e-e-e-e-e-e-e-e-e-e-e!"

.

Things with the band started stalling. We weren't going anywhere. I dreamed of arenas, but we were playing small bars instead. I wanted best-selling albums, but the boys were happy if the local radio played a song or two of ours. I wrote scripts for our music videos with helicopters and car chases, but I didn't have the money to buy decent guitar picks. I was so naïve. Stella accepted all this with an unfathomable understanding. She did not judge me. And I looked at life as if somebody somewhere had promised me something. I am asking myself now whether my craziness was contagious, or perhaps the daydreaming of

those first years of freedom from the communists had pervaded every-
one's minds, even the most skeptical of us.
    Or perhaps youth made things seem so inexplicably possible?

.

I shake the sand off my feet, put on my shoes, and head back to
the nightclubs and Friday mood. There's a long line in front of
every place. It makes no difference to me which one I choose. I
pause in front of one that is almost right on the sidewalk. Only
a tall plexiglass wall divides the table-filled yard and the street.

I can see everything happening inside. Gestures, waitresses,
customers, Bacardi, Jack Daniels, bartenders, TV screens, American beer ads . . . I get in line. Behind the glass are the pink tank
tops, the bare midriffs, the lower-back tattoos, the ubiquitous
California flip-flops, the silicone breasts, the chewing gum, the
laughs, the bleached teeth, the artificial tans, the searching eyes.

Soon the line behind me gets longer. Across the street, one
idiot gives another a piggyback ride. Both of them fall and start
rolling on the ground. The line laughs. A Jeep Wrangler drives
by and the three blonde girls in the back laugh and flash the
crowd. Large breasts gleam and disappear into the night. The line
screams its approval.

And then I notice the woman in front of me. More precisely,
I see her semi-profile. The beautiful line of her forehead, her
eyebrow. She shifts, slightly lowering her head to say something
to the girl next to her, and I see her arms folded over her chest.
There is something about the way she readjusts the jacket hung
over her shoulder. I see her left fingers slightly caressing the fabric of the dark sweater and pulling it over her breasts. It's not that
she is cold, but more a reflex left over from the years when she
had been embarrassed by her own body. Her pants are white and
free flowing. The fabric, light and see-through (cotton? linen?),

allows me to make out the line of her behind and her shapely thighs. Suddenly, she is aware of my stare and turns around to look at me. Our eyes meet briefly. I can't tell if she likes me, but she doesn't shut down.

Beautiful? In that particular way that seems visible only to me. In that particular way that urges me to reach for my camera. In that way that tempts me to pull out her inner beauty, the one others don't see. She is attractive but she has never quite believed it. No one ever told her when it was most necessary. Her friend is a scrawny brunette, with slightly dark skin, thin lips, perky little breasts, and a high, round butt. She throws a warning look at me and I read the subtitles: "Fuck off, loser!" They go in first, then I follow. I tail them to see which of the bars they are heading towards, and I pick another from which I can see them. The bartender is quick, but the orders are piling up. All of a sudden, next to me, four half-drunk women show up. They are all blonde, wearing tank tops, shorts, and flip flops. Three of them could lose at least twenty pounds and would still be chunky. The fourth is beyond help.

I exchange glances with the woman at the bar across from me at the very moment a broad-shouldered guy with a beer in his hand approaches her. These muscled morons have a distinct way of holding their beer bottles—grasped firmly like dumbbells. From this distance, by the way the young woman speaks with words, gestures, and body language, I can tell she's not American. And there is something about the way she keeps pulling on the sweater over her shoulders as if it's a shawl or a light blanket. Obviously, the conversation with the body builder doesn't go anywhere, as he is not the type to waste time talking, so he waves goodbye and approaches the next girl, as he would the next piece of exercise equipment.

The bartender leans over to take my order. I tell him what I want.

"Dirty martini."

"With vodka?" He says.

"*Absolute*-ly!" Where could this young woman be from?

"Olives?"

"Three." No, definitely not Europe. Actually, why not? Portugal, perhaps.

She could be Spanish. This quiet intensity in her. The bartender shakes the cocktail and pours the murky, greenish content into the chilled martini glass. I take a sip. Wonderful. I compliment the bartender. He thanks me humbly and asks if I want the ice from the shaker before he tosses it. Professional, a true professional. He asks me where I'm from.

"Bulgaria."

"Never been there."

"And you?"

"Michigan."

"Never been there, either, but I went to school close by, at Ohio State."

"Oh, Ohio State. The Buckeyes almost did it this year, huh?"

"Almost."

"Are you a bartender?" He asks.

"Used to be. It's how I put myself through school."

"You know what you want."

"I know nothing."

"I meant . . . the martini."

"Yeah, I know my martinis."

"What did you study in Ohio?"

"Photography."

"Cool. Is that what you do now?"

"No, I work for a pharmaceutical company."

"You take pictures for them?"

"No. I stopped taking pictures some time ago."

"So, what do you do now?"

"I monitor data from clinical trials."

"Well," he shrugs. "It pays the bills."

"It pays the bills." I say and order another one. I leave money for the two cocktails. He thanks me and goes to the other side of the bar to take a large order. I sip the second martini much more slowly. I feel its coolness crawling down my throat and penetrating my body, caressing my agitated nerves. I close my eyes and enjoy it. Nice. Maybe she's Latin American. Venezuela? No, maybe Argentina. The tranquil grace, the walk. The tango in her eyes. Argentina. Definitely, Argentina.

"What are you drinking?" I hear a raspy voice to my left. I turn. The fattest of the four smiles, leaning toward me. The strap of her top has slipped down her round shoulder. Her bra is green.

"Uhh, martini. What are you drinking?"

"Long Island Iced Tea." She manages to conceal her Southern drawl until the third syllable.

"Very good." I say and get down from my bar stool to pick up something from the floor that looks like a dollar bill.

"So what are you drinking?" She asks again and leans toward me, exposing an even better view of her cleavage.

"Martini. And what are you drinking?" It's not a dollar bill, it turns out to be a dentist's business card.

"Long Island Iced Tea. And you?" I decide to see how far I can go.

"Martini. And you?"

"Long Island Ice Tea. And you?"

"Martini. And you?"

"Long Island Ice . . . But you asked me already. Wait, what happened to your face?" Goddamit, I had forgotten about my bruise.

"I fell down the stairs." I take another sip of my martini and glimpse at the bar across from me. She is not there. Her friend is not there, either. I scan the entire place but she is nowhere to be found. I jump off my bar stool and start looking for her, climbing the stairs to the upper level. I can't find her. I don't see her around the bathrooms either, and I don't see her outside where the smokers are hanging out. I don't see her anywhere, ever again.

I return to the same bartender and order two more of the same. I drink them bottoms up. Then a blonde beauty enters the bar. She's wearing a mini-skirt, has huge, round, silicon boobs, and is slightly under thirty. I immediately set off toward her before the asshole in the monkey suit with the stupid beer bottle shows up. I get close to her. I have no idea what I say. Neither does she. My strategy is to hit on a woman who will never pay any attention to me, who will brush me off right away so I can leave and go to my hotel room before somebody beats me up again. Then, I can watch porn until I fall asleep, because I need to get up early. I have important business tomorrow. She, obviously, is drunker than I am. We shout to each other because the music is loud. She says she finds my accent very sexy. She likes my nose. We do shots of tequila and suck limes, sugar, and salt. I tell her about the Jack Nicholson movie; how his wife died and he went crazy. She tells me about her mother, who is also her best friend.

Staggering, we leave the bar. At the last moment, I remember to visit the condom machine in the bathroom. Grapes and raspberry are tonight's flavors. *Grapy* or *Berry?* Stella hates flavored or colored condoms. I hate them, too. *Grapy* it is. I catch a cab. The hotel is five minutes away. The girl falls asleep in the cab. I hardly manage to drag her out. I pay the driver. We go up to my room.

"I gotta pee," she stammers. Then she disappears for about ten minutes. I get nervous. My head is spinning. So is the furniture. I shouldn't have let her go to the bathroom. I should have undressed her passionately and stuck it into her. I've had this hard-on for about an hour now. I am debating if I should beat the monkey quickly, before she returns, so I can last longer. I hear the shower.

"Hello!" I yell. No answer. "Hello?!" What is she doing in there, shooting up or something? I don't even know her name.

What's her name—Stacy? Tracy? Daisy? The bathroom door opens and a perfect, wet female body enters the room. Look at that. This journey is beginning just wonderfully. Nine days without my wife and I score a drunk Pamela Anderson. She moves closer, looking me straight in the eye. She passes me and jumps onto the bed. She gets on all fours and shakes the mattress, as if trying to check its firmness. She presses her breasts down while lifting her ass up. She looks like a cat stretching and sharpening her nails. Her index finger gestures *come here* and points toward her waxed, perked-up pussy. I understand that I have to lick. I kneel on the floor, so my mouth is at the right height. I stick my tongue in her and start licking, sucking, biting, snorting, suckling, massaging with my lips, blowing, spitting, and growling. My hands glide across her tight belly (how many hours spent weekly at the gym?), caress her round breasts, return to her ass, grab her waist, spank the firm globes, slide under, and rub her clitoris. At some point, she starts moving more energetically. She thrusts herself harder in my mouth, pushes my tongue back, and gets into a rhythm. I lick, I lick, I lick, I lick, and lick. She becomes more aggressive with her thrusts. I go deeper with my tongue. I dig in tighter. The muscle under my tongue hurts. I stop licking and start sucking. I suck. I suck. I suck her, as if sucking the poison from a snake bite. I want to suck Stella out of there and spit her back—whole, beautiful and real, fragrant as linden blossom, salty as the sea, and silent as the night. I want her, I want her, I want her.

"Come here, big boy." Tracy/Stacy/Daisy looks over her shoulder at me, flips over, and pulls me between her thighs. "Come here." Her experienced hand grabs my cock. What I don't understand is what happened to my erection. There is a numb reptile hanging between my legs. She patiently starts stroking it with one hand, while rubbing her breasts with the other. Her eyes are half-closed. Blood vessels show through the flushed skin of her neck. Her nipples are big and brown. I reach across her body and switch off the reading lamp. Then I help her get back in her previous pose, so I can continue with my tongue and buy some time until the anaconda wakes up. In the semi-darkness, her body is sliced by the yellow street light cutting through the blinds. I try more energetically with my tongue but nothing really happens. Not only my penis, but my neck gets limp, too. I can hardly hold my head up. And then, who knows why, I decide to stick my index finger in her anus. She jerks away, pushes me off of her, and jumps off the bed. She collects her scattered clothes without saying a word.

Where are you going Tracy/Stacy/Daisy? Where did you come from, and whom are you trying to forget? A moment later, I see her silhouette wobbling through the bright rectangle of the door, which slams behind her. Her footsteps fade down the hallway. And then it's quiet. I get up and drag myself to the bathroom. I have no better idea of what to do before going to sleep. Plus, I always feel better in the morning if I drop a rope after a night of drinking. I ease my ass down on the wet toilet seat and look around for something to read, out of habit. I notice her thong in the bathtub. I reach over and grab it. I touch it to my cheek and close my eyes. I recreate her perky ass, her goose-bumped vagina, and the large nipples of her silicon breasts. I quickly wrap up my business, get out of the bathroom, and throw myself across the bed. With her wet thong in my hand, I masturbate, squirt it toward the ceiling, and fall asleep, unable to make it back to the bathroom.

•

For several years, my band cycled through members, my country—governments, and Stella and I—cheaper and cheaper apartments. Then suddenly everything fell apart. Our bass player took a job as a customs officer and left, the drummer married a pop singer and both of them took off on a cruise ship to earn a living, and, on top of everything else, the lead singer caught a disease of the larynx and became practically mute. I tried playing with a couple of other bands, but it wasn't working. I couldn't make myself play other people's songs at restaurants. I spent less and less time with the guitar. Stella and I both graduated and had to find a more dignified way to surrender to reality. She could become a school teacher, I—a journalist at some local newspaper, taking pictures and writing. With our earnings, we could choose to be either permanently hungry and live closer to downtown, or be only semi-hungry and live in one of the ugly, government-built projects outside the city. We chose the latter. It was winter. We moved our stuff in a friend's Opel.

The building was in a gray, concrete neighborhood, a safe haven for gusty winds. The one-bedroom apartment was on the top floor, the balcony faced northeast, the walls were moist, and snow blew in through the loose, uninsulated windows. There was no central heating and Stella hated being cold. It was so cold there.

The good thing about this concrete box was that it had a view of the airport. Low-flying airplanes would interrupt our conversations, reminding us that something better awaited us someplace else. From time to time, when Stella wasn't home, I'd warm my fingers on the brown electric radiator and pull out the guitar to play a little. My old songs, however, sounded somewhat two-dimensional, and no new tunes would come to me. I started getting used to the notion that maybe making music was not my calling. I doubted my talent. Did I even have any talent at all? In that cold apartment, however, it was impossible to think about those things.

I had to do something. I had to leave. We had to leave together no matter what!

I spent months looking for the best way to leave the country. The easiest way was to continue our education. We both knew perfectly well where we wanted to go: America. We were both tired of waiting for our lives to start.

·

After a night like the last one I can't sleep in, which makes the next day not only painful but also long. In the window, I see the bluish light of a morning I don't want to live out, yet can't postpone, either. I eat a few triangles of Toblerone and leave the rest for later. I stay in the shower for a long time trying to somehow arrange the events of the last two days in my head. The only proof of the reality of what has happened is the bag in my trunk. If I manage to trade it wisely, I'll make a decent amount of money, I'll buy myself some time, I'll buy the equipment I need, and I'll do only what I want to do. What do I want to do, though? What do I want to do? And would it bring Stella back? I step out of the shower. There are three chocolate letters left on the table—O N E.

·

−i've never seen you cry
−i never cry
−you don't want to?
−no, i just can't
−what if i die?
−if you die, i'll cry
−a lot?
−maybe not a lot
−a little?
−a little−yes
−but you'll cry
−of course i will
−cry now, then
−i can't, i told you

·

The car is cold and smells of coconuts. I've hung six air fresheners on the rearview mirror. The clock blinks 5:40 A.M. Until I have my first espresso, nothing good can happen, so I try to remember the location of the coffee shop from last night. I find it at the corner of Henderson and Grand. I park in front of it and wait in the car until the doors open at six.

I go in. I order two doubles. I sit near the window, take out one of the notebooks I bought yesterday, and quickly scribble the few sentences that are roaming around my sleepy head. I open the road atlas I bought from Walmart for $4.97. I unfold it. There are at least two major routes I can take to the East Coast. If I take I-15 to Utah and then Highway 70 across Colorado, Kansas, and Indiana, I'll reach Ohio. Then 79 to 80 and then directly to New York, which is my final destination. I have traveled this route already. I'm familiar with it, so I don't even need the atlas. It's picturesque and I like it a lot. That's why I take the other one—whatever's left of the legendary Route 66—Arizona, New Mexico, Texas, Oklahoma, Missouri, Illinois, Indiana, Ohio, Pennsylvania . . . to the East Coast.

•

I sold the Stratocaster. We got married. City hall, church, restaurant, guests, relatives, dancing, photos, videos—we went through all of it. We did it because we needed the money for America.

We were both admitted as graduate students at Ohio State University to complete our master's degrees in literature. We borrowed more money from friends and relatives, paid the first semester's tuition, and took off.

It was my first time on a plane. We first flew to the Czech Republic and then to America. Somewhere in the white clouds above Prague, I felt some kind of lightness, unfamiliar lightness. It was liberating.

We landed in Columbus late at night. The air was cool, innocently clean, and filled with unknown scents. In the sky above the airport, a two-tailed comet shared the night with myriad tiny stars and a few airplanes. This comet would be visible for two more weeks. Then it would go on its way and appear again in twenty-some centuries, explained the chubby cab driver while he helped us fit our luggage into the trunk of the yellow car.

The next morning we walked down foreign streets and inhaled the springtime air of Ohio. The earth was beginning to soften, the soil breathed out warmth, squirrels ran up the trees, wild geese swam in the ponds, passersby smiled at us, and we smiled back.

To my academic program, I added two photography classes. Stella would go to school early in the morning. She started working in the library in the afternoons and painting in the evenings in the loft of an old factory building that had been taken over by some fellow artists. I spent my days in the university and in the photo lab. Then, by pure luck, I found a bartending job. I started making decent money, which paid for my education. Besides, I was freelancing as a photographer here and there, which brought us some income as well. My only free hours—from midnight until eight in the morning—I spent in the uniform of a security guard at a Budweiser plant, dozing off—dizzy from the smell of hops and the immense scale of my own plans. I can't remember ever being busier. Stella and I hardly saw each other.

Then I met Ken. The money I made with him was enough to buy my first professional photo equipment and quit one of my jobs. I felt strong, bursting with energy. I knew that something glorious awaited me somewhere.

•

I find a payphone and call Danny again.

"Listen, bro. I need to ask you two things, right off the bat," he says.

"Go ahead."

"First, does Stella know anything about this?"

"Stella is not here."

"Does she know about this?"

"No."

"Do you understand what you're risking?"

"Oh, please."

"You should be shot."

"I know. Someone tried already."

"Is there a way to talk you out of this nonsense?"

"No." I answer. On the other end—silence. Then:

"OK. Let me tell you that I'll do this for you just this one time, OK?"

"OK."

"No! I really want you to promise me that this is a 'one-time-only' deal and that it will never happen again."

"I promise!"

"What do you promise?"

"It won't happen again."

"OK, then." Danny sounds as if he's trying to suppress his excitement. "I spoke with Boss."

"Oh, *the Boss?*"

"Yes, *the Boss.* His name is Boss. Victor Boss."

"Well? What did *Boss* say?"

"Well . . . it's serious."

"What is?"

"The whole thing."

"The whole thing?"

"Yes."

"Really?"

"It's serious."

"You just told me that."

"Listen, man, you normally don't buy things like that from

strangers. Who knows who you are? Plus . . . the guy has his own supplies . . . Plus, in this business everybody knows everybody. I'm at the bottom of the ladder. In principle, it's not impossible to take care of the whole thing at once, but . . ."

"What? How much money can we make?" I ask the most important question.

"That depends, demand and supply, the quality of the weed and so on. If everything's fine and the marijuana is as good as you describe it, we're talking about approximately fifty grand."

"Fifty?" I exclaim, slightly disappointed.

"Fifty, if everything's cool, if it's excellent! That's the high number."

"How about the low one?"

"I can't say until you come here. It might be twenty. It's between twenty and fifty. But there's also something else."

"What?"

"Victor is not in New York now. Something's happened and he flew to the West Coast yesterday. He's not coming back until the end of the week."

"Oh," I calculate in my mind. "Well, I thought I could be in New York the day after tomorrow."

"From California? In just three days?"

"Why not? I'm fast."

"You shouldn't be going so fast with what's in your trunk. You can come over whenever you want, but the guy won't be here before Saturday night." I can hear Danny turning the pages of a calendar in his apartment. "Saturday . . . is actually Halloween! What will you be for Halloween?"

"The Boogie Man."

"Zack . . . drive safely."

"Danny?"

"Yes."

"Thanks a lot!"

"Take care."

Danny and I go way back. I heard my first AC/DC song—"Dirty Deeds"—on his older brother's turntable. We smoked our first Dunhills together, and I was hiding in the walk-in closet of his room when he tried to have sex with his first girl. He used to draw these beautiful horses. He was a good artist and everybody knew it. He emigrated when he was eighteen and escaped mandatory military service.

•

Armed with good equipment, I started collecting a portfolio of images with which I intended to enter mainstream advertisement photography. I made up different products and took not only the photo ads for them, but also came up with whole advertising strategies—including logos, narratives, faces, imagery, and music. I spent every possible minute with the best photography books, learning from the biggest names in the business. I studied the techniques and images of photographers and artists from centuries ago to the present. I compared the light from seventeenth-century Rome in the paintings of Caravaggio to the light of mid-twentieth-century New York in the photos of DeCarava. I searched for what all the great masters had in common. I was most interested in the human face. To me, even the most boring face in Robert Frank's photos was more interesting than the most beautiful Ansel Adams landscape. What was it that could turn a face into a magnificent image? I diligently searched for the principles of iconicity. I knew they existed. I put my portfolio together carefully, going through hundreds of photo sessions, models, objects. Of course, Stella was in the silver emulsion of thousands of my negatives. What I wanted was to move to the West Coast as soon as we graduated from Ohio State. I started applying for positions in several places in L.A. and San Francisco. I exchanged e-mails, letters, and phone calls with art directors of fashion magazines who seemed interested in my images. Stella, on the other hand, had

scheduled a few job interviews with various universities. We knew our
time was coming and we had to make the leap.

Then we decided to visit New York for a couple of days before mov-
ing out West.

·

At seven I'm in the car because I have to leave L.A. before the
traffic really thickens. I take I-10 East. The sun is already up and
glinting on the backs of the cars in front of me. I try to find a
radio station that doesn't irritate me. I know that every ten or
fifteen minutes I'll have to deal with the next attack of ads—
something I have never learned to ignore after all these years in
America. Most likely I never will. The locals handle this as if they
have an implanted chip that switches their attention on and off
during commercial breaks. Maybe this mechanism is formed in
the first early years of television watching. I'm missing the "first
seven" in this respect. I grew up somewhere else, with a different
kind of television. There—I remember—we had similar reactions
to the communist propaganda, which, just like the commercials
here, kept the system going.

·

One of the reasons we went to New York was to see Danny. He and I
had talked on the phone a lot, but we hadn't seen each other in years.
I had told Stella so much about him and now I wanted to introduce
them. The idea was to fly to New York City, spend a few days there,
and take a train back to the Midwest. We arrived and the city was just
as we always imagined it—the greatest. We took a cab from LaGuardia
Airport to Brooklyn where Danny lived. And, there he was—the same
scrawny wrists, same smile, same crooked tooth, same walk, only his
eyes seemed somewhat muted. He and Stella clicked. Danny was the

epitome of a starving artist. He painted, took photos, created installa-
tions, and made a bunch of other things. He had this small camcorder
and took it everywhere, capturing thousands of hours of reality. For a
short time, he had worked as one of Christo's assistants, photographing
his installations. After that he started assisting Hito—one of the greatest
commercial photographers in New York. Danny also worked part-time
at Christie's warehouse, bubble-wrapping works of art that had been
sold during their auctions. He was a small-time drug dealer as well.
Danny talked quickly, intensely, and a lot. His thoughts jumped from
topic to topic, themes changed with the speed of his thoughts. Following
him was exhausting. We listened to Sun Ra, Miles Davis, John Coltrane.
At the end of the first night, he pulled out a big bong and we smoked
something. That was a first for me. I remember how his head became
more three dimensional than it actually was. Stella refused to smoke
with us. Later, I vomited endlessly and went to bed cursing myself.

The next day Danny suggested we go to a French painter's opening
reception. The invitation read:

BERNARD FOUCAULT
THE BEGINNING OF THE END
Contemporary French Painting

It was hot and humid. We wandered the streets all day long, visiting
galleries, tourist spots, coffee shops, and bars. I was fascinated by the
city in an inexplicable way. I had never thought that something like
this—being captivated by a place—even existed. I always look skepti-
cally at people who are in awe of San Francisco, London, Paris, Rome,
and Venice. Why?

In Manhattan, I took photos of streets, displays, sky, buildings, trees,
people. I tried to capture the entire afternoon. Fourteen rolls of black-
and-white film later, we stopped back at Danny's place, showered, and
went to the opening. The gallery was in Chelsea. It was crowded. The
wine wasn't bad; there were fruit and cheese platters, cocktail napkins,

toothpicks, grapes, and crackers. His paintings. Oh, his paintings were huge. Saturated, thick layers of oil paint with almost no imagery—only distant, cold colors—as if extracted from the intestines of extinct reptiles. Here and there, the eye managed—with great difficulty—to discern silhouettes of reclining men. A sense of something monumental, or rather minimally monumental (is there such a thing?), emanated mostly from the enormous size of the canvases. The paintings, however, hovered over me in a way I didn't quite like. The feeling deep down in my gut—the one that always jumped whenever I came across real art—was now dormant, leaving me indifferent. I shared that with Stella. She gave me a look as if I had farted in a church.

I continued with wine and cheese until, eventually, things started falling into place. At some point, Danny introduced The Artist—I had already labeled him that, because of his pretentious beard and his manner of speaking, that consistently annoying "u-u-uh" before uttering the most banal thought. I had my Leica with me. I photographed him. I photographed him and his paintings, him against a gigantic self-portrait as a background. He was very open to the idea of being photographed. He wasn't posing, yet he didn't give off that careless attitude toward the camera I have noticed in some artists. He just looked at the camera, his dark eyes hiding nothing and saying nothing. I remember that Stella moved slowly and pensively, as if in a trance. On our way out, I noticed tears in her eyes. After the show, Danny, the Artist, his manager, Stella, and I dove into a nearby bar. He was painfully sensitive each time the conversation shifted to his art, but the terminology he used to describe it was pathetic. And it wasn't because he didn't have a good command of the language—he had studied and lived in America much longer than I had and spoke excellent English with a slight French accent—but simply because everything he said was completely unoriginal. I aggravated him ceaselessly, assaulting him when he least expected it, mocking the clichés with which he shielded himself. I didn't stop fucking with his idea of high art, which I loathed and in which he believed. From time to time, my eyes would catch

Stella's and I read such astonishment in them—as if she had caught me
playing with a lamb with a knife in my hand.
   We stayed in the bar until they closed and kicked us out. We said
goodbye to Bernard Foucault and his manager, promising that we'd
see each other again. He kissed me, slipped his card in my palm, and
insisted that we give him a call if we were ever in Paris. Stella and I
stayed in New York for three more days, seeing anything and every-
thing we could in the galleries and museums, We went out in the eve-
nings, ate pizza slices for $1.50 by the metro stations, and spent all our
money on jazz clubs, CDs, and books.
   The last day in Manhattan, we walked and walked and walked,
and Danny followed us everywhere with his camcorder, filming. At
Penn Station we said goodbye, parted ways, and Stella and I got on
the train and left New York.

·

I step on the gas and open the window.

   I am in San Bernardino around eight. I decide to stop and grab
something to eat before I hit the desert.

   I see a mall in the middle of nowhere. The billboards have
been erected into the blue sky, each taller than the next and each
more annoying than the previous one. Gas stations, fast-food restaurants, auto dealers, shops all raise their hands so you spot them
first. I park in front of Henry's. The strong desert wind chases
empty shopping carts around the half-empty parking lot. I grab
one and enter the store. I fill the cart with nuts, chips, Toblerones,
and some other stuff. I pay and get out. At the other end of the
lot, I see a Bank of America branch—the bank where Stella and
I have our checking account. I go in, say "Hi" to the girl behind
the counter, and withdraw a thousand in new twenty-dollar bills.

   There are four gas stations at the four corners of the intersection. The food clientele is torn between McDonald's, Burger King,

Taco Bell, Chinchiladas, Taste of China, and Thai Paradise. I can imagine the confusion of those fat people with their stomachs constantly inflamed by hunger, standing in the center of this enormous parking lot, surrounded by choices they would rather not make. I keep looking around as I get in the car and spot the purple sign of a pawn shop reading JEWELRY WORLD AND LOANS. Underneath, written directly on the window pane in white paint is "We Install Batteries." There is a picture of two tiny bells. There is also a picture of two white doves carrying a sign in their beaks: GIVE HER DIAMONDS.

•

—will you hold this card in front of you for a second, i have to measure the light?
—what is this?
—a gray card
—i can see that
—eighteen percent gray
—eighteen percent gray?
—it's a term, eighteen percent gray
—why do you need this eighteen percent gray card?
—i adjust the light meter with it. here, see—i point it at the gray card, like this, and the light meter now "knows" that this gray is eighteen percent gray. so, it can calculate what is darker or lighter than this gray. you see, every light meter, no matter how precise, needs a starting point. the color value of this card here is the universal starting point for all light meters—it's eighteen percent gray . . .
—eighteen percent?
—gray. just don't ask me why it's eighteen percent
—i won't. it's a weird number, though
—the half-way point between black and white

—why do they call it *black-and-white* photography then? why not
gray?
—*gray* photography just doesn't sound right, i guess. even
though it is more fitting, since it reflects everything in nuances
of gray.
—do you still want me to hold this card?
—the beauty of every photograph, Stella, is in the development
of its middle values, in the gray. black and white are simply
extremes without which even the most interesting negative
seems to be lacking contrast. the life of photographs is actually
in their middle values
—i understand. so we keep going?
—we keep going

•

Ohio was as flat as a parking lot and almost equally as interesting,
compared to the sidewalks of New York with which Stella fell in love.
I, on the other hand, could not wait to accelerate my life in what I
believed was America's fastest lane: Los Angeles. We said goodbye
to our friends in Columbus, rented a U-Haul, packed everything we
owned, and set off for California.

If you are debating about whether or not to share your life with
someone, try getting in a vehicle and driving together for five days.
Had the honeymoon preceded the wedding, how many marriages
would never have happened, how many emotions would go unwasted?

The four days during which Stella and I crossed the continent were
some of the finest of our lives.

When we arrived in Los Angeles, a murky red sun was setting in
the Pacific Ocean at the same time that an impossibly big moon was
rising over the hills. We kissed between the two for a long time. It felt
like we were on a movie set.

The first couple of weeks, we lived in a hotel. Stella went to nine interviews with reliable employers who were supposed to call her at any moment. The moment stretched into weeks.

Things did not look much brighter for me, either. A few months after we moved, there was only one place left where I had not shown my portfolio. Two of the art directors I was absolutely sure would employ me did not even return my calls. Three others stood me up about eleven times. In the end, I was happy to be given a chance to show my portfolio to four more people, three of whom were receptionists. In two publishing companies, I was patted on the shoulder with the promise of a call "as soon as something comes up." Nobody had told me then that this was the way people talk in L.A. I had mistaken their words for truth. I had taken their small talk for promises.

In the waiting room of a small magazine—my last resort—I spent an hour and a half watching people go in and out. I was reading the Employment Opportunities *section of a forgotten Sunday paper. In the* Photography *section, there were five ads altogether—two for school photographers, one for a gig photographing dogs and newborn babies, and one for printing in a large black-and-white lab. Because the ads were in alphabetical order, my eyes were drawn to the previous section—*Pharmaceutical*—where the job openings were two pages long.*

"Fred, where are we going for lunch?" I was startled when I heard the familiar voice of the art director with whom I had had several very promising conversations when I was harmlessly far away in Ohio. I realized that I had been sitting there the whole morning. A slender, dark-haired man wearing an Armani blazer walked energetically out the door. We finally "met in person."

Steven.

He held my hand a beat longer than normal. His palm was small, dry, and a few degrees softer than mine. He looked me in the eye with a stare in which there was nothing even remotely resembling anything but indifference. We were in the hallway. I started telling him how long I had worked on this and that, and how we had just moved, and how I could not wait to . . .

"Zack," he interrupted me. "Do you have a web site?"

"No, but I have my portfolio right here."

"Zack, do me a favor. Leave it with Jennifer, will you? When I come back from lunch, I'll look at it and I'll call you later this week." Australian accent? South African?

Steven's cell phone rang, he picked it up, his face lit up, he dug in his blazer pocket, and waved goodbye to me, holding car keys on a BMW key chain. He turned around, and walked down the hallway, joyfully rushing toward his lunch with Fred. I watched his Armani getting smaller and smaller in the gray hallway. I wanted to be naïve then. I wanted to be able to trust people. Even people with soft palms, Armani suits, fake British accents, and empty blue eyes . . . oh, how I wanted that! I so knew that the phony would never call me. And he didn't.

•

Since I was a kid, I've always liked to look in pawn shops to see what people have left there to earn a few bucks. Now, however, I'm only interested in this place's music collection. The owner has just opened the shop. It's dim, with that typical stale smell mixed with the odor of carpet-cleaning products. I start digging through a bunch of tapes and CDs of jazz, soul, rock and roll. My trip will be long and—I hope—uneventful, so instead of searching the radio stations, I want to listen to music I choose myself. The owner looks at me with a blend of suspicion and suppressed curiosity. Perhaps he is waiting for me to start looking over my shoulder toward the door before reaching into my back pocket and pulling out a golden ring for sale. Instead, I grab a few albums by Sting, Louis Armstrong, Joey di Francesco, Al Di Meola, U2, Thelonious Monk, Tupac Shakur, and Paganini. I had just pulled out a twenty dollar bill to pay when I notice the camera display. Cheap, two or three pixel digital cameras, old broken film junk, Polaroids, cracked flashes, scratched, odd-sized filters . . . What catches my eye, though, is a deeply scarred Nikon FM body with a crooked prism and a worn-out 50 mm lens. What has this guy been through? Who's left it here? I ask if I can take a closer look. The owner unlocks the display and hands it to me. Up close, it looks even worse. Sad, lonely, and distrustful is this Nikon. As if he understands that he doesn't belong here. But even if he had not been in this prison, he would not have found a place for himself in this silicon-operated, digital photo-universe with countless automatic functions. He is one aging analog model with an ordinary lens and a manual focus—too much of past, a sad present. No future.

I try its shutter speeds one by one—they seem just fine. It even has a working battery in the light meter. I point it outside and it seems to measure the light accurately—f 8 at 1/16 of a second. At this time of day, with 100 film, that's what I would expect. The shutter blades sound like they should—with that barely perceptible metallic ring. The manual focus is not that great, but still, it's OK. How much? One hundred and fifteen dollars. I don't even try to negotiate. The owner swiftly grabs the crisp bills from my hand before I change my mind. I ask where the closest photo store is. He steps outside to show me which way to go and how many blocks to drive south before turning right. I find it easily. The store clerk is an old-timer with thick prescription glasses. By the register, there is a large bin full with out-of-date film stock on sale—seventy-five cents a piece. I buy a few color Fuji's and twenty-five black-and-white, long-expired rolls of Ilford and Kodak. I ask if the store carries developing chemicals. The clerk laughs—who deals with developing nowadays? Everybody shoots digital. Why don't I buy a digital camera? These right here, for example, are on sale.

No, thanks.

.

After failing to find work as a photographer, I decided to look for a job in a photo lab. One of the most famous ones on the West Coast was The Black and White. *I went there on a hot afternoon with my portfolio in hand. Bob Evans, a disciple and friend of Ansel Adams, had been the owner of the place for fifty years. A bell above my head rang as I entered the store. Bob himself appeared. A gray beard hung down over his blue, rubber apron. He carried an enlarged digital print of a snowy mountain.*

"How can I help you?"

"Yes. I'm looking for a job."

"Fill out an application."

"Mister Evans, could you, please . . ." I tried to take out my portfolio to show him my work—everything in this folder had gone through my hands—photographing, developing negatives, printing.

"Fill out the application first and we'll call you if something . . ." He interrupted, without looking at me, carefully placing the snowy mountain against the wall.

"Could you . . . ?" I opened my portfolio and laid it before him. Only a flick of his eyeballs and he would have seen my masterpieces. He, however, didn't take his eyes off the stupid mountain. He wrinkled his nose, squinted his eyes, and pointed toward a pile of forms in the corner.

"The applications are over there." I stared at him for a while. What if I had grabbed him by the beard and swept the floor with his old fart ass? The phone rang, he picked it up. I snapped my portfolio shut and slammed the door behind me. The bell kept ringing as I crossed the parking lot.

●

I leave the store with that feeling of a job well-started. I need these kinds of feelings the most now. On my way to the car, I note that I haven't been sad about Stella for almost an hour. I feel like screaming. I load the Nikon with color film and shoot it quickly, choosing different light situations—as much I can in a San Bernardino parking lot—I need to check how well it works. I pull out the roll of film and go into the closest CVS with a photo center—a big machine which every cashier operates when they are not busy with customers. I leave the film with a lady in a checkered uniform and roam around the store while I wait for the results. Thirty minutes later, I hold the warm pictures in my hands. Wonderful. I smile, jump in the car, pat my new friend, make him comfortable on the passenger's seat, and head toward the sun.

•

About fifty miles east of Los Angeles, I enter the California desert and my rock station is interrupted by the voice of an evangelical preacher from the airwaves of a local Christian radio station. For a while I drive between the frequencies, U2 in one ear, religion in the other, Stella in the middle. I notice that I'm running out of gas. I realize I have to refuel soon as I adjust the seat to make it more comfortable. There are very few cars on the road, so I fly at over ninety miles per hour. Then I remember what's in the trunk and slow down—it's time for me to start taking that into consideration.

. . . your sins, your transgressions, he took upon himself . . . the . . . z-h-z-h-h-z-h-z-h-b-z-z-b-z-b-z-b-z-z-j-j-j-j . . . our sins . . . z-z-z-z-z-z-z-z-z-z-zd-z-d-z-z-z-zz-z . . . Christ died on the cross for . . . z-b-z-b-z-z-z-z-b-z-b-z-z-b-z-b-b-b-z-z-b-z-z-z-z-z-z-z-z-z-z-z-z-z . . . let us repent for . . . f-f-f-f-f-ff-f-f-f-f-f-f-f-f-f-f-f-f-f-z-z-z-z-f-z-f-z-f-f-f-z-f-f-z-f-f-z-z-z-z-z-z-z-z-z-f-z-f-z-f-z-f-sin . . .*'s gonna ride your wild hors-e-e-e-e-s?* z-s-z-s-z-s-z-s-z-s-z-s-z-s-z-s-z-z-z-z-z . . . enter the Kingdom of Heaven . . . *Who's gonna drown in your blue sea? . . .* s-s-s-s-s-s-z-z-z-z-z-z-z-z *. . . hey hey sha la la, hey hey.*

•

—hey zack, I know what we have to do
—what?
—i'll tell you, but first put the camera down and massage my bootie
—with pleasure. so what were you saying?
—we have to conquer the world!
—when?
—right away
—you and me?
—me and you
—why?
—why what?
—conquer the world?
—for . . . fun
—massaging your bootie is fun
—yes, it is fun
—so why conquer a world in which there is no bootie sweeter than yours?
—you're not conquering the whole world for just one bootie, silly
—then why conquer it?
—because you have to
—i have to?
—hell, yeah!

•

. . . sha la la, hey hey sha la la who's gon-n-a ride your wild hors-e-e-e-s, who's gonna drown in your . . . d-z-z-h-g-h-j-j-j-j-j-j-j-j-z-z-z . . . are born in sin . . . *hey hey, sha la la, hey hey, sha la la.*

I squeeze the last chords of music from the radio just before I pass the sign for Sun City (population 56,327)—I am now entirely on the preacher's frequency.

He finishes his morning sermon with the parable about a master who, upon leaving his home to travel, calls his servants and entrusts them with his property. "Now, to one he gives five; to another, he gives two talents; and to the last, just one—to each servant, according to his ability. According to my dictionary here, one talent in those days would be between ten thousand and thirty thousand dollars now. Let's agree on ten. It was a lot of money then. It still is. So, the first man starts a business and makes five more talents. The second also manages to double his talents. The third one decides to play it safe and buries his talent in the ground. Then, after some time, the master returns and asks to settle accounts with the servants. The first one returns ten talents. The master says "Great job, servant. Come, sit next to me, enter into the joy of your master." The second gives the master two talents more than he had left him. The master is pleased "Well done, trustworthy servant. Enter into the joy of your master." The third servant says "Look, master. I know you are a difficult man, reaping where you haven't sown and gathering where you haven't winnowed. So, I didn't want to risk anything. I was afraid of your anger and that's why I hid my talent in the ground. Here, you can have it back." The master says: "You wicked and slothful slave! You know that I reap where I don't sow and gather where I have not winnowed. If you didn't want to use your talent, you should have at least invested it with the bankers, so I could collect it with interest when I came back." The servant shrugs his shoulders because he doesn't know what to say. "Now," the master yells, "take his talent from him and give it to the one who has ten. For, to every one who has, more shall be given, and he will have abundance. But from him who does not have, even what he has, will be taken away! And throw the useless servant into the outer darkness, where there will be weeping and gnashing of teeth!"

The pastor quickly interprets the parable and reminds us that he'll be expecting us in church tomorrow. Whoever has to work can purchase tomorrow's sermon on audiotape for $29.99 or on compact disk for $39.99. God bless us. I turn off the radio.

·

After about two months of futile efforts, I let down my guard completely and started working in a small camera store called Super Photo, located in an open mall. They hired me because I lied on the application that I didn't have the necessary education or experience but am a fast learner. The owners were a tiny Korean guy and his wife, with whom he constantly quarreled. His name was William, and his wife's— I don't remember. He paid only ten bucks an hour, still better than nothing. There wasn't too much to do anyway. After the first two weeks of training, he began letting me work on my own. The most humiliating aspect of this enterprise, however, was that I had to suffer William's attitude toward my work. The pictures I printed for my customers were scrutinized and showered with criticism. He found them either too dark or with too much yellow and blue, either the contrast was not right, or something else was off. As time passed, I realized that his disapproval had nothing to do with me or my printing but, rather, was an emotional vent for his relationship with his wicked wife. She always had her hair and nails done, she protected herself from the sun with an umbrella, and for lunch she ate food with too much onion which made her breath unbearable the second half of the day. The customers who came to the studio liked my work and complimented it in front of

William. Since I worked fast, they would leave their film in the store, go shopping in the mall, return later, pay, and go home pleased, only to come back with the next finished roll. William gradually adjusted his vision to mine, and his nagging became more subdued and less irritating. His wife started buying me sandwiches for lunch and giving me some extra money at the end of the week.

Stella also found a low-paying job at a private art school, but kept looking for a position as a college teacher. During those first difficult months in California, I remember she painted light, small watercolors and left them on the balcony to dry. The warm wind blew gently on them. They sometimes flipped over, fluttering. I liked those ethereal creatures, I collected them, some of them I framed and hung on the wall.

Things had just started looking up, when one day there was a complication. It showed up in the negatives of a cheery, redheaded gentleman with a mustache and hairy forearms, holding a heavy automatic rifle and stepping with his boot on the head of a dead African elephant. Several black men with rifles also were looking at the camera, smiling. I printed several pictures in disbelief until I confirmed that the elephant was real and the pictures authentic. I jumped up and showed this barbarity to William, who was sifting through the mail. The Korean narrowed his eyes, threw a reproachful look over his spectacles and, with the electric bill in hand, pointed me back to my work.

"William," I said. "This here is an African elephant. Is it not an endangered species?"

"I don't know," said William, continuing to browse through the junk mail.

"William," I insist. "We have to notify the authorities. The African elephant is in the Red Book."

"Are the prom pictures ready?"

"William, listen, this is illegal and atrocious. To kill an animal and photograph yourself with the body, in this case, a Red Book cadaver..."

"Don't meddle in things you don't know anything about. What happened with the prom pict...?"

"This man is a monster, William!"

The Korean suppressed his reaction and said, "This man is Mister Richard O'Reilly. He lives in Rancho Santa Fe and builds shopping malls just like this one." A broad gesture with his arm followed. "For fifteen years, Mr. O'Reilly has been developing negatives from all his safaris here alone. He brings in hundreds of rolls. What do you want me to do?"

"You do whatever you want, William, but I cannot sit here and make color corrections of the negatives of a serial killer!"

"Why do you say that?" He asks cagily.

"Don't you see him posing with murdered animals?"

"So?" He leans closer to me. "So? Who says he was the one who killed them?"

"William," I snapped. "You know very well he killed them. Why would he pose with them if he didn't?"

"That might be, but how are you going to prove that he killed them himself? Huh? What are you going to do? Sue him? Who are you? You think his lawyers won't crush you to pieces because you've decided to spoil the weekend of a respectable American citizen just because he decided to pose with a dead African elephant?" Pause. "And you better change the chemicals in the developer before the machine jams up again!"

"I changed the chemicals last Tuesday!"

"Change them again!"

I sat down back behind the printing machine and selected one of Mr. O'Reilly's negatives. In the "quantity" box of the touch screen display, I typed in 1000. In "size," I put 8x10 inches, and pressed the start button. I got up and methodically began organizing my work area. William stopped looking at his mail and, for a while, just observed me.

A group of school boys and girls entered the shop and started checking out the small digital cameras on display. I was expected to ask them if I could help. I didn't. William threw me a murderous look, quickly got up, and went over to the kids, forcing a smile. I continued to

silently and slowly clean up around myself. William was split between
the group of kids and me. I gathered my things, put on my jacket, lifted
the small divider, and got on the other side of the counter. William's
face tightened:

> *"Hey, hey, where are you going?"*
> *I didn't answer.*
> *"Hey, come back here and finish your work!"*
> *I didn't even look at him.*
> *"Hey! Hey, wait!" The kids, sensing the conflict in the air, looked at*
> *me, then at him, then back at me. I waited to be sure the printer started*
> *spitting out the first enlarged photos of Mr. O'Reilly stepping on the*
> *big, dead animal. I left the store, lifted up my hood, and shoved my*
> *hands deep in my pockets. It was cloudy and was getting chilly.*

•

The sun is high already. I turn the AC on and start thinking about
the weed in the trunk. This, for sure, is the most absurd of all the
schemes in my life so far. I don't even know how to roll a joint,
yet I'm on my way to sell dozens of pounds. I know I have to keep
it moist and fresh so it'll be more expensive—I know that much.

I remember, some years back somebody had brought some
marijuana to a party and there were lemon peels in the zip lock
bag. To keep the weed moist, they explained. In this heat, I should
probably do something like that now, too. My gas level light has
been blinking bright red for at least twenty minutes now. I take
the next exit to Pamona.

•

> —what are these feathers?
> —wings
> —do you have to photograph me with them?

—yes

—zack, i've seen a million pictures of naked women with wings

—yeah, me too. now please, turn around so i can figure out how

to attach them

—they're heavy

—stop complaining

—i'm not compl . . .

—stella, please!

•

Pamona is a small town ten miles from the freeway. I pass farms with tractors and combines, decaying buildings with rusting tin roofs, chicken farms, grazing cows, horses, and tall eucalyptus trees. At the first blinking red traffic light, I stop to make way for an elderly man in a cowboy hat pulling three llamas tied to a rope behind him. They glide across the zebra crosswalk. The last one stops for a second and looks me straight in the eye. I reach for my camera but the cowboy tugs at the animal. It blinks heavily and lazily moves on. At this moment, I realize that from now on the Nikon will always be loaded and within reach.

Llamas . . . I must have been seven or eight at the time. The circus would come in our town every summer. So, there we were. My mom and I were standing in front of a poster which claimed that we'd see "tigers, lions, and *lamias*."[1] I wasn't that interested in tigers and lions; I had seen them jump through burning hoops before. My imagination was tickled by the word *lamia*. In my juvenile imagination, these were mythological creatures—the dragons from the illustrated fairy tales I would read over and over tirelessly. My mom bought tickets, we sat in our seats, and I

---

1   *Lamia* is Bulgarian for "dragon."

waited for the performance. How intense was my disappointment when, instead of three-headed fire-breathing *lamias*, they pulled several scrawny, sheep-like creatures with long necks and sad eyes on stage. Llamas.

.

We ran out of money. Stella found another job at a center for mentally challenged children. I continued ironing a fresh shirt each morning and making the rounds at advertisement agencies, studios, and photo labs, with less and less success. Then I started selling my lenses one by one. In the job section of the Sunday papers my attention was inevitably drawn to "Pharmaceuticals" as it was closest to "Photography." Then I found work in a wedding photography studio. The owner, Madam Solomon, was a five-hundred pound Jewish woman who wore a wig and crimson lipstick on her gargantuan mouth. As soon as she hired me, she began training me in her own trademark method of photographing weddings. I had to watch hours and hours of her training videos, memorize a set number of compulsory poses, and strictly adhere to her manual. Madam Solomon's plan was to create a standard mode of photographing brides and grooms who, regardless of circumstances, were to always look the same. For this purpose, Madam Solomon had hired many photographers like me who had to shoot with the same cameras, the same settings, the same lighting, and the same printing materials. The goal was for all of us, regardless of who we were, to achieve absolutely identical results. Madam Solomon had set up shops in seven states, but her goal was, in seven years, to open seven times as many. This was just the beginning, though, because America was simply one of the markets for her wedding business. Madam Solomon was determined to become the McDonald's of wedding photography.

I swallowed my pride and shot six weddings for her. She hated my photos and swore not to pay me because my stubbornness was "beyond belief." Nothing of her "standard expectations" had been met. Her methods had not been applied at any of my weddings. The customers, however, loved my pictures and the monster didn't fire me. She just held my money until "I learned how to take photographs" according to her manual. I shot five more weddings. After the last one she finally agreed to write me the check I needed so much. Just before she did, Carla Solomon suffered a massive aneurism in the restaurant of the Bellagio Hotel in Las Vegas, watching the water fountain show.

She died with her wig stuck in a plate of fried calamari.

•

The town looks deserted. I find the store I'm looking for. Its name is Orchard and it's located on the only main street. I park in the scorched lot and enter the store. It's cool inside. The prices are laughable compared to those in Los Angeles. I buy ten lemons for a dollar. Add a gallon of water. I move toward the register when I see the cherries. Big, red, and *lots of them*. I haven't eaten cherries for years, I realize, and these look as if they have just been picked from the tree. I try one. My mouth waters from sweetness, coolness, and childhood nostalgia. I buy four pounds. The clerk is around thirty years old, pushing two hundred pounds, short, with peeled-off nail polish, a wedding ring, dark circles under her eyes, and a badge with the name "Melody" on it. She asks me what I'm going to do with so many lemons. I pause for a moment before answering:

"Lemonade."

"You're not from here." She says, packing the fruit.

"No."

"Huh . . . and where are you from?"

"From far away."

"It's probably beautiful there."

I take the bags. "It is." She fixes a bleached strand of hair over her forehead and hands me the change, muttering, "It's probably nice."

I take the dollar thirty-six. "It's nice." I shove the money in my pocket. "Melody, is there a coffee shop somewhere around here?"

"A coffee shop?"

"A coffee shop. Where they serve espresso?"

"They only sell donuts here." Her face somewhat brightens. "There's no *expresso* here."

"No espresso, huh?"

"Nope."

"How about close by somewhere?"

"There's a fancy coffee shop in Ramona. On Main and Seventh. They make *expresso* there."

"Ramona?"

"Ramona. A little town nearby."

"Where is Ramona?"

"Go straight on Main Street until it becomes 67th, you get out of Pamona and ten miles down is Ramona."

"So, I leave Pamona, drive down 67th, and get to Ramona."

"Yes, sir."

"Thanks very much, Melody!"

"Sure thing!"

"Take care, Melody!" I'm just about to leave, but she points to my face.

"Does it hurt?"

"Excuse me?"

"Your face . . . the bruise . . . what's it from?" She inquires with genuine compassion.

"Oh, this?" I touch the skin under my eye ever so slightly. "Nothing serious. I fell down the stairs." Good girl, good person. I'd rather not think about her right now. I know that if I start thinking about her life in Pamona, about her no-fewer-than-three kids, about the husband with his wife-beater and a can of Budweiser in front of the big-ass flat screen, about her hidden bottle of vodka in the garage, about her Prozac . . . There we g-o-o-o-o . . . there goes my craziness again. I don't care about Melody and her misery. I don't care about Pamona and Ramona. I don't care about any of this. I care about a double espresso. What a surprise, I'm angry again. Well, now, let's eat a lot of red cherries. I get in my car, open the bag, set it on my lap, and start driving down the only street in the deserted town. I don't eat—I shove cherries into my mouth, spitting pits all over.

•

Back to the Sunday paper, back to CAREERS, where I'd find two or three ads under the PHOTO section and whole pages with "WANTED" under PHARMA. Unwillingly, I started peeking at them. The job opportunities were abundant. All one needed was an appropriate education and several years of experience. After reading the ads more closely, I started noticing that for one of the occupations—Clinical Research Associate, known also as a "monitor"—there was a far more liberal attitude toward the required education and experience.

I sold two of my four Carl-Zeiss lenses, as well as five Nikkors, in order to buy a used Toyota.

I started searching the Internet and gathering information about a monitor's duties. I acquainted myself with their experiences and the problems they encountered. I registered in their Internet forums and joined their discussions. I learned that a big pharmaceutical or biotechnological company invests an average of five billion dollars before a new drug developed in a lab reaches the market. Once a new heartburn drug, for example, has been discovered and developed by scientists, and enough satisfactory information has been gathered on its quality and non-clinical safety, then the FDA may grant approval for a clinical trial involving humans. The company developing the drug (also called

the "sponsor") then outsources the job to a clinical research organiza-
tion, also called the "investigator." The investigator, over the next five
or six years, recruits volunteers with predetermined characteristics,
administers the treatment, and collects data on the patients' health.
Some of the volunteers are treated with the new drug, some are given
a placebo, some are assigned randomly, some studies are blinded, some
double-blinded, so even the researchers don't know what is a placebo
and what is not. Then the data is sent back to the sponsor. The sponsor
analyzes it and decides to go ahead with the drug or not. The monitors
work for the investigators. The monitors oversee the clinical trial. The
monitors spend half their days in hospitals comparing data collected
from the subjects of the study, checking if signatures are in the right
places, making sure names match. Monitors have the easiest and most
boring job in the CAREERS section in the paper. They also make
between fifty and a hundred and fifty thousand a year.

I sold another Carl-Zeiss and one Nikon body. California swallowed
up my equipment, plans, dreams, and ideas one by one. California
cooled down my eagerness, sucked up my energy, and in just a few
months stripped me down to despair.

California—it became clear—had no use for me or my images. What
California needed was the next drug.

.

I drive out of Pamona. Large stratus clouds, blue skies, dried-out
trees, hills in yellow and brown, cacti, round rocks. San Pasqual
Valley—the *only* battle the Mexicans won in the Mexican-Amer-
ican War—took place right here. Only about twenty people from
both sides were killed in the battle. Man, they must have run
up and down these stony hills like goats. Rifles must have fired,
blood must have turned black on these very rocks, vultures must
have circled up in the blue sky. I pass an ostrich farm and enter
Ramona. I find the coffee shop. It's called Packard's and it turns

out to be a trailer with an awning over the sidewalk. I go in. It is cramped and unbearably hot. There's an old espresso machine. Behind the counter, a girl is filing her nails. I ask how much a double espresso is.

"The espresso is a dollar fifty, so—three dollars for two."

"I don't want two espressos, just one double."

"I still have to run two. Two times one-fifty is three dollars."

I take a deep breath and try again, calmly.

"You got a manager here?"

"No."

"I want to talk to a manager." She leans in and without a word points with her nail file at a pay phone on the sidewalk across the street. I don't move. I stare. Long pause. Why don't I just pay for two espressos and leave as soon as possible? It is what it is. There's no Starbucks around, there's no Pete's Coffee—one-fifty single, a dollar seventy-five double, a smiling, fast grad student with a pierced tongue behind the counter, helpful manager around somewhere, wireless internet, sepia photos on the walls, styled leather lounge furniture, air conditioning, intelligent music, and well-intentioned people. I left all that behind, in the big city.

I turn around and slowly walk out. I go to my car. I reach through the open window and pull out the Nikon, a notebook, and a pen. I take a few wide shots of the trailer/coffee shop. Then I go back in and without asking for permission, I start taking pictures of the girl. At first, she's stunned. Then she remembers that she won't look good frowning, so few shots latter, she starts smiling as she thinks she is supposed to if she wants to be in a magazine. She even tries posing. The window to the right above her provides a diffused, almost Rembrandtesque lighting. I snap a dozen shots and order a double espresso. Almost disappointed I wrapped up so quickly, she asks: "For the paper?"

"Which paper?"

"Our paper."

"No."

"Three dollars."

"Three dollars." I give her three dollars and fifty cents. Why am I doing this? Because I'm a good guy, that's why.

"That's it? Fifty cents?" She exclaims, disappointedly handing me an unclean ceramic cup. "Fifty cents for the pictures? Can't you be more generous, man! Go-ss-sh!"

I give her an annihilating look, throw the camera over my shoulder, and, without a word, cup in hand, I leave. It has a faded lipstick mark on the rim, and the espresso looks thin and sour before I even try it! I pick one of the four plastic tables on the sidewalk and sit down. The table shakes and half of the liquid spills. Great. It's going be awful anyway. I sip. I was wrong. It's not awful. It's disgusting.

What did I expect from the only espresso machine between Pamona, Ramona, and who knows how many more towns around here? What did I expect from rural America? What did I expect from this life anyway?

I look around. Three plastic flowerpots with artificial geraniums hang over the tables. They tremble with a breeze coming from who knows where. It's hellishly hot outside and the air above the long, empty street stands still, but here in the shade, there's a gentle breeze. Strange. Under the tent hang sun-bleached, fly-spattered, tiny national flags: Canadian, Danish, Italian, Japanese, Australian, French, one more Italian, and another one I don't recognize—horizontal stripes with red on top, yellow in the middle, and red underneath it, with a coat of arms I can't make out. On the other side of the street is a gas station under construction, temporarily enclosed in orange plastic nets. Across from it is a motel with a big illuminated turkey above the front door, The Turkey Motel. Under the turkey it says: *Dances—every Friday and Saturday.* So, people here do dance. A little further I see the sign,

La Cocina, Mexican food. Next to it is a drug store which sells all sorts of things, and catty-corner from it, there's a somewhat large restaurant named The Old Telephone. I bend over my hundred-page notebook and start writing whatever comes to mind.

·

Although I was sure no one would ask for my original diploma, I invested two hours in Adobe Photoshop creating a new, fake diploma out of my old Bulgarian one. It looked pretty decent. The black-and-white copies looked more than authentic. I chose to have graduated with a degree in neurobiology from Sofia University. The odds that any of my prospective interviewers would've studied that same field were very slim, and it would make me less vulnerable to questions about it. It turned out I was right. After I was done with my education, I searched the Internet, copied the biography of a Hungarian doctor and started putting together my own monitor resume.

I made up a Bulgarian pharmaceutical company named ALPHA-PHARMA where I was supposed to have worked for several years. I created a website for this fantasy business using retouched pictures of buildings in New Jersey. I invented a Research and Development Department which dealt with clinical research. My imaginary boss was a picture of a moron I downloaded from Google images. I named him Dr. Ivan Draganov. As for my own photo, I went to a Party City store on Claremont Street, bought a white doctor's coat for $19.99, and kept the receipt. I photographed myself smiling and then returned the merchandise. In the "References" section, I wrote a few Bulgarian phone numbers that I was sure no one would call. To ensure the American references, I bought three Motorola phones and opened three mobile telephone lines with different area codes in various parts of the country. So whoever called would have only these numbers from my job applications, and I was prepared to give references for myself.

The first job interview was scheduled around Christmas. I spent the week before that in the library, reading whatever I could about the human body, studying medical terminology—I had graduated with a degree in neurobiology after all. At night, trying to cram as much as I could about a monitor's job responsibilities, I fell asleep on my PC. The big day came and the interview lasted three hours. When it was over, I was sweating and trembling. I felt relieved the next day when they called to inform me they had chosen another candidate. The second and the third interviews were easier, shorter, yet still unsuccessful. The fourth one went well, but ended with a conference call in which I almost fell apart under a cross examination by a German working for Lindhau Research and an Indian-accented woman, her voice amplified by speakers and soaked with suspicion.

Every interview after that was a breeze. And there were many.

A month later I had offers for second interviews from several companies. After my excellent performance at two of them, both offered me positions. I asked for an absurdly high salary at the first one, ICONIQ (honestly hoping they would turn me down), and a modest one at the second (so I could turn them down). I wasn't sure what I was doing. Both companies agreed to my conditions.

I chose ICONIQ, a global, multinational corporation with headquarters in France and offices all over the world. The closest one to L.A. was in San Diego, so we had to relocate to the very border with Mexico, an hour and a half away from Los Angeles. Stella and I didn't mind moving to San Diego; in a way it reminded us of our hometown, Varna.

We rented a two-bedroom apartment in the north of the city and moved our stuff over the weekend. On Monday I was in the Human Resources office, filling out paperwork. Two hours later, the thickset HR manager stood me in front of a digital camera, I said "cheese" and the machine spat out my ID card. On it, I saw my name underneath a black-and-white photo fit for an obituary.

Then I realized why they hired me so fast—they desperately needed

monitors for the development of a new generation of drugs for treating
clinical depression. After billions of dollars and years of work had
been invested in that study, they now had information that a rival
pharmaceutical company was on its way to releasing a similar drug
on the market. ICONIQ was racing against the clock.

I was assigned to the team of a short, bald guy, with a pencil mus-
tache and the face of Inspector Clouseau. His name was Scott. Scott the
manager.

•

—c'mon, please, you make it better
—i'm busy taking pictures
—and i'm posing for you, so you make the coffee
—OK then, when we finish I'll make coffee and you'll fix the
bed
—if you do the dishes first, 'cause the sink is full
—right, we had company last night, i forgot
—well, you got drunk
—i didn't get drunk!
—yes, you did
—i did not
—who fell asleep on the floor?
—i wasn't sleeping. i was listening to your conversation
—what did we talk about?
—you talked about a-a-a- . . . art
—you were snoring, zack
—i was pretending
—is that why you farted?
—me?!
—loudly
—shit! what would . . . how am i gonna look those people in
the eye?!

—we had a lot of fun last night
—yeah?
—you were really funny
—really?
—they were dying of laughter
—what were they laughing about so much?
—your stories
—well, i'm a clown
—you were so funny . . . and when you jumped and started up
dancing with the coat rack . . .
—i honestly don't remember that at all
—funny!
—tsk, tsk, tsk . . . how could you let me sleep on the floor
—you're funny even when you sleep
—but of course! especially when i happen to fart . . . jesus, how
humiliating!
—well, it's human
—all too human
—m-m-m-m-m . . . baby . . . i love you
—farts and all?
—i was kidding, zack, you didn't fart
—i didn't? really?
—really
—phew, thank god!
—now go make some coffee, will you?
—you little fox, you . . . wait, hold it right there. just like this,
half-turned
—zack . . .
—yes, stella . . .
—if you ever stop making me laugh, i'll leave you
—you'll go looking for another clown?
—no. i'll just leave you

●

I've no idea how long I was sitting there at the plastic table at Packard's, but I am pulled out of my daydream by the loud noise of a backfiring exhaust pipe. The noisiest and shiniest cheap motorcycle I've ever seen parks a few feet away from me. A tall, skinny man dressed in black leather dismounts. He is wearing a military helmet with a swastika on it, a sparkly chain in place of a belt, and big leather riding boots. In his right boot, the handle of a knife. The eyes of this rider are hidden behind mirrored, deep-purple shades reflecting the emptiness of the whole street. When he takes them off at last, I realize that he can't be more than nineteen years old. He has a goatee and a slow stride, with which he arrogantly walks past me and enters the trailer coffee shop.

From the drugstore across the street two girls come out and head toward the coffee shop. They cross the street and sit at a table on the corner. The first one is blonde and pretty—pony tail, cut-off jeans, a little red tank top revealing her navel, blue flip-flops, oversized sunglasses, sucking a milkshake from a large plastic cup with a straw. The other one, chubby, also wearing sunglasses, starts reading something aloud from a fashion magazine. The biker in black reappears from the shop with a Coca-Cola in hand and slowly approaches his motorbike. I now notice that he has a knife stuck in his other boot as well. The chubby girl lifts her greenish-yellow mirrored glasses from the magazine and looks toward the biker. I can't see his response because he is already in front of the bike with his back toward me. He just stands there sipping his Coke. Then, in the middle of the scorching intersection, another kid appears. He crosses the street unhurriedly and stops at an empty table. His hair is fair, parted in the middle, his face covered with red, agitated pimples. He is wearing an Iron Maiden T-shirt, camouflage pants, and white sneakers. He drags up a chair, sits down, and starts monitoring the intersection carefully, without ordering anything. For one much extended moment, all of these figures are still and silent. I have the feeling that I am in someone else's bad dream. I choose to leave it and get into my car. From there, I manage to snap a few shots of the still-unmoving figures and head back toward the freeway which will take me away from here.

•

My training with Scott lasted a week. I knew most of the stuff in theory and wherever the theory came up short, I shrugged my shoulders and said that we had done things differently at ALPHA-PHARMA. I asked Scott how he wanted certain procedures done and he was glad to explain everything. Scott liked being asked. After the training, I was assigned to assist a senior monitor whose wife had died not long ago, and who had bad stomach problems. He was silent, sighing, swallowing pill after pill. I learned a lot from him. Three months later, I was given a laptop with several programs installed and was attached to a guy named Mike. Mike and I clicked instantly. Mike was easy to talk to, funny, and Scott-intolerant. Everything I needed to know to be ready for inspecting on my own, I learned from Mike.

I was handed a list with the hospitals and health centers participating in the clinical research. I was given the contact information of the physicians who received fat paychecks to work with us. What was expected from me in those early days of my new career was to inspect the study documentation. The overly swamped doctors sent their assistants, who were even busier. So after a brief handshake, they slammed thick folders down on my desk, with forms signed by the volunteers participating in the clinical trial, and disappeared. I retired into some empty office and compared the data. Had the patients filled out the questionnaire properly? Did their symptoms match? Were they the right age? Were the drugs taken as prescribed? Were there any complications after they were taken? All I needed to do was compare data. Data, data, data . . . endless strings of data.

•

On one of the cross streets, just before the exit sign for Ramona, I see something picturesque. It's a dirt road lined with more than fifty mailboxes; they're attached to wooden posts and stuck in sand-filled paint, cat food, detergent, fertilizer, and other such tin or plastic containers. Some of these mailboxes are old and rusty, some brand new, others painted over, some crooked and with holes in them. Every one is different from the next one. And, where the dirt lane meets Main Street, there is a large empty space that recent rain has turned into a muddy puddle. The street sign reads HOPE. I take a few quick, wide shots of this cross-roads. Then I go over to the mailboxes and shoot vertically and horizontally, getting the name of the street in the picture. Now I squat down and carefully compose the shot. I focus on one with a weathered American flag on it (Mr. and Mrs. Miller), which is next to the Hansens (orange hippie sign). I open the aperture, to get the shallow depth of field I need, and I click the shutter. Now, again, the same shot, but only this time, I close down three stops to include HOPE reflecting in the puddle. One, two, three, four clicks. Great. And then, just when I think I'm done, I hear the sound of an approaching vehicle behind me. A white pickup truck splattered with mud enters my frame, goes through the puddle, exits and stops abruptly in a cloud of dust by the mailboxes. A white cowboy hat emerges from the window and an arm wrapped in bandages like a wounded soldier's head reaches out to open a mailbox. Now I realize how much was actually missing in my shot. This is it. The mud-splattered truck bed, the cloud of dust, the red stop lights, the cowboy hat, the American flag, the street named "Hope," the mailboxes, the intersection, and the hand grabbing the fat pile of mail puts all of this together. I squat a little more, looking for a lower angle and just then the cowboy hat pokes out of the cab, turns my way, and shoots me a disapproving look. O-o-o-o-p-s. I get it. I've got no business here, holding a camera, crouching by a puddle. I bend over and pretend I'm tying my shoes. Brilliant. The cowboy hat slowly retracts; only the elbow remains sticking out. The pickup truck pulls away.

And then, as I'm squatting, I feel the sudden sharp pain in my stomach. Ou-u-u-u-u-u-c-h, it hurts. What's happening? Something pierces my lower abdomen. The pickup truck makes a turn around the first corner. O-u-u-u-u-u-u-u-u-u-c-h-h. Somewhere down there in my viscera, a ball of snakes starts wriggling. Pain, pain, pain. Then I remember. The cherries. Goddamn you, unwashed, dirty bastards! Goddamn you unwashed, dirty, and who-knows-how-chemically-enhanced motherfuckers! I knew something would go wrong. I knew it. I ate three pounds of filthy cherries and had that god-awful espresso—what good could come out of that? You don't *buy* cherries, you stupid moron. Cherries are love. You either grow cherries or *steal* them. That's what you do. If you are that desperate, you'll spend a couple of bucks to recall the taste, but NOT STUFF YOUR FACE LIKE A GOD-DAMN PIG!

I'm already in the car when I feel the call from behind. I know what will follow . . . I step on the gas pedal. Faster, I need to find shelter. Pamona is six, seven minutes away but given the critical condition I'm in, I'm not sure whether this is close enough. O-u-u-u-u-u-u-u-c-h! It's far. To the left and right are only newly harvested fields, earth burned by the sun, barbed-wire fences, no shelter. There are no ditches along the road, nothing resembling a hill; as far as my eyes can see, there's not a tree or a bush, nowhere to hide my ass. You, harvested, rural California, do you have the slightest idea of the storm in my stomach? Down there everything is moving, pulsating, and writhing in pain. Am I giving birth?

There's the sign for Pamona—five miles. It's impossible to hold on, just impossible. I start twisting in my seat like a ganglion. It's unbearable. I speed up. Slow down, Zack. You don't need to get pulled over. Not now. A little more, just a couple of miles. Ouch . . . Pamona. Aw-w-w-w-w-wful. I'm so close. Here—Pamona. Is there any salvation? Here's the empty main street, if only I hold it one, two, thre-e-e-e-e more seconds, h-o-o-o-o-o-nestly, I'll be saved. No, I won't, no-o-o-o-o-o-o-o-o-o, it's u-u-u-u-u-u-u-nbearable. I can't stand it any longer. For a split second, I loosen the aperture back there to let go of at least part of the pressure but I realize that along with the released gas, a thin streak of liquid has leaked out. No! No. Stop. Thank god, I manage to tighten up before I'm up to my eyeballs in my own shit. I see a TEXACO sign. With screeching tires I make a sharp turn into the gas station and hit the brakes next to the pumps. I jump out of the car and run inside. Behind the counter is a tall young man in overalls.

"Key to the bathroom." I manage to say.

He silently points toward a sign: Restroom For Customers Only.

"I am a customer." I raise my voice.

"How can I help you?"

"The bathroom key, and fast, please, before I make a mess here."

"I can't sir. It's for customers only."

"Here . . ." I reach in my pocket for money, paining my stomach even more. "Here . . . twenty dollars . . . for gas."

"Would you like anything else, sir?"

"No."

"On which pump?"

"One."

"Number one is out of order."

"I don't care, you . . ." I snatch the greasy ring with the restroom key to paradise from his fingers.

I think the first geyser seriously soils my half-pulled-down jeans. The second one unloads everywhere on and around the toilet bowl, which I'm still trying to get to. The third wave splashes where the previous two were supposed to break.

My eyes closed, I experience the most intense moments of cleansing I've had in years. This palette of pain, relief, pleasure, and sudden healing makes me believe in rebirth.

Then I lose all sense of time. I sit there for a long time, listening to the sounds gurgling beneath me. At some point, I realize that it's all over. After delaying as much as I can, I open my eyes and look around. When I finally do, I understand there was a reason why. Everything around me, except the ceiling, is sprayed. Floor, walls—in smaller or bigger splashes and drops in nuances of greenish brown, with reddish dots of peelings and even cherry pits. I close my eyes again. Under my lids—fire circles and golden stains. I open my eyes—shit all over.

.

In my job I conducted myself as a trustworthy and hardworking employee. One-third of our time I spent in the grey cubicles of ICON-IQ, monitoring in-house, and the other two-thirds of the time I had to visit the sites. My workdays were the same as the workdays of every other person. If you had to watch them on TV, you would choose to kill yourself. I simply put up with them and then went home. Stella, for a long time, tried to make me tell her what I did for a living. I managed to avoid her questions with half-lies, promising her that all of this was just temporary. Once we get on our feet in California, I would return to my photography. She was used to accepting my entrepreneurial spirit when we were hard up. She was familiar with my adaptive gene. I think she believed me.

Then, the first hefty paycheck came. Then, beginner's luck—to investigate irregularities in a small clinic that was working with clinically depressed patients. Several of the volunteers enrolled in the study did not match the criteria—it was clear they were doing it just for the money. One of them was a drug addict going from research study to research study, faking syndromes, getting treatments; there was also a case of a pregnant young woman who hid her condition and enrolled in the study without even properly signing her consent. Scott was very pleased with my watchfulness and praised me in front of my colleagues—this is what it means to work with an experienced professional.

ICONIQ, however, started pressuring us with the deadlines. We had to speed up before our rival company flooded the market with their version of the drug.

•

I wipe myself off somehow, leave the restroom, and slowly walk among the shelves of merchandise, pretending I'm looking for something. The tall kid in overalls is watching me carefully. Why is he doing that? He's acting as if he knows something I don't. What could you possibly know, dumb ass, that I don't, huh? Huh? Every now and then he quickly looks at a small monitor in front of him. Is there a surveillance camera in the bathroom? Shit. Impossible. But, then again, who knows? Some of the scenes from a few minutes ago run through my head. I bet I would have heard him laughing had there been a camera. I keep pretending to be studying the junk on the shelves as I approach him. I am careful to walk in such a way that the insides of my pants touch my thighs as little as possible. There's a reason for that.

"The water in the restroom doesn't work." I yell from a distance. I can hardly contain my anger.

"I was gonna tell you," he says, without taking his eyes off the monitor. I've noticed that sometimes other people's wickedness has a calming effect on me. Just a minute ago I was wiping shit-smeared bathroom linoleum with my own underwear because I'm a nice guy, and now—such a lack of appreciation. None. I'm already standing in front of the kid. I hand the bathroom key back and suddenly lean forward to see what's on the monitor he keeps looking at. Split into four, the black and white screen shows different angles of the building. No camera in the bathroom. In the upper right corner I see a car exactly like the one I drive, only . . . all of a sudden, tires screeching, it shoots out of the gas station, turns right on Main Street and . . . Is this my car? Stella's car? It can't be. My car?

"I think that's your car." Overalls points an index finger. I run out the door. The white beauty gets smaller and smaller. I can't believe my eyes. It gets smaller and smaller until it disappears into the middle of the afternoon on Main Street, Pamona, California. I look left and I look right. Dead air. I run back inside. I kick the door open and jump over the register with my fist in the air. The gangly kid pulls away as far as he can: "Don't you touch me!" Falsetto. I reach out, trying to smack the loser in the muzzle. He quickly squats down with arms over his head. My hand whizzes above him and grabs the phone receiver. I won't dirty my hands with this jerk off.

"Don't touch me-e-e-e-e!" Overalls cowers even lower.

"I'll break your fucking head open, you fuck!" I dial 911. "Don't move, I'll brea . . ." And then it crosses my mind what could possibly happen if somebody at the other end of the line picks up.

The police sirens. The excitement. The trigger-happy cops in a small town where nothing ever happens. The screeching tires. The car chase. The panic. The turns. The chase. The getting closer. The loudspeakers. The rollover. The sirens. The open car doors. The broken windshield. The gaping trunk. The bag. The marijuana. I notice one of Overalls' eyes through his interlaced fingers. I grab the telephone receiver by the cord and hit him in the fontanel. His head shrinks back between his shoulders like a turtle's. The receiver jumps back into my hand.

"Ooooh," he bellows.

"I said don't move!" In the receiver, I hear a female voice. ". . . emergency, your names and teleph . . ." I hang up. "You fucking shit! Go clean the bathroom! Right now! Go, go, go!" I don't even wait to see if he reacts. I get out. I look around. Nothing. I drop my arms and sit down on the curb. Stella. Where am I, Stella-a-a-a? The loud noise of a bad muffler lifts me back to my feet. A beat-up brown Dodge, ugly as hell, is driving toward me. I wave and, of course, it passes me by. If it were me, I'd pass myself by, too. Just look at me. Shitty ass. I'm calling the cops, whatever. I'll . . . well, look now—the Dodge slows down, stops and backs up, rumbling. I run toward it. I open the door and . . .

"Melody!" I yell. Still in her uniform, weary but smiling, she—my guardian angel—cleans pizza boxes, McDonald's bags, Pepsi cans, Penny Savers, and the like off the passenger's seat. I reach out to hug her. "Drive, Melody, drive. They ran away. Disappeared. Motherfuckers!" She's looking at me with her wide-open, bad-makeup-day eyes. In disbelief.

"What happened?"

"They stole my car, Melody! Go, please, go." She accelerates down Main Street. "I was at the gas station and somebody . . ."

"I can't believe it. Here? In Pamona!" Melody shakes her head incredulously.

"I know." I shout.

"Where should I drive?" She presses the gas and narrows her eyes, ready for the chase.

"Just drive."

"Where?" She yells, driving as fast as she can.

"Straight ahead!" I try to imagine how far my car could be. I look left and right at every street intersecting Main Street.

Something, however, tells me that we have to keep going. Not more than ten-fifteen minutes—that's how much time I give the stupid fuck who complicated my life. The fuel level warning light was on and that's exactly why I got myself into this mess in the first place—I needed gas and lemons for the load in the trunk. Ten or fifteen miles, no more. Then I notice that after the initial shock, Melody has been throwing me odd looks. She looks at me weird. She sizes me up from head to toe . . . oh, no . . . not this, Melody. Her eyes shoot down to my . . . You thinking about love, woman? Melody? In a moment like this? Wow. Is that what you are thinking about? And just then my sense of smell returns. I stink. I roll down the window.

"The bathroom in the gas station . . . Someone shit all over . . . I slipped on the floor and look what happened," I say.

"Why didn't you call the police?"

"About the shitter?"

"About the car."

Then I see something white in the distance.

"Right there, Melody." Stealing a car from a gas station, huh? Great idea. There's a reason it was there, moron.

•

A monitor's job is simply common sense and concentration. A well-trained seventh grader could do it. I grasped the routine in a couple of months and managed to finish my weekly load in just a few days. The job required me to travel throughout California. Because I worked quickly and efficiently, Scott started sending me to other states as well to help short-staffed teams. This was a sort of unspoken promotion and it brought me a great bonus at the end of the year.

Stella found a new studio space in the industrial zone and painted a lot.

•

—zack, you really understand nothing about the world
—nothing
—absolutely nothing
—and you?
—i understand everything perfectly well
—why don't you explain it to me then, stella?
—because you have to understand it on your own, my dear
—you tell me and I promise I'll forget everything and then
understand it by myself
—you promise?
—move to the left a little, please. no, left, your left
—like this?
—yes. now hold still

•

The white thing in the distance is a sign reading FOR SALE: 74
ACRES. BY OWNER. I almost start bawling like a baby—I was so
damn sure that I had the bastard. After the sign we keep going for
about five more miles until I'm convinced that we are not going
the right direction. It's impossible that I had that much gas left
in the tank. Before I give up, I decide to do what I've heard that
good detectives do. I close my eyes and try to imagine that I am
the thief. There—I steal my own car. What do I do now? What do
I do? I drive as fast as I can, get on Main Street, I put the pedal
to the metal, jerk the wheel toward the first electric pole I see
and . . . finish with this comedy once and for all. I open my eyes.
"Melody."
"Yes?"
"Stop." She stops. I jump out of the car, I walk alongside the
road, search the ground until I find four dry wooden sticks, then
I shape them like a square in the dust.
"What are you doing?" She stands behind me.

"S-h-h-h-h, quiet, please," I say without lifting my head, focused on the magic. Actually what I am doing is *closing up the little devil.* I know this magic from my grandmother. Every time I lost something as a kid and I tried to find it and couldn't, I'd get angry and be impossible to calm down. My grandma would tell me to *close up the little devil.* You close up the little devil with whatever is at hand—tree branches, pencils, or what have you. The important thing is to make some kind of a square and to imagine the little devil inside it. Then you find whatever you've lost. This magic works flawlessly. Always. And I'd forgotten all about it for almost twenty years. I stand up quickly: "U-turn!"

"Excuse me?"

"Let's go. U-turn."

"Are you sure?"

"No." In a few minutes we are back in Pamona. Before the last turn on Main Street I tell her to turn left. We drive to the first big street running parallel—Henderson. We take a right and another right, and drive in the direction opposite of the one I saw my car disappear in. We are now heading not toward the freeway, but toward Ramona. Before the end of town, we take a right again and get back on Main. We drive east and about three miles down the road, off to the side, between the asphalt and a corn field, in the shade of a lonely tree is my car. *Stella's* car. Stella's white Mercedes. Even from a distance I can see there's a man in the passenger's seat doing something I really doubt would please me. My adrenaline surges, my heart races like I'm sprinting, my throat dries up instantly. I recognize these symptoms.

"Melody!" I scream. "That's it. Stop right behind it. Right behind the car!" Melody speeds up and at the same time, who knows why, puts on her turn signal, and makes a sharp right. We edge toward the car with a roar. I swear I see Melody hitting the brakes but the effect is minimal. Her face stiffens, her eyes grow wide, her mouth opens with a scream "Oh, M-y-G-o-d!" I pull the hand break and spin the wheel to avoid the crash. Unsuccessfully. Stella's car jerks and turns ninety degrees. A cloud of dust and the trunk gapes open. I jump out, throw myself over the car, grab the door handle, but it's locked. I jump across the hood to try the other door, but it's also locked. And then I see the Iron Maiden T-shirt. The motherfucker stares at me with his gray eyes exactly like he did at the intersection in Ramona an hour ago—without emotion. Only his pimples seem riper. I guess he ran out of gas right here, and just so he didn't leave empty-handed, Iron Maiden is busy with the stereo—half pulled out, wires sticking up.

"Open the door, idiot!" I scream. He just sits and stares. The maiden from the T-shirt glowers, axe in her bonny hand. "Ran out of gas, huh, fuckhead?" Now I feel my anger engulfing me completely. This isn't good. Not good at all. "Open the door, you stupid fuck! Open the door and get out." I register the damage on the rear of the car. The bumper is a little messed up, the left tail-light is broken and the trunk might be hard to shut. I walk around in circles cursing, Melody walks around me, apologizing. She begs me not to get angry, she'll help me fix my car, and she knows a guy who fixed her husband's pickup, but . . . "Get out!" I start boiling over, it's more than I can hold in. Melody doesn't stop clucking around me for a second. "Open the . . ."

"I'll clean the trunk a little bit," I hear Melody saying behind me and see her head disappear in the trunk where clothes, plastic bottles of water, tools, miscellaneous Walmart stuff, and the lemons from Orchard lie scattered. There is also the bag.

"Don't touch anything!" I shout, terrified. This startles her. She jerks back, hits her head on the hood of the open trunk, then gives me a guilty look. I pull her aside and slam the trunk. It doesn't shut. I slam it a couple more times, harder. It won't shut. I see that Iron Maiden has twisted his skinny neck back and is watching me. I gather all my strength and try one more time and manage to shut the trunk. Melody looks scared. So does the thief inside my car. A-ha, I'll pull some emotion out of you, huh! He gawks with his little rat eyes. "OK. Here is how it's gonna go down. First, I'll break the windshield, then I'll break your stupid head, because I'll be very pissed off that I had to break the windshield." This seems to make him think a little faster.

"I ain't gettin' out!" He can actually talk?

"Get out!"

"I ain't gettin' out!"

"It will hurt!"

"I ain't . . ."

"I'm getting exceptionally angry with you, boy!"

No reply.

"OK, listen," I pause. "Let's make a deal. I won't hurt you!" He doesn't believe me. If I were in his place, I wouldn't either. I take a deep breath. I start slowing my breathing down. I have to get out of here as soon as possible before a police car or some friend of his passes by—I remember a certain idiot with a swastika helmet and knives in his boots. Something makes me believe that this Iron Maiden is not in it alone. Most likely, at this very moment, somebody is filling up a container with gas for the car and will show up any moment now. I've got to split. I have to be reasonable from now on. Not eat unwashed cherries, not leave my keys in the car, not think about Stella, not get drunk in Mexico, not pretend to be a good Samaritan, a playboy . . . I've got to be reasonable if I want to survive in this chaotic world. I've got to . . ."Listen, prick," I say calmly. "Here is the deal." He is all ears. Big ones, too. "Put the stereo back where it belongs. Then get out of my car and out of my sight. OK? Put the CD player back. And I won't hurt you. Got it?" I see him wrinkle his forehead. Thinking, maybe. "Come on. Put it back. Just like it was. Exactly as you found it. OK? And I won't touch you. I promise." I have to get out of here. This little shit is buying time until the motorcycle Nazi shows up any second. Melody babbles on around me, this guy is from Ramona, not

Pamona, she knows his sister, the older one, the one who married the dentist, they gave birth together, not Melody and the dentist, Melody and the dentist's wife gave birth, but her baby was . . . "Did you hear what I said, Iron Maiden?! I'll count to three and if I don't see you putting this stereo back, I'll start looking for a big rock." This obviously convinces him to get to work. I've noticed that with some people you've got to be more descriptive about your intentions, otherwise they don't get it. Iron Maiden bends over and starts putting the stereo back surprisingly quickly. Pretty soon, while I circle around the car listening to Melody's nonsense, he knocks on the window. I get closer to examine his job. Everything looks right. "Now, turn it on so I can hear it." He slides a CD in and turns up the volume. "Good. Now—the radio?" I hear the radio, too. "Press button number one." He does. Country music. "Now—press button number four." Smooth Jazz 103.5. "Now—get out!" Still hesitant, he unlocks the door and slithers out. I meet him with a punch between the eyes that knocks him on his ass.

"But, you said . . ." he cries.

"You messed up my preset buttons, you moron! I said exactly *as you found it*! That does not include country *or* smooth jazz." His hands are raised defensively. His eyes are foggy from my jab, his body shaking uncontrollably. He gets to his feet. "Get the fuck outta here! Run! Run!" I yell, stomp my foot, and observe him melting away toward Ramona. I look at Melody, who is finally silent. In her look I read a mixture of amazement, admiration, and some kind of disappointment. Apparently, I am not so different than the rest. Well, I'm not, I guess.

After I lock the car, Melody drives to the closest gas station. On the way there I learn that her husband is a truck driver who comes home for the weekend every other week. That her kids (by three different fathers) are very nice, and her sister helps her however she can. I buy a small gasoline container and fill it up. I grab a bunch of air fresheners—for her car, which I stunk up. I buy candy for her kids (three, eleven, and thirteen) and we head back to the Mercedes. While she's talking, I'm looking at the desolate street. The sense that people have deserted this town in the heat still lingers in me. Before I take off, Melody politely offers to let me go to her place if I want, to take a shower and change clothes. The idea of water over my body is very tempting. I thank her, but I have to go. I don't even want to think what might happen if out of the blue, a semi pulls up to her house while I'm there and her man jumps out of it, and I'm in the shower. One of those *it's-not-what-you-think* situations that I really don't want to deal with. I'm proud of my decision, damn it. I'm proud. There, I can be reasonable when I use my head. I give Melody a hug, thank her one more time, and we go our separate ways. She gets back into her car, waves good-bye, makes a U-turn, ferociously turning the steering wheel, brushes something off her eye, and drives off, tires screeching. She can probably see me in the rearview mirror. What is her bleached head thinking now? Melody.

•

Stella kept on working with kids who needed help. Sometimes she'd tell me about them, and I tried to listen. I hadn't seen any of her paintings in a long, long time, but I knew she had been painting. When I came back from work, tired from staring at names and numbers, I didn't feel like talking about anything, and on the weekends I just didn't have the energy to drive downtown to her studio. I had given myself a break from art, photography, writing, philosophizing. I decided to spend at least one year of my life dedicated to work, financial stability, and TV. I avoided any kind of serious conversation with Stella. Over time, I invented mechanisms to do that. I didn't feel like talking about my work (she still wasn't sure exactly what my occupation was) and I certainly didn't want to bring up art. The word future *made me sick to my stomach. My attitude toward Stella did not change; I just freed it from a few unproductive aspects.*

•

I get in the car. I'm again reminded of how good you feel after you lose something for a while and then find it. I get on the freeway with a full tank and a painfully empty stomach. I am hungry after the excruciating diarrhea. And, of course, I am aware that no matter what I put in my mouth, I'll suffer. I'll starve, I decide. I'll starve until my head clears up a little, until I get my thoughts in order, until my emotions abate. I'll starve my sorrow for Stella. I just need to leave California.

•

I started traveling often. The company paid me ninety dollars an hour for my business trips and the time I spent out of town. So I started choosing more indirect flights.

In order to get to Illinois, for instance, I'd fly to Texas, which added eight more hours at airports and planes. Money-wise, this was more than my grandma's annual pension back in Bulgaria. The thought of it was absurd, but also entertaining in a way.

I'd fly to Florida through Chicago, which extended my journey by six to seven hours, even though there was a more direct flight from L.A.

To New Orleans I'd take a layover in Sacramento.

The longest way to New Jersey was through San Francisco.

I spent less time with Stella and our silences.

The company policy was that travel time shouldn't exceeded seventy-five percent of the time spent at home. I began to appear as an exception. Scott the manager did not miss an opportunity to mention my professionalism and loyalty to the company. In fact, I felt fine in this

*new endeavor of mine—among people who needed my expertise, with
employers who appreciated my efforts, and with a bank account which
for the first time in my life looked promising. I felt strangely fulfilled.
This was it—fulfilled. For the first time in years, I liked the idea of
calling my mom and chatting with her. I'd mostly do it from airport
coffee shops between flights. Those conversations were gifts from me,
and she was happy and proud that I, her only beloved son, traveled
so often, that I was succeeding professionally in America, while my
friends* back home *could hardly make ends meet. Of course, I would
conveniently neglect to mention the reason for my frequent travels,
and it never even crossed her mind that I would be anything other
than a photographer, writer, or artist of some kind, at the epicenter of
something exciting. I don't know how she would have taken the truth
that I was visiting clinics, collecting data, and writing business reports
instead of stories.*

•

I'm driving southeast. Eventually the populated areas yield to
vast wheat fields. The prices of the newly built houses advertised
on the billboards along the freeway become lower and the landscape—more desolate. On the road I'm always fascinated by the
ever-present wooden utility poles, the barbed wire fences all along
the way to the East Coast—evidence of an America I fell in love
with so long ago. Far, far away on the horizon rise murky, bluish
mountains that don't get any closer, even though I've been driving
toward them for a while now. Between them and me lie acres of
farmland. I pass huge yards where all sorts of combines, tractors, machinery, cement trucks, caterpillars, bobcats are covered
in gray dust. Places like these frighten me. Further on, I pass an
outdoor enclosure with enormous concrete pipes piled on top of
each other, colored green, red, yellow, blue, and black like a huge
art installation. Here and there to the left of the road, satellite

antennae jut into the air, beneath them stand small houses, trailers, and bungalows. Alongside the asphalt there are yellowing patches of grass, burned thorns, tumbleweed, gravel, blown-out tires, beer cans, broken bottles, papers, shattered stop lights, oil stains, plastic bags waving in the wind—the remains of passing humans. From time to time, tall trees appear—slim, with light-gray dolphin skin and small, hard leaves, in groups of three or four. I don't even know what these trees are called. I drive for a long time through uninteresting, flat places. No matter how unpopulated everything looks, though, from time to time I see the unavoidable Taco Bell, Shell, McDonald's, Burger King, even Walmart, Pizza Hut, In and Out, Dunkin' Donuts, Mobil, and Chevron—corporate calluses surrounded by tall palm trees, imitating oases.

I now figure that for the last couple years, I had been working hard to make my bank account pretty and my days unbearably boring. I know that this is also the case with all my co-workers and their co-workers' co-workers. I haven't met interesting people in a long time. I haven't read a book in a long time. In fact, I now think that Stella had begun leaving me long before I saw her off last week. I had noticed those shadows of absence—first in her gaze, which withdrew from mine more quickly than before. Then, in our most intimate, still-occurring moments of closeness, one invisible part of her would remain half-turned away, as if to see whether someone was calling her. In our now rarer kisses, I'd feel that trace of coldness, like the breeze at dusk in late August. As a kid, I remember the old fishermen in my hometown saying that *the sea was turning.* Stella's physical projection left me last week. But the larger part of her had left before then. And that's the part I miss most.

I exit the freeway and pull over. At the foot of a yellowish hill scattered with large oval rocks, the shadow of a utility pole has cast a dark, elongated cross. A group of slender, dark green cypresses stand to the side like sentinels. I take the camera and carefully compose the picture in the viewfinder. I finish the roll, take it out, put it in my pocket and load a new one. I get back in the car.

An hour later and it's still California. As far as my eyes can see, there are different nuances of yellow. The foreground is a freshly harvested field, as bright yellow as a punk hairdo. The hay bales are lined up in long, neat rows. A little further on is a murky-brownish field with huge heaps of straw dozing in the late afternoon. The air is yellow-brown, dyed by the desert wind. Yellow. Brown.

Then, from a dirt road adjacent to the freeway, a white convertible appears with a woman dressed in white, wearing a fluttering white scarf and dark sunglasses. Behind the car, a yellowish dust trail stretches for as long as my eyes can track it. I try holding the steering wheel with my left hand as I take a couple shots with my right. For a short while, the convertible and I drive at the same speed, and I get the feeling that I'm on a train, following my favorite movie star through the window. I'm not on a train. And the woman out there is no movie star, but perhaps the wife of a small-town accountant. Whoever she is, a moment later she turns right onto a perpendicular road and drives away. Drive away as much as you want, unknown lady. I will go on.

The foot of the mountains starts turning dark violet and the peaks—milky orange. Imperceptibly, it has begun getting dark. I pull off the freeway and stop in front of a small motel named Mirador. It's quiet. A girl with a Spanish accent and a name tag that says GABRIELA checks me in. The motel is almost empty. I take the key and find my room.

I get in.

I turn on the light.

I toss the Nikon on the bed and flop down on the bedspread.

I get up and check the bathroom. Well, it needs an intervention, there's no getting around it. In most American bathrooms, there is a fan in the ceiling. It's usually connected to the light switch. So, every time I go into a bathroom and turn on the light, the noise these fans make drives me nuts. No comfort or intimacy whatsoever. I pick up the receiver and dial 0.

"Hi Mr. Kara . . . bash . . ." My name shows on a display apparently, but she can't pronounce it.

"Hi."

"How can I help you?"

"I need a screwdriver, please."

"May I send our maintenance man, Mr. Kara-sh . . ."

"It won't be necessary, Gabriela. I just need to tighten something here on my suitcase. For just a minute."

"No problem, Mr. Ka . . ."

"You can call me Zack and you don't need to do it all the time."

"No problem, Mr. . . . errrrrr . . . Zack."

"Thank you, Gabriela." I hang up. In a minute, a guy brings the screwdriver and leaves. I pull up a chair, go into the bathroom, step up on the chair, unscrew the four screws of the small vent on the ceiling and unhook the fan's wires. Now I can spend some time here without feeling like airplanes are constantly flying over my head. I throw my soiled clothes in the garbage, strip off whatever else I have on, and jump into the shower. I close my eyes, standing still for a long time. Then I open my eyes and start observing how water behaves. I see how the drops hit the tiles, turning into small streaks, intertwining, continuing on down, making unexpected turns, and running into bigger streams. Enchanting.

I feel much better after the shower. Still undressed, I lie on the bed and study the ceiling for a long, long time. I can't remember ever doing that. I've always thought that was just a cliché for depressed types, but I was wrong. No ceiling is just a ceiling if you have the eyes to see. A gallery, a film, a book, a concert, a bas-relief . . . To me, it is now an etching of Dante's *Inferno* with all its demons, suffering, and torture.

Stella, Stella, *Lama Sabachthani!*

I have no idea how long I spend like this, but at some point I realize that there's nothing above me to look at anymore, because it's completely dark outside. I have to get up. I put on a pair of jeans and go to the car. I drag the bag into the room. I go back and get the lemons. Are there enough? Well, there better be. I pick up the phone and dial 0 again.

"Hi, Mr. Kara-ba . . ." The familiar voice starts energetically and stumbles on the third syllable again. They all do. "Hi."

"Gabriela, how are you?" I say.

"I'm OK, thank you, Mr. . . ."

"Zack."

"Zack."

"Gabriela."

"Yes, sir."

"Thank you for the screwdriver. I needed it."

"I'm glad. What else can I do for you, Zack?"

"Gabriela."

"Yes?"

"I need a knife."

"A knife?"

"A knife."

"A set of utensils?"

"No. Just a kitchen knife. A sharp one." A pause at the other end.

"A sharp knife?"

"Yes, very sharp."

"May I ask . . ."

"I'm thinking about slitting my wrists."

"Oh!"

"I'm kidding, Gabriela," I say. "I'm kidding. I need it for something else."

"Of course, sir." She sighs with relief. "I'll send somebody over in a minute."

"Gabriela?" Hesitantly.

"Yes, sir?" Somewhat warmer.

"Did I scare you?" Reluctantly.

"Yes." Serious.

"I'm sorry." Quietly.

"It's OK." More quietly.

"Have a nice evening." Even more quietly.

"You, too . . . Zack." Whispering. Very carefully and slowly, I hang up the receiver. There–I can still awaken someone's emotions! Not all is lost. Perhaps not.

Somebody bangs on the door–a plump Mexican woman in a blue uniform with a huge knife in her hand. She silently gives it to me. I read the badge pinned to her enormous checkered bosom–Juanita. The knife's blade flashes, and for a split second I see in it Juanita in her home village somewhere in Mexico, a knife in one hand, a chicken in the other, walking confidently toward a stump. Dust, cackling, feathers, blood . . .

Why don't you chop off my head, too, Juanita? Slaughter me, Juanita.

I am a dead man already, but I'll bleed.

I thank her, give her a few bucks, take the knife, shut the door behind her, lock it, double lock it, fasten the chain, check the windows, and fully close the curtains. I untie the bag. This is the second time I've done so since it fell in my hands. And this time I'm sober and relatively calm. Until this moment, somewhere in me the thought was alive that perhaps all of this is just some mind-trick. Some kind of half-dream and half who-knows-what. Deep inside, I guess I've hoped that this isn't happening. Too bad, because it is. The first thing the fucking scent of the marijuana does is land me in a meadow in my childhood. I'm about five and I'm rolling down a hill flecked with wild flowers. Before my eyes, a tall, blonde girl with a wreath on her head and a dark, long-haired man with a beard emerge and disappear. She's running, laughing and waving her long straight hair, he's reaching out, trying to catch her, and a German shepherd jumps around them with its tongue sticking out. From time to time, the man catches the girl and they both tumble into the tall grass; the dog bounces around them, nudging them with his wet nose, then runs toward me. I scream and roll down the hill even faster. This is the first time I've seen people kissing. It attracts me and appalls me at the same time. So I shut my eyes while they do it. The dog's name is Smoke. The man and the woman are Christo and Teresa. He's my father's cousin, and she's Polish. Christo goes to Warsaw for a month. They meet there and fall in love. They find that puppy by a dumpster and take him in. Then they return to Bulgaria. They had taken me with them for a walk in the woods that day and they were kissing, picking wild flowers, and weaving wreaths as I was running with Smoke. There must have been some kind of wild cannabis plant in that meadow.

I take a lemon, I thrust the blade into its thick skin and it squirts me straight in the eye. I rub it for a long time, then open my eyes and wait for the circles to fade.

Christo and Teresa got married in the cafeteria of the machinery plant where he worked. Teresa became a seamstress in a factory. She gave birth to a boy and a girl within a few years and her face faded to gray. One winter evening in the middle of the seventies, Christo came home from work and found the girl crying alone in the empty apartment. Neighbors had seen Teresa with a suitcase and the young boy at the bus station early in the morning. It must have been November. They must have been wearing overcoats.

Christo went to Poland many times to look for Teresa. He couldn't find her, or so he said. He never remarried. He raised the girl she left behind and the girl was more beautiful than a children's fairytale. There was no sadder father than Christo in the whole world. He started drinking. The girl grew up and turned into a very attractive sales associate at a lingerie boutique, and after that—people say—into a prostitute. Maybe they said such things just out of spite. But maybe they were right. You never know with people.

.

—hey
—you're *hey*
—hey
—what?
—i want you to write a book about me, zack
—i will
—promise?
—lean toward me a little, like th-a-a-t, look at the camera
—do you promise to write a book about me?

.

I start peeling the lemons into small, martini-ready lemon twists. Then I drop them into the bag and shake it. I should have bought more. On the other hand though, the weed seems fresh, moist, and it should stay like that for quite some time. This bag contains thousands of joints. God willing, in a few days I'll be in New York and it should still be as fresh as it is now. I just have to get my act together if I want to finally turn the tide. It's about time. It is time. It has been for a long time now.

"Hello, Gabriela."

"Yes . . . sir."

"Thanks for the sharp knife."

"You're welcome."

"You can send Juanita over."

"She's already off. You can leave it in your room. Housekeeping will take care of it tomorrow."

"A knife in my room? I don't know, I don't think it's a good idea, Gabriela." I say. "Who knows what I might do . . ."

"Of course, sir." She stiffens up immediately.

"I am joking, Gabriela! I'm joking. I'm calling for something else, though."

"Yes?"

"I need to find a guy, but I don't know his number."

"Do you know his last name?"

"Yes."

"If he's listed in the directory, I'll be happy to help you find him." I spell his name to her and in a minute Ken's voice is on the other end.

"Hello?"

"Hey, Ken! How are you?"

"Zack? How are you doing, my friend?"

"I'm OK," I lie quickly—what are friends for? "I'm on my way to the East Coast."

"When's your flight?"

"Uh, I'm not flying. I'm driving."

"Oh, even better! Driving through the great American wilderness. You'll stop by, right?"

"That's why I'm calling."

"Is Stella with you?"

"Stella's not here . . . I'll be by myself. Are you and Linda still together?"

"Yes."

"Is she living with you?"

"Well, it's complicated. I'll tell you all about it."

"I'll be there in a couple of days, amigo."

"Great. Drive safely."

"OK."

"Check in from time to time from the road!"

"Sure thing. See you later, Ken."

"See you later."

I hang up the phone. Yellowish light from the reading lamp, wallpaper with a floral pattern, a brownish table with a glass of water on top, a wet towel on the floor. I'm naked, on my back, alone, here and now. That's it. Nothing but me. No Stella. No mother, sister, father, friends, tribe, pets. Naked. Foreign country, foreign motel, foreign bag with foreign marijuana. Alone, stripped to the skin, to the blood, to the marrow . . . to pointlessness.

I almost reach for the remote control but stop. Why fill this room with foreign images? Why fuck up this perfectly lonesome moment on top of the covers of a cheap motel room?

Suddenly, for a split of a second, I separate from this male body and look at it from above, from the corner of the room. I also see my consciousness, my thoughts, my anger, my . . . jealousy. My jealousy? Did I mean *jealousy*? Instantly, I am back here and in myself. Jealousy? Impossible. I am not JEALOUS. I was not jealous. Jealous of whom? Another man? I've never been jealous. Jealousy is for . . . jealous people. Insecure people. People who cling to someone else. To something that doesn't belong to them in the first place. Jealousy is fear of losing love. Jealousy *is* fear.

Is this possible? Is it really possible that I am handcuffed to this motel bed by a feeling that has used me up and left me dry and helpless? Is it possible that I have been guilty of the biggest betrayal of any true love—sleeping with jealousy? Have I been sleeping with jealousy this whole time?

•

We closed on Valentine's Day. It just happened. It was the second house we saw that morning. The realtor's white BMW pulled in front of a two-story house painted in light-peach with a RE/MAX sign stuck in the dewy lawn. The realtor, a skinny woman in her late forties, opened a folder with printouts and spent some time informing us about the neighborhood—schools, daycare centers, shopping, demographics . . . things we didn't really care about. The lawn sprinkler squirted water onto a decade-younger version of our agent, who was smiling against a background of red, white, and blue balloons on the FOR SALE sign. The house was actually bigger than what we needed—two levels, three bedrooms, spacious garage—but I guess we let ourselves be convinced that this was the best deal at the moment. We were supposed to be getting more house for less money. While the agent cornered Stella and chattered on in that unbearable tone of voice adopted by supposedly successful, independent American women, I walked away, wandering through the empty rooms. I could lightproof one of them and turn it into a black and white lab where I could hide and pretend that digital photography didn't exist.

There was a garage and a tool shed that could be turned into a studio for Stella. She would then have a place to work anytime she wanted. The owners of the house were Koreans who had relocated to Chicago. They were asking a very reasonable price. The unpleasant part was that the empty rooms had soaked in an unfamiliar, sweet and sour smell, and dark spots on the beige carpet gave away the damaging presence of small children and pets. The real estate agent was quick to reassure us that there was some odor removal spray—she would tell us where to buy it—that does miracles in getting rid of absolutely all sorts of smells. There was another one, too—for carpet stains—in case we should decide to keep the carpet instead of changing it. But if it were her, oh, she would "change it in a heart beat." She showed us the back patio, which overlooked a canyon choked with greenery. There was a tangerine tree, a tall palm tree, and lots of bushes. She winked at us conspiringly, grinned, and with a flick of her wrist literally unveiled

*the house's last bonus—ta-da-a-a-a! From under a vinyl burgundy
cover, she uncovered a Jacuzzi in a corner of the yard near a rose bush.
Its chlorine eye reflected a piece of the blue sky above. Neither Stella
nor I would ever spend a minute in a hole in the ground filled with
hot water, so we just smiled at each other and shrugged—we could still
read most of each other's thoughts. The realtor, if she detected our lack of
interest, did not show it and continued, most professionally, talking us
into buying the property. Then we went out to the street. All the houses
were painted in subtle variations of peach. The sky—trivially blue and
empty. It was strangely quiet—still and uninhabited, as in the after-
math of a hydrogen bomb. We did not look any further. Out of courtesy
to the agent and fairness to ourselves, we saw several more properties,
but all of them made the Korean residence seem more and more attractive. We made an offer that same afternoon. We were approved for a
mortgage and, within a month, we moved in. It was easy.*

·

I glimpse at the digital clock on the night stand. 11:09. It is 11:09
here. Stella, where are you? Are you just waking up? I loved being
there when you woke up—with your bleary eyes, messy hair, and
pillow-traced face. I love watching her wake up. You know that
you are truly in love with someone when you want to wake up
together more than you want to fall asleep together.

·

*The den on the ground floor was supposed to be my darkroom. I hired
a contractor to connect two large, stainless-steel darkroom sinks and
print washers to water-supply and drainage lines with shut-off valves
and PVC traps, in accordance with all the existing codes, the whole
deal. I securely light-proofed the windows with black asphalt paper.
I installed exhaust vent hoods (once I had passed out in a darkroom*

133

without one of those after breathing in photo chemicals for ten hours). I covered the floor with rubber mats and bought a nice-sized print drier. I bought a big Durst enlarger equipped with a Schneider lens from eBay. On Craigslist, I found functional darkroom casework from some defunct industrial photo lab. I spent weeks shopping for containers, shelves, and cabinets to furnish the lab that was supposed to take me back to photography. I was creating the lab of the future. I didn't use it once.

.

I get up and stand by the window. The moonlight oozes through the blinds in long stripes. Banal. I look out at the empty parking lot. I look at the full moon. There is a strong wind. Banal. Everything is so banal. Then I see the headlights of an approaching car pulling up in front of the motel. A girl and boy get out of the car, hugging and staggering. He stops under the lamp and starts fumbling in his pockets for a long time. She bends over to pick something up off the ground. The wind blows her long hair in all directions. He also squats down. They start kissing right there, squatting, leaning against each other—wobbling and funny.

I move away from the window and lie down.

.

1988, Varna

An empty apartment, late spring, lots of people, cheap gin, tonic. We were twenty and wild. Van Halen, Pretty Maids, Krokus, Kool & the Gang, Metallica, Judas Priest, midnight, jumping up and down, knocking over furniture, screaming from the balcony, dancing, pillow fights, soccer in the kitchen, infuriated neighbors, and the police. End of the party.

Outside was a full moon. The night was silvery. I took her by the hand and we walked. She didn't know where I was taking her. I didn't know what I was doing. We passed the last few buildings on the fringes of town and crossed the railroad tracks. She grew silent, but kept following me without asking questions. We jumped over a small brook and kept going up the dirt road. Two shadows, hand in hand, as if in a trance. The gate was locked. I kicked it open. We went it. I led her through the dark, short rows. Only a few graves away from the fence, I threw myself on her. I remember she was wearing tight jeans and it took me some time to unzip them. I pulled her T-shirt up. Her breasts were white in the moonlight. I didn't have time to look at them though. I entered her with a strong thrust, painful for both of us, and crashed over her soft body in a few seconds—guilty, dirty, and disgusted with myself. I wanted the grave upon which I had desecrated her to open up and swallow me forever.

She lay under me with eyes wide open, looking at the moon over my shoulder. The scent of lilacs suddenly filled the air. The crickets started chirping unbearably loudly. She pushed me off her. She got up, pulled on her jeans, and zipped them. I looked up toward her outstretched hand. The full moon around her head. She helped me get up.

Then she gave me the world's hardest slap.

•

I hear a squeak.

I am tangled in a hazy net of images. I dream that my teeth are disintegrating. First—the right eyetooth. Then the next one. And then all the rest. They crumble like river limestone, like chalk. In their place, I can see only small, rotting stumps. I don't have teeth anymore. I am horrified by the fact that I am losing them, that my mouth is turning into a big, moist wound. I'm crying? I never cry. I haven't cried since I was a kid, since . . . I wake up with a low, muted growl. My jaws are numb and hurt from clenching.

Tears wet my cheeks. I can't figure out where I am. Then reality slips into my thoughts. Discovering that my teeth are right where they belong doesn't make me feel better. I want to cry even more. I cried in my dream, clenching my teeth until I woke up. I lie on my back trying to calm my breathing. Is this night endless? I turn on the TV. Idiocy and old movies and infomercials and country music and wild fires and ads and no love anywhere. God, what am I doing here? What's happening, God? What's the point of all this? What's the point of me even looking for a point? Is there anything I might have missed, God? Anything I have to know? Am I going bananas, God? Am I going nuts? And if I am, why? And if I'm not, are you sure? God, what if I decide to put you to the test? What if I put you in a situation in which you would have to make a decision? Huh? Huh? Huh? Huh? A situation in which YOU will have to decide between:

(a) your devout servant in this motel room, or

(b) your stupid principles of non-intervention.

What if I fill the bathtub with water, plunge in, and slit my wrists beautifully—all the way down—with Juanita's big knife? Who's gonna bring me back to the living then? Who? That's what I thought, too—no one. NO ONE. No one, I tell you. No one. N-o o-n-e. No way.

God, I know . . . I have to do something. I have to write. I can't check out of this world before scribbling out a few sentences. It's not cool. It's not me. There was some blank, white paper and pens somewhere here. I have to write a few lines for my little sister, for my mom. This has nothing to do with you, my darlings. Zack will just retire for a little while. Nothing personal. Nothing that . . . I'm looking for a piece of paper. I open the drawer of the nightstand. There's no paper there, only a Bible. What's an American motel without the Holy Bible? Aha . . . Here's a pen "Dear," I begin writing. "My dear little sister, when you read this . . ." The pen is running out of ink. The pen is running out of ink at the beginning of the most important letter of my entire life. So much for good luck. I start shaking it furiously. "... don't know how ..." What do I want to write, actually? How ... what? What? I need a break. I pull the Bible angrily from its spot and open it to a random page. My eyes fall directly on "... there will be weeping and gnashing of teeth." Goosebumps. I read it again word for word.

And then suddenly I feel the chill. A real, physical chill. It comes from nowhere, but it is especially for me. It's some kind of personal chill. It wraps me in its icy veil and pulls me somewhere. My face quickly gets numb. I feel my muscles freeze one after another. My lips withdraw toward my teeth. My skin thins out and stretches over my cheekbones. Underneath it, invisible nails grasp my skull. I start shivering all over and my teeth chatter uncontrollably. The Bible starts shaking in my hands and falls to the floor. I hear a snarl from my stomach. I'm trembling.

Then the sudden chill releases my body as mysteriously as it came. However, the sense that the male body here in this motel room belongs to me returns far more slowly, so it takes time for me to remember how everything works. I put my body, my feet, and my arms back on and shake my shoulders. I bend over slowly and pick up the small Bible from the floor. It had fallen open to "... weeping and gnashing of teeth ..." This is the most precise description of the state in which I woke up. I awoke to the gnashing of my own teeth. And to my weeping. Weeping? Oh, weeping. Weeping. I put the pillow back on the bed, sit down, lean back, and start turning the thin pages.

"... *there will be weeping and gnashing of teeth. And when he said that, he shouted: Whoever has ears—let him listen!*"

Listen to what? To whom? I read the lines above.

"*And cast the worthless servant into the outer darkness; there will be weeping and ...*"

I know this already—"*gnashing of teeth.*" What is "*outer darkness,*" though? I keep reading further above.

"*For to every one who has will more be given, and he will have abundance; but from him who has not, even what he has will be taken away.*"

Serious business.

"*So take the talent from him, and give it to him who has the ten talents.*"

Is this the parable of the talents? The same one in which the master goes abroad and calls upon his servants to entrust them with his property? He gives one five talents, the second one two talents, and the third—one talent.

"*. . . to each according to his ability.*"

According to his ability, huh?

"*He who had received the five talents went at once and traded with them; and he made five talents more. So too, he who had the two talents made two talents more.*"

And the one with the single talent buried it in the ground.

"*Now after a long time the master of those servants came and settled accounts with them. And he who had received the five talents came forward bringing five talents more, saying, 'Master, you delivered to me five talents; here I have made five talents more.'*"

Sucker!

"*His master said to him, 'Well done, good and faithful servant; you have been faithful over a little, I will set you over much; enter into the joy of your master.'*"

The same thing goes for the second servant as well. But then comes the third one, who says: "*Master, I knew you to be a hard man, reaping where you did not sow, and gathering where you did not winnow; so I was afraid, and went and hid your talent in the ground. Here you have what is yours.*"

How does the master treat his faithful servant who did not want to take a risk?

"*You wicked and slothful servant!* . . . *You ought to have invested my money with the bankers, and at my coming I should have received what was my own with interest.*"

And he punishes the servant. But why does he give five talents to one servant and less to the others in the first place? Why doesn't he give them equal amounts? The one with the five talents worked with them. But I guess it's easy to take a risk when you have five talents. You can afford to lose one and then win it back. The pastor on the radio this morning explained that one talent is about ten thousand dollars. So, even if you lose ten grand, there's a chance you'll be alright, because you are still left with forty. Now, the other guy with the two talents seems braver. He risks more: fifty-fifty. Definitely braver. But the third servant? The third one. Just one talent: now what? If he loses it, he's toast. That's why he doesn't risk it. Why should he? Yet the master sees his caution as laziness.

And what is it then, if not laziness?

I don't know, I have to think.

What is there to think about?

I have to think about it.

Wicked servant, you anger me!

I'm sorry.

What is it then, if not laziness?

What?

Don't pretend to be stupider than you are, sly one! Don't you put on an act with me!

I'm not putting on an act.

You are putting on an act.

I'm not. Who are you anyway?

It doesn't matter.

What do you want?

Why didn't you try to do something with the talent I gave you?

What talent?

What talent?! Now you really are pushing it, wicked one!

Oh.

Tell me why.

Because . . .

Yes?

Because . . .

I'm listening.

Because I was . . .

What?

Afraid? Is that you want to hear? I was afraid to lose what I had.

What you have is not yours, stupid! You have nothing . . . Nothing! Understand that and go out into the world, before you anger me so much that I take back everything you think you have. It's not yours. It's mine! I've given it to you to use. Not to bury it in the ground, you ungrateful one. Get out. Out!

Please don't be mad. I have one little question.

I'm not mad. This is how I talk. What do you want to ask?

Isn't there at least one servant in the parable, maybe a fourth one, who is not mentioned, who might have tried to do something with his talents but lost them? Between the first servant with the five talents and the second one with two, there might have been two more—with three and four talents, respectively, I think.

You're thinking too much!

Please tell me what happened to the fourth servant.

What do you want to know?

What happened to him?

How should I know? I don't keep track of those who lose, but of those who don't win!

How about the losers?

There are no losers! The talents are mine!

I wake up. My heart pounds in my throat. The voice still echoes in my head. I don't remember ever hearing it more clearly. Five talents—fifty thousand dollars. Two talents—twenty thousand. Danny said that the grass is worth between twenty and fifty. God, which one of those servants am I?

•

The smell of the previous owners never left the house despite our efforts, including changing the carpet, repainting, and countless attempts with professional-strength cleaning products. The odor was most repulsive in the studio, where it smelled like rotting vegetables, perhaps garlic. Stella didn't even bother taking her easel in there. For a while, she tried painting outside in the yard, but she said the sun was too bright. She didn't like painting outdoors. She felt like she was being watched from all sides. She couldn't get in the right mood. It didn't work, it just did not work . . . She couldn't stand the traffic on her way to work, she didn't like the neighborhood with our invisible neighbors, and she detested the house even more than that repulsive flat in Bulgaria with the noisy planes flying over it. Stella was not happy in our new home.

•

I wake up to a slamming door. Startled, I jump. My heart races wildly. There's no one in the room. I get up and look out through the blinds. A man in the parking lot slams the trunk of a huge Lincoln, gets in, and drives off, screeching his tires. Strange. Even stranger than that is the light. I look at the clock. Eight in the morning. Outside however, it seems to be a different time. It's dusk. Sunset. Orange. Golden twilight. A strong wind is bending the palm trees around the little pool. I decide that the clock is broken and I've slept through the entire day. I go outside. The smell of smoke hits my nostrils, and I see the flying bits of ash. The air really is golden-orange. All of a sudden I realize what scares me the most—the silence. It's silent. Silent almost as if in a dream. In the parking lot there is only one car, mine. My first instinct is to run to the reception desk, but instead I grab my camera and load a roll of color film, the most light-sensitive I have. I take pictures of the empty parking lot, the bending palm trees, the orange horizon, the American flag reflected in the orange windows of the motel . . . I feel like I am in the quiet belly of an orange balloon, which will burst any moment now, and I will see the world in the colors I remember. I take a few more shots, not knowing—and not even wanting to know—whether I'm dreaming or whether a nuclear war has actually started.

I load my belongings in the car calmly, shove the sack of marijuana in the trunk, and open a Toblerone. I bite off two triangles, and, with Juanita's knife in one hand and a chocolate bar in the other, I head off toward the reception desk. War or no war, one must remember what needs to be returned and to whom. Then I see the fire trucks. And the police cars. A man in uniform, Sergeant Somebody, blocks my way. His glance is fixed on the big knife in my hand. I explain that I have to return it to the receptionist and pay for my stay in the motel. This area, he says, is an evacuation zone and you have to leave immediately. That damned Santa Ana has blown the wild fires all the way here. But . . . I have to return this. You have to leave immediately! I promised to return . . . Next time—the sergeant interrupts me. We are just a few miles shy of the most severe fires in California. Don't you watch TV?!? He tells me that I can use this road and that road before they are shut down. I-8 is blocked, 63 South is jammed. A state of emergency has been declared.

I finish up my Toblerone in the car, put the knife under the driver's seat, and take off.

•

I must have made the decision to buy that house subconsciously, hoping that its fireplace would warm up our relationship. At first, Stella was totally against the whole idea of buying a house, but then she gave in and let me do whatever I wanted. I regretted this. I had allowed the real estate propaganda to lure me in, cash out its commission, and then ditch me in this frigid house.

One of the reasons we didn't sell it right away, once we realized that we couldn't live there, was that we would have lost a load of money—the real estate market was growing bitterer by the minute. The other reason was the canyon next to the house. A creek bubbled through it and, depending on the year, it would reach the ocean, or disappear amidst the rocks a few miles down. Birds chirped in the bushes and trees, and cicadas buzzed incessantly in the grass. At night, the soundtrack was taken over by choirs of squalling frogs. The proximity to this amazing oasis, even though it was surrounded by dull, identical suburbs, made us inclined to keep the house a bit longer.

Stella kept her studio in that dilapidated building downtown. Her paintings were stored away, actually piled on top of each other, dusty and covered with bed sheets. I made her promise time and again to bring at least a few home so we could hang them in the house. She never did.

As if she had anticipated the fires.

As if she had seen them.

As if she had provoked them.

•

On one side of the road, more and more houses are engulfed by flames. Over the hills in the distance, I see burning avocado farms, blackened orchards, smoldering fields. I refuse to photograph them. Instead, I take a few shots of the marshlands on the other side of the road, the deserted trailers, and the old rain gullies. I pass a trailer park with erect antennae sticking up toward the sky. They look like enormous caterpillars with their legs randomly pulled out. I photograph that, too. Then I keep driving east.

I can feel the desert now, even though I'm still driving by harvested fields filled with hay bales. At one point, the traffic stalls completely. The cars crawl one at a time under a giant pillar of smoke hovering over the highway. It's my turn now. I pass under the dirty rainbow.

•

We met with the Artist one more time. Those days I had started giving Stella expensive, and often useless, gifts which she accepted with feigned enthusiasm. After two years of working for the company, I managed to scrape together a few days off, used the many thousands of free miles on my MasterCard, and surprised her for her birthday.

It was fall in Paris. We roamed the city all day long. It seemed that I had never seen so many people kissing. I had brought my camera but felt no need whatsoever to look at this city through the rectangular eye of the viewfinder. Everything looked boring, banal, and oh-so-déjà vu. We spent the afternoon at the Louvre. Later, I pulled out Bernard Foucault's business card, and, despite Stella's protests, called him. She didn't want me to do it, insisting that he had invited us only out of courtesy. It didn't mean that we should actually call him three years later. Besides, he would hardly remember us. But I had the feeling that the cold weed creeping through my relationship with Stella had sprouted during our first menacing meeting with that man. Something made me believe that I could turn our life back if only I settled the score with him at another meeting. That is, if I could only manage to tame my overwhelming urge to annihilate this unsuspecting man. I had spent months preparing for this rendezvous. I had spent countless hours rehearsing my lines. I had to present myself as a loving husband, a fan of the Artist, and a devout art aficionado.

We met at a small family restaurant somewhere in Montmartre. I behaved myself all through the second bottle of cabernet. But then the Artist started talking about art, acts of creation, and such, and everything went to hell.

"You know what Bernard . . . romanticizing the act of creating a painting is the same as exalting the flight of a bird."

"And . . . uh, Zacque, what's so bad about that? Why not look at the world from a bird's eye view?"

"Monsieur Bernard, birds don't fly because they desperately need to see the world from a bird's eye view, but simply because they cannot find what they are looking for on the ground."

"And what is that, Zacque?" I loathed, absolutely loathed, the way he pronounced my name, adding that short, soft "que," that diminutive suffix fused with garlic breath.

"Bernard, listen to me! Are you listening? Listen now, the creative act of an artist and the flight of a crane or a blackbird have one sole purpose—survival. Survival!"

"And why do you think, uh, so?"

"Even the most beautiful bird, Bernard, doesn't fly for pleasure, but for practical reasons. And actually, Bernard, I'm talking about true art, the art of your own countrymen—Rimbaud, Baudelaire, Mallarmé, Gauguin, Matisse . . . about true art, not some kind of post-postmodern, neo-minimalist, monumental shit."

"Everybody creates art the best they can." Bernard tries not to be hurt.

"Excuse me!?" I'm already furious. "Bernard"—I slam my fist down on the table—"art is not doing what we can do! Art is doing what we can't not do! No matter how well we do it. Actually the better you do it— the worse! This turns us from honest amateurs into jaded professionals. It turns us into craftsmen, tailors, bricklayers, shoemakers. What? I'm

making no sense? Of course I'm not. What makes me happy? What about ha . . . ? Happiness? O-o-oh, happiness, shmappiness, love, God— these are all probably functions of the liver. Or the brain, same fucking difference. Simply pheromones, hormones, chemistry . . . It's been proven. Read scientific literature!"

I spilled wine on my shirt, ordered one last bottle, stuffed my face with crème brûlée, paid the bill, and we left.

The full moon outside energized me even more. I somehow remembered a verse by François Villon, shouted it in Bulgarian, and three youngsters in leather jackets cussed me out, I lunged at them to fight, Stella and Bernard stood between them and me to separate us, he told them something, and his soft voice managed to calm them down.

Then he walked us to our hotel, we said good night, he kissed me (French, how French), and I headed up the stairs wobbling, expecting Stella to say good-bye and follow me. Disgusted with myself, I went into the bathroom right away to take a shower and stood under the warm Parisian water for a long time. When I got out, Stella was not in the room. I sat in the chair next to the bed for several endless minutes before I dared peek through the curtains down at the little courtyard where I left them. The cobblestones of Montmartre bluishly reflected the ample moon light.

And then I saw the Artist and Stella pull away from each other. She shot a quick glance up toward our window and disappeared into the shadow of the entrance.

•

I turn on the radio. Every station is broadcasting the fires. Apparently they started yesterday. The first flames had been noticed at daybreak in Potrero, a small town north of the Mexican border. Some David Finley called 911 and said that he could see flames at a neighboring ranch, which was uninhabited. He also said that he'd stay to protect his home if things became critical. Twenty minutes later the fire was out of control. David Finley burned to death in his ranch along with his handicapped son. Forty miles north of there, a little while later, another fire had been spotted. A few miles to the west, the forests of Witch Creek blazed up, those flames were heading to the southwest, after just an hour they had reached a height of fifty or sixty meters and were moving so fast that no living creature in their path had even a prayer of escaping. In Steel Canyon, another fire was raging across the country, picking up speed, and, if it had reached Descanso Valley, hundreds of homes could have been destroyed. Bandy Canyon, Rainbow Canyon, San Martos Canyon, Palomar, Sorrento Hills, Pomerado . . . Highway 15 in northern San Diego is experiencing traffic delays because of low visibility due to the smoke. The Harris Fire roared west all morning across Rancho Bernardo and Poway, destroying hundreds of structures and forcing thousands of people from their homes as it followed the same path taken by the disastrous Cedar Fire a few years earlier. Tens of thousands of people have been evacuated. Those fires—I come to understand—are being pushed by strong Santa Ana winds. The same winds are expected to ground firefighting aircraft for a second straight day. The Santa Ana winds make taming the fires impossible.

People who have lost their homes call the radio stations.

An out-of-breath, raspy voice: ". . . the Devil's wind, the Devil's wind came . . . Not Santa Ana, it's *Satana!*"

A calm voice: ". . . have no idea where I'll spend the night. I have to be in court tomorrow morning, but all of my suits are gone."

A high-pitched voice, a little crazy sounding: ". . . the most important thing is that we managed to save Becky . . . Becky, say 'Hi,' say 'Hi,' Becky, say . . . *ruff, ruff* . . . Good girl!"

•

What happened between Stella and me in France was as sudden as
love at first sight. We spent the second night in Paris avoiding each oth-
er's glances and behaving matter-of-factly like accountants who have
worked together at the same company for a long time. On our way back
to the States, at the airport, we read magazines. I was secretly spying
on her over the pages to make sure that I wasn't imagining things.
She was staring at an article that she was either reading for the tenth
time or hadn't started at all. Her face was impenetrable. We boarded
the Boeing. I remember I was looking at the small green airplane on
the screen before me, swallowing hard on the airplane food. While
we were climbing above Paris, everything still seemed as serious as if
it were make-believe. As if we were playing some kind of a game for
grownups. And if one of us had started laughing, the other one would
have immediately joined in, as had always happened during all of our
years together.

This time, however, neither she nor I would give in. We both felt that
this time, it was different.

While the little plane on the screen was over England, we still
seemed to have a chance to avoid everything that would follow.

I tried to take a little nap over the Atlantic.

I woke up over Iceland, only to find her staring at the back of the
seat in front of her.

Over Greenland, the suspicion that things had irrevocably changed
settled silently between us.

Over Canada, I knew for certain that down below a cold and alien
continent was waiting for me.

After all those hours in the air, we landed in California like two
strangers who merely helped each other with their luggage.

•

On an adjacent dirt road, against the background of some distant bluish mountains, I notice a dense swirl of smoke with a

motorcycle flying in front of it. This fascinates me for some strange reason. I pull over on the shoulder abruptly, hit the brakes, and jump out of the car with the camera. A cloud of dust engulfs me. I snap three or four shots and run out of film. I reach in my pocket for more.

•

—have you ever been unsure about whether a memory, story, or dream belongs to you or me?
—no
—yesterday, i started telling something and suddenly i hesitated. i wasn't sure whether it had actually happened to me or if i'd heard it from you
—darling, i know my memories
—mine seem like memories of memories. ghosts. as if i'm made out of ghosts
—stella?
—yes
—i'm in love with you
—you're in love with my ghost, silly
—you just can't be a ghost with these goose-bumped boobs, this long, tousled hair, these lips, and these blue eyes. you are sweet as milk and honey. there are no such ghosts
—there aren't?
—no

•

After our return to America, Stella fell into something of a fever. She spent the first twenty-four hours in her studio, didn't come home at all, and finished eleven paintings. She painted during every single minute of her free time. She came home exhausted, spattered with paint, and distant. At night, she stayed up late in front of the computer, writing. She withdrew, disappeared into her inner self, and, without giving off any negativity whatsoever, she began leaving me and everyone else around us. I noticed that she started walking straighter somehow. Her skin, despite the sleeplessness, was firm. Her face radiated softness—an unaddressed, different softness. Her eyes were both lively and cold at the same time. Stella explained nothing and wanted nothing. She painted. She didn't talk. I, on the other hand, tried to find peace on my business trips. I monitored clinics that were recently visited and found reasons to conduct more and more site visits. I took up extra work and started moonlighting as a private consultant for another firm, thus violating my work contract with ICONIQ. I zealously chose to go to more and more distant and dull clinics. I spent hours and hours at airports, staring at TV screens, tuned in to the compulsory CNN. The same old news from the Near East. The same old dark stringy arms holding AK-47s above their heads. The same old white men getting off airplanes, wearing expensive suits. The same old explosions, same old anger, same old analyses, same old real estate problems, same old stock markets, same old natural disasters, same old advertisements of the same old companies that made sure everything was the same old same old.

When two people turn their backs on each other, one usually looks ahead and the other—to the past. I was staring at CNN.

•

"There must be better places to photograph than this wasteland!" A low male voice startles me. Right behind my car, a big, black, shiny police motorcycle has pulled up. No! I'll just never wise up. "There must be better places, huh?" Behind the uniformed giant's mirrored aviators, there are probably irises, a retina, a cornea, optic nerves, humanity . . . I don't see any of that. The cop is on his motorcycle, inches away from a big bag of marijuana and three yards away from a jackass with a camera.

"Uh-h . . ." Nothing comes out of my mouth.

"You didn't signal before you pulled off the main road." The cop stirs in his seat. He keeps staring at me. He pulls off one of his gloves and moves his fingers. Should I start running? Should I . . . "This is illegal, you know." Every American cop loves uttering the word "illegal." "It's illegal." I want to murder him. A man unwittingly starts behaving like a criminal simply because he is driving with a load of marijuana in the trunk.

"I'm sorry, sir!" I mumble, while the cop takes off his other glove. Is he going to give me a ticket or what? "I'm sorry!" Cops like to see that you are sorry, that you are very sorry. "I'm very sorry." And that you respect them. "I respect the law, sir. I'm sorry." You can save yourself all sorts of trouble if you just keep your head down.

"Me, too. Drivers license and registration, please." Maniac. This one's a maniac. "Yes, sir. Of course, sir." In moments like this I understand why you need an unregistered gun in the glove compartment. I take out the documents and approach him.

"Are you from the newspaper?" There we go. Am I from the paper? What's the right answer? To *be* or *not to be* from the paper? There was a trace of friendliness in his tone. Perhaps even more? Perhaps. What if he is on very good terms with the local media? What if he *is* the local hero in the battle against human and drug trafficking? Has he been on the front page?

"No, sir. I'm not from the paper."

"That's what I thought." The cop turns away slightly and pulls out a bottle of water. He unscrews the cap carefully and takes a long sip without shifting his sunglasses from me. My nose itches. I scratch it with the hand holding the car insurance policy slip. Stella's name flashes before my eyes. "That's what I thought." The cop takes off his glasses, pulls out a small white handkerchief from his top pocket, and starts wiping them carefully without even glancing at the papers in my hand. *Gestapo* blue eyes, nothing human. "Take your pictures and drive safely. It's a danger zone out here. The fires. Have a nice day." The cop puts his shades on and starts his engine. My legs are shaking. "Next time, signal when you pull over!"

•

I met Ken in Ohio. At the bar where I worked there was a regular customer who was thirty-something. She would show up from time to time, order a pint of the local amber, sit at the corner table, and stare blankly at one of the TVs. I didn't know her name. I remembered her face, just like I remember the faces of everyone who has ever ordered something from me. So one night she showed up with someone. He had light blue, glazed eyes and a receding hairline. He was a little chubby and wore a shirt buttoned-up to the top with no tie. She ordered the usual brew, he—a Coca-Cola. He attempted to pay the bill but she stopped him and firmly paid for her own drink, which made him uncomfortable, I think. Then, she made the surprising move of introducing us to each other. My name was obvious to everyone because it was pinned on my vest, but she created the illusion for him that she had known me for a long time. His name was Ken. Hers was still unknown to me. Pleased to meet you, pleased to meet you. They sat at the most distant table and for a while I forgot about them. In an hour, she came to the bar and thanked me for being so kind to her. I glanced at Ken over her shoulder and noticed that he was staring at the glass between his nervous palms. I suspected, by now, that his Coke had warmed up like a cup of bad coffee. She introduced herself—Linda—and explained that she had met the guy just recently and didn't know of any other place where she would feel safe. This reminds me of a home I once had, she said.

I thanked her for that and poured another pint of draft beer. Two weeks later, I saw them again. They looked more relaxed with each other, although Linda still paid her bill separately. Then they started coming every week—usually on Wednesdays. I suppose the idea of meeting on the weekend seemed too involving to her. The way they treated each other made me think that he had been widowed for a long time and that she had never been engaged. Later, I would learn that I had almost been right.

It must have been a Thursday, because Friends *was on when they came back in. She ordered not her usual beer, but vodka and orange juice (uh, big night?), he asked for a Coke again, and they sat at a table by the window. At this moment, they were the only customers I had. I remember that during a commercial break, I decided to run to the back for more white wine. When I returned, holding a few bottles of chardonnay and sauvignon blanc in my arms, I saw Linda, stiffened, clasping the arm rests of her chair as if trying to get up but staying glued to the seat. Ken, across from her, was frozen with some kind of a half-assed grin on his face—a leftover from the last moment of an interrupted conversation. They looked like a still from a paused video. I left the bottles and quickly ran over to their table. Ken still couldn't peel that stupid grimace off his face. Linda, rolling her eyes, pointed to her throat. I grabbed her from behind, crossed her arms over her chest and shook her. A moment later, she noisily inhaled, started coughing, and her face eventually regained its color. She had choked on a piece of pulp from the orange juice.*

Ken claimed that I had saved the love of his life, for which he would always be indebted to me.

•

Before leaving California, I cross a vast field with hundreds of huge windmills, lazily masticating the desert air. Behind them is a row of hills, softened by the distance and the haze and spotted with white, round rocks like a leopard.

And then, at that moment, in the dry sky with no trace of a cloud—I see the rainbow. Seven small, mother-of-pearl brushstrokes, and not in the usual pastel colors, but in their saturated versions—from electric blue, poison green, and golden yellow to tangerine orange. If God has painted this—I smile and adjust my sweaty ass, which is stuck to the seat—he is nothing but a child. There are a couple more cars sharing the long drawn-out highway, but I get the unerring feeling that this rainbow is meant for me. This cutout up in the sweltering sky is absolutely out of place. At the same time, I'm sure that I'm not hallucinating and that it is not an illusion. I don't even bother photographing it—some things are not meant to be captured on film.

•

Six months after we met the Artist, Stella bought a ticket to Paris. "I can't stand this any more, Zack. I have to find myself and I have to do it alone." I didn't know what to say. There was nothing I could say. Could I stop her? When somebody is getting ready for their personal trip, the only thing you can do is help with the luggage. My pain in those last few days was unbearable, but I think I managed to conceal it. The morning before she left, we had coffee, I sent her off to the airport, and went to work. When I came home, I noticed her coffee cup with the pale lipstick mark on the rim. I didn't wash it. Why did I put it away unwashed? She had left everything here—her paintings, her poems, her youth, everything . . . Why did I make a fetish out of this particular trace of her? The two weeks during which she was gone, I spent my time at airports and in hotel rooms. I stayed late at hotel bars drinking martini after martini. I listened to strangers' bullshit, then went up to my room, watched porn, CNN, and fell asleep hugging the pillows. During the day, I perused protocols and data, looking for the tiniest discrepancy to catch. Around that time, I started eating Toblerones.

•

If I were to travel long enough in one direction, I'd pass through deserts, mountains, and seas, and get back to the point where I started. The spaces—even this road rushing toward the horizon—no matter how flat they look, are, after all, parts of one globe which can be walked around. We know that. But what about time? Does it still remain so incomprehensible?

In the distance, on the roof of a wooden building, I see a big white sign reading: JESUS CHRIST Is LORD. Smaller letters underneath it read: *Pumpkins and corn for sale.*

And what if we just have the wrong idea about time? More precisely, about the direction we are moving in it. We have been taught to believe that life begins with birth, goes through maturity, aging, and, inevitably, ends badly. According to this universal outlook, things move from new toward old, from pleasure toward pain, from passion to indifference, from beauty to rotten teeth and Alzheimer's. In this *natural* order of events, every relatively reasonable, thinking individual would have to be a pessimist, since that is the only possible attitude given the system in which we exist. In this *natural* order of events—birth, childhood, youth, old age, death—any more optimistic theory would have to be regarded as a sign of a psychological disturbance, or fiction. It wouldn't have been in unison with nature. But what if all of it is wrong? What if we actually live our lives backward? What if we live in—let's call it—the principle of *backward* time? What if everything starts with death, whose cause we choose, goes through old age (in most cases), sickness, habits, middle age, crises, youth, disappointments, love, adolescence, hopes, childhood, and ends up in the womb? What if *this* is the natural order of things and optimism is a residue of one *natural* way of thinking? What if what they taught us in school is simply a *superstition*? It's been clear to poets who have predicted their own deaths down to the last detail, to artists who painted *future* cities and machines, to psychics describing events with incredible precision, to prophets of all kinds of religions all over the world. And if this isn't enough, children cannot be wrong. Babies, for example, cry when they are born. For no other reason than they are mercilessly clear that their lives are just ending. With time however, they become used to the rules of the game. They pretend to understand backward living, they learn to forget who they are, and only from time to time, at a playground, you can hear a kid starting a story with the words, "Once upon a time, when I was a grownup . . ." What if we live not our real lives, but a reflection of them, in which everything is upside down? Maybe, with every new decision we make, we try to correct events from the past, which is impossible, and thus we are sentenced to failure. Every single plan we make for the future is inadequate because it's pointed in the wrong direction.

Under the principle of backward time, everything has already happened.

•

America is still one of the few places in the world where a person can make a decent living with honest work and perseverance. I did it otherwise. Here is what happened. After the choking incident, Ken and Linda became more frequent visitors to the bar. Something like a friendship started to form between us. And while she was still reserved, or maybe embarrassed by the episode, Ken stared at everything I said with his blue eyes wide open and a smile ready to glide toward his old-fashioned sideburns at any moment. When I talked to him, he had the annoying habit of moving his lips, as if he were listening to me with them.

One evening, Ken showed up earlier than usual, looking nervous and excited. Linda arrived at the regular time and they withdrew to their table in the corner. Ken never stopped glancing at me, as if he were afraid I might leave. Then they left. I was surprised later to see him entering the bar just before closing time. He said he had something important to tell me. The information he wanted to share with me was "extremely important." I kept on doing what I was doing—closing the bar and listening to him inattentively. Ken was the chief buyer for an upholstery-producing factory, how important could that be? It was a small business, quite conservative. The son of the owner had just taken over the company and had been promising serious changes. No one, however, expected them to be this serious, said Ken, signaling to me to come closer and listen carefully. As far as I knew, Ken didn't drink, which made this otherwise inebriated gesture somehow significant. I leaned over the bar.

"Don Simons," whispered Ken, "the new boss, has signed a contract with Honda." I didn't know what to say, so I shrugged.

"Well, good."

"For supplying the interior upholstery of the new cars made here for the American market."

"So?"

"Don signed the contract for the new model, which means that we have to increase our production by at least five hundred percent. He doesn't have that much capital. That's why he's selling the business to an investment company in Cleveland."

"What do you mean, selling it?"

"I mean, selling it—with all its assets."

"What about you? What about the workers?"

"Listen. Only a few people know this, believe me, only a few. You don't need to know how I know it. What you need to do tomorrow is go to the closest stock exchange, or do it over the Internet. Now . . . listen to me carefully. The investor company is called INSTALLMATIC. Buy as much stock in INSTALLMATIC as you can. Their index is . . . get something to write with . . . their index on the New York Stock Exchange is JPI. You got it? JPI. So right now, their stock is selling at about four dollars a share. The day after tomorrow they will be worth at least three hundred percent more. At least. Zack, you understand? Do this. Do it for yourself and your wife."

"And how about you?" I ask. "Are you gonna do it?"

"No, I can't. If they catch me, I'll go to jail. This is no joke." I start wiping the counter for a while.

"Ken," I say. "I have a better idea. I'll scrape together some money, but I don't have a lot. If you lend me some, I'll buy stocks for you, then we'll share the profit."

"Three hundred percent, Zack. I'm telling you."

After closing the bar, I went home and spent a sleepless night. Without telling Stella, I gathered up everything we had in the bank. I pawned the car and the few valuables we owned. Before noon I had eleven thousand dollars, with which I bought shares of INSTALL-MATIC. I borrowed twenty more from Ken, bought more shares and started waiting. The next day, Don Simons announced the sale of his company. The shares went up. Not by the predicted three hundred percent. Five hundred.

Two days later I sold the shares, walked into the photo store on High Street and bought all the photo equipment I needed. And for Stella, I bought the biggest easel from the art store. I went home and told her everything. That night, we went to a fancy restaurant, we ate the most expensive steaks, drank expensive wine, expensive cognac, and champagne as the city lights sparkled in the quiet waters of the Ohio River. We went home late, staggering and undressing each other up the stairs. We made love slowly and passionately, falling asleep embracing, woke up, and made love again. We were winners. It was delicious.

·

—aren't you sometimes afraid that this will remain here between us? all of these words, thoughts, silences . . . all this will remain unshared?

—is that why you're taking pictures of me?

—maybe

—no, i'm not afraid.

•

I catch up with a red pick-up truck. In its bed, two plastic black and white bags, whipped by the wind and speed, violently beat the crap out of each other. After a few moments of combat, one prevails and the other flies out and sticks to my windshield, right under the left wiper blade. I turn on the wipers to shoo away the intruder and switch on the radio, hoping to distract myself from my thoughts. I search the stations and I pause at a country song, "pray, pray, pray" sings the man, lamenting over his nights without his beloved woman. I step on the gas so I can pass the red pick-up. Just a second before I leave it behind, I notice the weathered bumper sticker that reads PRAY. What is this? Yet another coincidence? Or yet more proof that everything is just a set up. Why did I have to listen to country, a style I never liked, and what are the odds of *hearing* and *seeing* the same word at the same time in the middle of the desert? Do these coincidences play into the backward time I was thinking about before I caught up with the red pick-up? Is it possible that this *synchronicity* is another reminder (like confusing *déjà vu*) that I don't think straight? What is straight, anyway?

I take the exit toward a small town. I need to eat something. At the second light, the street narrows—one of the lanes is under construction and some pipes jut out of the asphalt. I drive slowly past sign that reads MEN AT WORK. Then I see the men at work. My eyes are drawn to one guy, who is ferociously beating the asphalt with a sledgehammer. I'd like to be a worker now, too; with a sledgehammer and an orange helmet; with a sweaty, once-white T-shirt and jeans worn out in the crotch. I want to take a hammer and beat the earth with it until it cracks open and I find Stella. Then I won't mess up my head with theories anymore.

On the desolate, squalid town square I spot a Mexican cantina and pull up in front of it. Fans, hanging from the ceiling. turn in the air slowly, a boom-box plays *corridos*, and the smell of burned grease fills the room. A customer in a plaid shirt and suspenders, with a mustache and a white sombrero, sits under a faded, fly-specked Frida reproduction and eats a fat burrito. Two chubby kids with backpacks lean over quesadillas and drink from a Fanta bottle with two straws. Behind the counter, a dark Mexican smiles at me, his hair bluish-black like a crow's feathers.

"A-a-a-a, señor, cómo estás?"

"Nada," I reply and start reading the chalk-written menu above his head. I don't feel like talking to Mexicans right now.

"No, no, no, no, no-o-o-o-o, amigo. Cómo estás mean *How are joo*. You don' say *nada*. Nada mean *nothing*. OK? You gotta say, *Muy bien, gracias! Y tú?* Da means, a-a-a, I am well. How about joo? When joo say *nada*, joo say *nothing*. OK, now again: Amigo, cómo estás?"

"Nada. Nada means nada. I'm not well, amigo. I am nada!"

"Ay, ay, ay, senor. Why joo don't eat sonthing, drink *una cerveza* and everything will be all right."

"Give me one *carne asada gordita*. No onions, please." The Mexican writes my order down with a pencil and hands it to the invisible cook behind him. I open the dirty fridge and pull out a green bottle of beer. I drink two of those while my food is cooking. Then, I attack my fat *gordita* hungrily. Pieces of meat, lettuce, diced tomatoes, and bell peppers fall from the edges, but I gather them with my fingers from the greasy table and shove them into my mouth. Tasty. I feel much better when I leave the joint.

I get into my car and open the windows. My belly is full. Right next to my spot, a rusty brown Datsun comes to a halt with a screech. Behind the wheel is a stringy, fortyish guy with a goatee in a black muscle shirt. Two scruffy bleached-blonde girls, high school age, grin in the back seat. The three of them stare at me.

"Dude," says the Goatee. "Your car smells good. Very good."

"Really?" I say as I turn on the ignition.

"You can smell it from outside." One of the girls licks her upper lip and passes a joint to the other one. Both of them keep staring at me and grinning. Goatee's hair is short in the front and parted down the middle, but long in the back, falling over his shoulders. It is definitely an odd attempt at a mullet. Some of his teeth are bad and some missing. "It smells like . . ." There is something overtly sexual and sickening about this trio. With my right hand, I feel the car seat for my sun-heated camera, pull it up in front of my face, and quickly take a few shots. All three of them burst into wild laughter. I shoot again. "You wanna take pictures, huh, dude?! You wanna take pictures?! Well, how about this!" The Goatee holds up the blondish head of a third girl whom I hadn't noticed before because she had been bent down in his lap. Her lipstick is smeared. She has last night's make up on and her look is as blank as the sky above this empty parking lot. I take one last shot while the two girls laugh hysterically and jump out of the car, running toward the cantina. The Goatee flips a tattooed finger at me and pushes the third girl's head back down. I step on the gas pedal. The bunch of coconut air-freshener trees dangle beneath the rear view mirror—the smell I wanted to chase Stella away with.

•

Stella came home from France. On our way back from the airport, she opened the car window, took out a packet of menthols, and lit one. She had started smoking. I tried to say something about how unnecessary this bad habit was, but she interrupted me with a gesture. She felt like smoking and that was that. I could hardly swallow my exasperation. I felt offended.

I tried to convince myself that all this was temporary. She also made efforts to keep up a somewhat civilized coexistence; we were both learning to live pragmatically, like everybody else around us.

She started buying larger and larger canvases for her paintings—which I had less and less of a desire to see. When I actually had to, I found less and less meaning in them. In the beginning, everything she painted was close to me, and we talked about her art for hours. As time passed, though, her paintings became less interesting and more incomprehensible. Her last pieces were nine-foot squares in gray oil which told me nothing. Stella's first exhibit in California was a group show with one other painter and two sculptors. It was in a small, new gallery in San Clemente. On the day of the opening, I was busy conducting a site visit in Earlstown, Iowa, where, while tracking files and the database, I found two somewhat significant violations of the protocol. From the hotel room that night, I had a view of vast corn fields. The sky over them was leaden. It was the beginning of fall in Iowa. I watched the tall corn, ready for harvest, and wondered whether we, too, had our seasons. Does love have seasons?

•

I arrive in the Valley of the Sun—I guess that's what they call Phoenix—in the late afternoon. I park in front of a tourist information center and get out of the car to stretch my stiff body, pick up a map of the city, and use the telephone book. In it, I find one of the few surviving professional photography stores that carry chemicals for black and white photography and processing equipment. I call to make sure they're still in business. They are. Just before closing time, I manage to find the store. The owner is an old-timer wearing a blue vest and thick prescription glasses, with a crooked mouth and dwarf's beard, who scuffles amidst the shelves to the sound of his flip-flops. I buy Kodak film developer D-76, Ilford's rapid fixing solution and stop bath, a canister, a few one-gallon bottles, and some film negative sleeves. For a moment, I hesitate as to whether I'll need a thermometer like the one I used before (twenty-five dollars), but pass on the idea. I pay and leave with something vaguely resembling a smile on my face. I stop on the sidewalk and see off the last third of the sun setting behind the brick building on the west side of the street. Suddenly, the temperature drops. I cross the street and enter a supermarket. There, I buy a kitchen thermometer for five bucks, clothes pins (which I will use to dry negatives and pictures), several Tobelerones, and a bottle of scotch.

I find a hotel close to the freeway. My room is on the third floor, overlooking the dense trail of red and white car lights. After the Mexican food, I'm still full. I start in with the chemicals. I dissolve the chemical powder in water and get ready to develop the rolls of film. I go into the bathroom. I lay out my improvised tools, memorize where everything is, and turn off the lights. In the darkness, I crack open the first roll of film with my car key— God, it's been a while since I've done this—and I feel my hands trembling with excitement. I take a deep breath and try to relax a little. The lid of the first roll drops to the bathroom floor. I grope for the film, caress it, pull it, unwind it and let it hang down. I use my teeth to tear it from the spool. I love this delicate moment of violence. The instant when, with a short bite—I always use my teeth, never scissors—I free the film from the prison of the cassette roll. I fumble in the dark for the developing tank and start rolling the film onto the reel. My heart beats faster. I manage to load the reel, place it in the tank, and close it. I take another breath and make sure that everything is going well. I turn on the light. I pour some developer into the container and start the process. The first fifty-five seconds I shake the canister like a martini. I let the film rest for thirty seconds, and then shake it for five seconds each minute. For twelve minutes. I pour out the used developer, stop-bath it, turn on the faucet, and let the water run into the canister to wash it. I fix the film for another twelve minutes then let the water run over it for a long time. I continue with the hypo-bath, washing it again. I open the tank to check on the result and my heart starts pounding. Here they are—the negatives of everything I shot today. Here they are. I lift the film up to the bathroom light and stare at the little rectangles for a long moment. At a particular angle, and only for me, they come to life. I pin up the film to dry and jump in the shower.

My motel is too cheap to have a restaurant. Across from my room however, I can make out the big red "M" of a Marriot shining in the inky sky, so I decide to check it out. My plans for the night include a few martinis. I go out and inhale the desert night. I cross the enormous parking lot and go into the hotel. I nod to the girl at the reception desk and find the lobby bar, lush with plastic greenery and despicably lit like a small-town bus station.

"Good evening," I say, sitting down next to a gentleman in a plaid blazer who is reading the *Wall Street Journal.* He glances at me, nods, and keeps on reading while the bartender finds a second to take his eyes off the baseball game on the TV and nod in my direction with a *how-can-I-help-you* look.

"A dirty vodka martini," I say. The bartender is a tall, clumsy guy in a badly ironed shirt with a haircut that needs attention. He doesn't cool the martini glass, shakes the vodka in the shaker only a few times, doesn't add any dry vermouth, and pushes the glass toward me. I can't help but notice his dirty nails.

"Anything else?" I don't answer and don't reach toward his masterpiece. He shrugs his shoulders and is about to pull away.

"May I have a dirty martini, please?" I push away the glass. I don't like making scenes. All I want is a dirty martini, not just chilled vodka in a martini glass.

"This is a martini, isn't it?" the tall kid snaps.

"Can you make it dirty?"

"How?" He grunts.

"Well, first you make a martini, and then you stir it with your index finger." He involuntarily looks at his hand, then at me, and gets red in the face. The gentleman with the paper bites his lips. Now I feel bad that I offended the kid—after all, he had the decency to ask me like a man.

"Sir . . ." He starts.

"I'm kidding." I say. "I'm kidding. Just drop two or three drops of dry vermouth right here, pin three olives on this little sword, then pour a little bit of the brine right from the olive jar and it will look dirty. No big deal." The tall kid does as I say. I down the glass and before he manages to disappear to the safety of his corner closer to the TV, I gesture to him to repeat the procedure. The second one is far better because I asked him to mix the ingredients before shaking the vodka in the shaker. The third martini is almost perfect. The outlines of the world begin to soften up somehow. Phoenix, Arizona . . . I look in the direction of the guy with the paper, but his nose is deeply buried in pages filled with columns of small numbers. I'm getting bored. Should I go up to my room and write something? What should I write? A diary? What do I need a diary for? So that one day (if I choose to live without her, that is) I can read my own drivel? But I'm trying so hard to forget it right now. What should I write? A novel? If what has happened to me hasn't happened to you, there is no way you can imagine it. And if it has happened to you, there is no point in remembering it. Who needs another book about a separation? Who needs another sad book? Who needs another book at all?

"A beer." A voice startles me. To my left, a guy in a baseball cap and an orange shirt has wobbled up to the bar. He looks around, narrowing his eyes to focus on the setting. "Phoenix, fuckin' Arizona, man!"

"What kind of beer?" The bartender asks.

"Who cares?" The bartender shrugs and pours him a glass of Bud Light. "I am," yells the man with the baseball cap "getting married next month."

"Good for you," I say.

"What happened to you?" He points at my face.

"I fell down the stairs."

"Aha." My new bar-stool neighbor grins. "I, on the other hand, am getting married"—he looks at his watch—"in twenty-nine days and . . . eight hours." This time the guy with the *Wall Street Journal* murmurs, "Good for you," without lifting his head from the paper.

At this moment, a woman of undeterminable age with a pretty, but somewhat tired face walks toward the bar, and having heard the last sentence, says, "Congratulations."

"I," bellows the soon-to-be married man to my left, "lived in a tent for five years." Pause, during which he finishes his beer. "In Alaska!" he adds and bangs the bottom of the bottle on the bar. "I had hair this long and a beard down to here. And I lived in Alaska for five years."

"Was it cold enough for you?" says the gentleman with the paper. The woman orders a Chardonnay.

"And I was a radio DJ. Do you know what my show was called?"

"What?" asks the paper.

"I had a heater."

"*I Had a Heater?* That's an interesting title."

"No—I'm saying that I had a heater and I wasn't cold. But my show was called *The Hour of Enlightenment.*" He confirms what he just said by banging his fist on the bar. "*The Hour of Enlightenment!*"

"Fascinating." The gentleman shuffles his paper and keeps on reading.

"Fascinating, indeed!"

"Are you still a radio DJ?" asks the woman softly and sips her wine.

"No. I'm a flight attendant now, for United."

"And what about the radio?"

"There is no radio anymore. There is no *Hour of Enlightenment* any more. Only darkness. Dark darkness. I am a flight attendant. Give me another beer. Please."

"The same?"

"No."

"What beer then?"

"It doesn't matter. I'm from Minnesota. From Bob Dylan's hometown. Do you know Bob Dylan's real name?" The flight attendant turns to me. I tell him what Bob Dylan's real name is. "Great! You know. What are you drinking? Very few people know that Bob Dylan's name is not Bob Dylan. But you know. There is no independent radio in Alaska anymore. It was bought by corporate bastards and now they play the same six songs they play everywhere else in the world . . . No *Hour of Enlightenment.* Cheers! But I'm getting married in a month. My fiancée is sweet. We're gonna live in Jersey. She's a flight attendant, too. In the beginning, we'll see each other every other week. Then I'll tell her: 'Listen, you stay home and take care of the kid, and I'll fly and take care of you.' Two flight attendants make for an impossible couple. The marriage will . . ." Here a downward gesture of a falling airplane follows, accompanied by the appropriate sound effect. *"B-h-s-h-s-h-s-h-s-h-s!"*

"You have a child?" the woman asks.

"She's got a kid. Thirteen years old. I studied history in college. I wanted to become a historian. But there was no one to tell me, to even mention, that in the whole state of Minnesota there were only three jobs for historians and they were already taken. Five years in college, five years in Alaska in a tent, hair and a beard this long, *The Hour of Enlightenment,* and my ratings were this high . . . Now I open Pepsi cans on an airplane." He pauses. "Another beer, please." He gets his beer. I order a martini.

"Sign a prenup," says the *Wall Street Journal* man, completely out of nowhere.

"We're getting married in Vegas."

"Do you know her well?" asks the man to my right.

"I love Elvis Presley."

"Good."

"Angie is a good person. She said *yes*. A good person. I asked her half an hour ago. And she said *yes*."

"How did you ask her?"

"On the phone."

"On the phone?"

"On the god-damn phone."

"Tomorrow you call her and tell her you were drunk and don't remember anything."

"I am drunk."

"That's right."

"But I remember everything!"

"I used to call my ex-wife *the plaintiff*," says the gentleman to my right. "Yeah, I called her *the plaintiff. The plaintiff* did this, *the plaintiff* said that . . ."

"You're divorced?" Sincerely surprised, the flight attendant takes a sip from his beer.

"Just recently."

"Wow!"

"For the third time."

"Was it expensive?"

"What?"

"The wedding?"

"No."

"Really?"

"Well, not compared to the divorce."

"And how about the divorce?"

"The divorce was expensive. Especially if it's your third."

The flight attendant scratches his head. "I own Bob Dylan's sink."

"Excuse me?"

"I bought it from the antique store in town. With a certificate. Guaranteeing that it really is from his house. From . . . uh . . . the house he grew up in . . . before he changed his name to Bob Dylan. His name is not Bob Dylan. I bought it and threw it in the back of my pick-up, tied it up with a rope, and drove it home. Now it's in the basement. It must cost a fortune on eBay. But I'm never gonna sell it."

"Why?"

"Because I don't need money. And I'll tell my wife, my future wife, the same thing: I don't need money. I want to be happy!"

"That's right." The *Wall Street Journal* turns to another page.

"I want to be very happy."

"Good."

"In Vegas. In twenty-nine days . . . seven hours . . . forty se . . ."

"Why Vegas?"

"Because that's the only place where a priest can dress as Elvis Presley."

"I see."

"I have to buy her a wedding ring. How much was yours?"

The gentleman looks away from the paper and thinks for a second. "Well, my first wife's wedding ring was ten thousand dollars, but the *plaintiff* left with an eighty-thousand-dollar one. The divorce was in the millions."

"Wow, what do you do for living?"

"I'm an attorney."

"Oh, a lawyer. I knew a lawyer in Alaska. But he, you know, used to paddle on both sides of the canoe." A wink.

"Excuse me?" The lawyer doesn't understand.

"He paddled on both sides of the canoe." The flight attendant winks again, making the *soft wrist* gesture.

"Oh!" The lawyer starts roaring with laughter and finally sets his paper aside. "He was gay. Both sides of the canoe . . . I'll remember that."

"If I need money, I'll sell Bob Dylan's sink."

"Young man," the lawyer prepares to get up. "I have to go. It was a pleasure talking with you." Then to the bartender, "One more pinot noir and the bill, please. I'm going up to my room. Can I take it with me?"

"Yes, sure."

"How much do I owe you?"

"Twenty-seven dollars." The attendant jumps from his seat and extends one hand toward the lawyer, and takes the check with the other one.

"Sir, it's been my pleasure. I'll take care of this."

"OK," the lawyer says without a trace of hesitation.

"My name is Steve Simon. *Steve Simon and the Hour of Enlightenment!*" says the flight attendant in his radio voice.

"Richard Brockman. Pleased to meet you, Steve. Thanks for the wine."

"Don't mention it." The lawyer puts the paper under his arm, takes the glass, and sets off toward the elevator. We all look in his direction. The flight attendant scratches his head, puts his baseball cap back on, moves closer to the woman who has been sitting there, away from the conversation, and smiles at her with his widest smile.

"I bet you are very, very juicy." She smiles bashfully, looking down, but I can see that she doesn't take the compliment as an insult. "And very tasty." My hero keeps going. "If I needed to, I'd sell Bob Dylan's sink." A long pause follows, in which he attempts to peel off the beer label with great determination. Suddenly, he puts an end to his silence and smacks his forehead. "What just happened now?! I paid for his *three* glasses of wine? And he said *OK.*" Pause. "Well, it is what it is." Then he leans toward the woman. "If I need to, I'll sell Bob Dylan's sink. So what, the hell with it." The woman asks for her bill. The flight attendant offers to pay it, she refuses, he insists, and she finally accepts, leaving the two of us alone. We stay silent for a moment. I ask where the restrooms are and leave the bar. I find the pay phone by the restrooms, in the lobby across from the reception desk. I dial the hotel's number and hear it ringing. I see the receptionist set her magazine aside to pick it up.

"Thank you for calling . . ."

"Hi. This is Richard Brockman. I'm trying to get into my room, but my key isn't working."

"Oh, I'm sorry to hear that, Mr. Brockman . . ."

"Can you send me a new key? I'm in 1608."

"I'll send a new one now, Mr. Brockman. Actually, wait a moment, sir?" I can see her looking in the monitor. "B-r-o . . ."

"Brockman, first name Richard?"

"You are at the wrong room, Mr. Brockman. Yours is 2106."

"Thank you!" I hang up and go to the restroom. On my way back to the bar I pass by the front desk and smile at the girl. I order one more martini and a beer for the flight attendant. It's getting late. Maybe I have to eat something. No, I'm not going to eat, it's better if I throw up.

On the TV, the game has ended and now they are broadcasting *live* from California. The sound is muted. A reporter in yellow overalls, a mask, and goggles waves her arms animatedly in front of a background of tall flames twisting up toward the dark sky. Strong winds bend the sequoias next to her. The fire has engulfed the entire southern part of the state. The Santa Ana winds carry them westward. California is in a state of emergency.

"Steve, I want to buy you a drink. What's it gonna be?"

"Champagne! Working-class champagne. The champagne of the fucking flying working class. Champagne the color of piss. Beer. I need to piss. That's the thing with beer. You never buy it, you just rent it, damn it." Steve, staggering, gets up and sets off toward the restrooms unzipping his pants as he walks. I make a gesture to the bartender to come closer.

"Do you have Dom?"

"Excuse me?"

"Do you have Dom?"

"What dom? Listen, man, I'm not even a bartender," The tall kid says. "The real bartender called in sick today and they asked me if I could cover his shift, since it was supposed to be real slow. I'm a bar back. I can open beer and pour wine, but you've been asking for all sorts of weird shit all night."

"I'm sorry, dude," I say. "Dom Perignon is a champagne from France. Do you have champagne here?"

"Yes, we do." He sighs with relief.

"Dom Perignon is usually in a box."

"Is it expensive?"

"Well . . . yes."

"They keep the expensive stuff in the liquor room in the back."

"Do you have a key?"

"I'll bring it right away." He grabs a chain of keys from behind the counter and returns in a minute with a bottle of Dom. He takes out two champagne flutes. I tell him to pull one more out for himself. Steve Simon, the flight attendant, emerges from the restroom, unzipped, and climbs onto the bar stool just before the formal opening of champagne.

"What's this?"

"Champagne."

"I want beer."

"You'll drink champagne."

"May as well." I pour some in his glass, in the bartender's and in mine. We drink up. I close my eyes and allow the elixir to tickle down my throat, sink into me, find its way into my body, drench my bloodstream, and reach my heart. Stella, Stella, Stella, why didn't we drink Dom Perignon together? Ever? Why, Stella? Why didn't we have time for champagne and strawberries covered in Cointreau, for baskets of baguettes and French cheese on the cliffs of La Jolla? Why didn't we watch sunsets together while waves crashed on the rocks beneath our feet? Why didn't we roll in tall grass or swim in white-water rivers? Why, Stella?

"Champagne from France," says the bartender and smacks his lips. "Not bad."

"The French are chickenshit motherfuckers," Steve says.

"They are," I say.

"If you and I put on a couple of Nazi helmets and jump in a motorcycle with a sidecar . . ." Steve has a harder time enunciating his words now. "You and me, man. We'll take over Paris in a heartbeat. The French are cowards. We'll say: *Halt! Hände hoch!* And we'll say, *Frenchies*, we'll destroy your cultural heritage!"

"Hände hoch!"

"Surrender! Surrender quick! Hände hoch, motherfuckers. And they will surrender. The Frenchies are scared that if I fart," Steve lifts his ass off the seat, strains, and issues a loud fart, "like this, I'll destroy their cultural heritage. Cheers! You're not French, are you?"

"No, I'm not." We lift our glasses in a toast.

"You have a big nose."

"Thank you."

"And an accent."

"I'm a man with an accent."

"And bruises on your face."

"Oh, it's some face I got here . . ."

"Cheers. We are in motherfucking Phoenix, man," yells Steve the flight attendant. "Phoenix, fuckin' Arizona!" We kill the champagne. I announce that I'll pay the whole bill. Steve resists. I manage to convince him that it's a very special occasion for me. Then I ask the bartender to put the charge on my room since I'm staying here. He hands me the bill. I fill it out. Where it says *room number* I neatly write *2106*. I print the name Richard Brockman underneath and then I sign the check. I leave the bartender a fat tip, say good-bye to the creator of *The Hour of Enlightenment,* and leave. I cross the parking lot and go back to my hotel. In my room, I turn the TV on, mute the sound, watch the wild fires in California, open a Toblerone, suck on a few triangles, and take a sip of scotch. Then I undress, get in bed, and toss and turn for a while until I find the right position in which I feel the least sick from the alcohol and myself. I close my eyes and count sheep.

•

—what are you thinking about, zack?
—nothing
—tell me
—about time
—it's summertime. it will be sunny tomorrow with sca . . .
—about the category of time
—ah. and how much time do you need to finish one roll of film?
—that depends
—let's wrap it up, zack, OK?

•

I stand under the cold shower for a long time.

When did I actually begin to perceive Stella through my own thoughts about her and not through direct observation? I've watched her through layers of confusion and anger instead of seeing her as she was. Why have I viewed her through the monocle of my bitter ego?

I step out of the shower and dry myself off. I cut the film from last night into seven strips of five negatives each and carefully put them into the plastic sleeves. In the daylight I once again inspect the density of the exposure; I put away the film and leave the hotel. I buy coffee, grab a bite to eat, and drive off.

Phoenix, Scottsdale, New River, Black Canyon City, Camp Word, Rim Rock, Moons Park . . . Then the road starts climbing up, up, up, the cacti yield to short bushes, the short bushes to short pine trees. On the northern side of the road, tall green firs appear. Then I have to turn off the air conditioner and turn on the heat because here, in the dense, chilly mountain, it is already winter.

Flagstaff, Arizona. I don't even bother stopping in the little, snow-covered town, or, for that matter, anywhere else on this small mountain, dropped as if by mistake in the middle of the desert. A geographical paradox with white snow caps.

I drive westward on I-40, toward Winslow, Joseph City, Holbrook, Petrified Forest, Chambers. Somewhere there I hesitate for a moment, tempted to drive north and take a look at the Grand Canyon. But instead I step on the gas pedal—what is there to see? A hole in the ground.

And so, farewell Arizona. I cross the border into New Mexico. The fatigue from driving comes not from moving in space, but from not moving while it happens. Motionless, in a glass jar, you maintain your speed while the world around you flies in the opposite direction. The highway across New Mexico is gray and stretched like an army blanket. Dusty bushes, tall cacti, Joshua trees on both sides. From time to time along the road, I pass by little white crosses in the dirt with plastic bottles of water and withered flowers tied with rags—sanctuaries of loss.

In the distance—the Llano Estacado desert. Like in an old western, tall reddish formations rise high up in the sky out of nowhere. They are now sliced horizontally by thick power lines.

I drive by exits to Church Rock, Gallup, McCann, Wingate, Piraeus, the Top of the World (McGeehan County), and Wrangler Road. Somewhere around here is the Continental Divide, but at this moment, I don't care about seeing a line where some of the water runs east toward the Atlantic Ocean and the rest—west toward the Pacific.

I notice an exit to a gas station off the freeway and take it. I drive further down the road, where I see a cluster of brownish adobe structures with satellite dishes sticking up off the roofs and pick-up trucks parked outside. In front of some of the houses, brown-skinned kids play soccer or chase scruffy dogs. The skies above hand heavy and dark gray. At the gas station, I pay a plump man in overalls. I inquire about the people living in those houses. Navajo, he explains. Oh? And how about the kids, where do they go to school? He silently points in the direction of a white trailer with a tall pole adorned with the waving American flag. I ask him if I could spend the night somewhere around here. Sure. Where? You take this road here to the right about ten miles; there's a lake and a campsite. There's also a *pueblo* near by. Oh, I cheer up a little. Good idea, I'll step away from civilization for a while, I'll see Indians. I buy a bag of chips, a bottle of Coke, and a half gallon of milk. I leave a tip of a dollar something, I don't know why. Just before I close the door behind me, the guy says:

"Watch out for your hubcaps."

"Excuse me?"

"The Navajo steal hubcaps and car batteries from tourists who spend the night around the lake. When you wake up in the morning you might find your car on wooden blocks."

"Seriously?"

"Seriously."

"And what are you?" I ask him. He says he is half Pueblo, half Irish. I thank the *mestizo* and walk out.

No Navajos, no Pueblos! The Indians I grew up with, and who made me fall in love with America, were noble warriors and brave hunters—not small-time thieves.

I check the oil, then the tires, and turn on the ignition.

I began discovering America in my grandparents' basement. Ever since I was a kid I have read everything I could get my hands on. In that basement, though, I discovered the old Wild West. Once, fumbling through the heaps of old junk stored in the damp, darkish place, I stumbled upon a wooden chest filled with all sorts of ancient periodicals, pamphlets, yellowed fashion and pulp fiction magazines. Amidst pages full of recipes, sewing and knitting patterns, and pre-World War II fashion, I encountered the novels of Karl May, published in consecutive issues. I had already read Mayne Reid's *Osceola, The White Chief,* and other such books, so I had a decent enough idea about who the *redskins* and the *palefaces* were. Since the American Old West stories were serialized in pulp magazines and many of the issues had disappeared, a lot of the chapters were missing and important story elements had been lost. So I had to imagine what might have happened, connect the dots and *co-write* the story in my head. I would try to picture the missing parts, what the characters might have done or said. I would make up whole chapters of the pulp novel, rework the main characters, and would even create allies and foes that helped *my* story move forward. Huddled up on the hard, cool ottoman under the little basement window dimmed by thick cobwebs, I got lost in the American Wild West. I roamed its missing pages.

Traveling in different directions makes me think differently.

When I drive west, I dream big dreams, an eastbound journey takes me back to my memories, the north makes me think of work, and the south about wild things.

It's getting dark. In the distant purple sky, I see the city lights of Albuquerque, New Mexico. I take a look at the map spread out on the empty passenger's seat and try to decide whether to spend the night here or keep on driving as long as I can today. I don't really have to rush—I have three more days to reach New York. I keep staring at the map as I try to open the bag of chips. On the other hand, though, I can't wait to cross this continent.

I remember back there in the basement, in the fireplace, which sat unlit for decades, I had discovered a carefully hidden old musket, wrapped in rags. Crazed by the excitement of my discovery, I ran outside to show it to my grandpa. He put down the pitchfork he was using to unload hay from the bed of his truck, glanced in the direction of our neighbors' fence, drew me close toward the hay shed, and told me that this rifle was very old, from the time of the Ottomans, and that I shouldn't say a word about it because it would get confiscated by the communists. It had been his grandfather's; he had also left two pistols with mother-of-pearl handles, but my uncle Krastyu had stolen them, sold them and *drunk them up*. I had no idea how Krastyu could *drink them up*. I knew he drank a lot, but I couldn't believe that he could even drink guns. I tried to imagine him like a circus artist—swallowing sabers, knives, and now guns with mother-of-pearl handles. On top of everything, I didn't even know what a mother-of-pearl handle was, but I imagined it was something quite exquisite. Later, somebody showed me that mother-of-pearl was—that glossy finish next to the bass keys on a Weltmeister accordion.

•

Scott entered, carefully closed the door behind him. We shook hands, he frowned in that concerned way he had and sat behind his desk.

"Zack."

"Scott."

"I asked you to come here because . . ." Scott paused and drummed his fingers. I got goose bumps.

"I'm listening."

"Please don't take it personally."

"Shoot." Scott took a deep breath, got up, went to the water dispenser, took a little plastic cup, and filled it up.

"Water?"

"Yes, please." Scott poured one for himself and one for me, too. There was a knot in my stomach. I had the feeling that I'd been found out. I wondered if I would only get fired or . . .

"You know how much I value the education some of our staff members receive overseas." I lifted my cup so as to conceal my reactions. That could be my last cup here . . . "So I'll be direct. Zack, we are required to monitor the work of our employees." Scott's window offered a view toward a parking lot and other office buildings. If I had to spend every day in a room with a view like this one, I'd probably behave like he does, too. "We inquired about you and your work." I drank the rest of the office water. The knot in my stomach hardened. "Zack, the amount of education you've received in . . ."—Scott's helpful memory obviously omitted where exactly I was from—"in, uh, your home country." Scott sighed, relaxed his arms, changed his tone. "Before you came on board, we had a very good employee from Rio De Janeiro. He, unfortunately, went back to, uh, Argentina . . . Anyway, with him, we also had," Scott spread his arms apologetically, "so to speak, a problem. All I wanted to say is that the education you get overseas is very thorough and serious." Scott paused again, finished his water, and dropped the cup into the trash can. "Maybe that's why some complications occur." Pause.

"Scott," I wanted to spare him this beating around the bush, so I decided to attack. "What are you talking about? What about my education?"

"Zack, I really respect your attention to detail in your protocols. Maybe that's how you've been trained over there. And that's how it should be in health services. But . . . there's a but here . . . we, Zack, are simultaneously a health organization and a for-profit company. So, it's delicate. Here at ICONIQ, we care about our patients, it's true. But *we also care about our shareholders, the people who pay our salaries. We, Zack, are not simply doctors or businessmen. We are artists. And we have our competitors. Five years of development, six billon dollars in expenses, and we are on our way to winning second place in a race for two."*

"How can I help to accelerate the process?"

"There you go. You've understood me right away." Scott smiled. "You and I can understand and listen to each other instead of having to repeat the same thing over and over again like we do with Mike from your team. When I have similar conversations with Mike, it always turns into an argument. You see, Zack, ICONIQ doesn't pay a lot to," Scott leans over his desk, making finger quotes, "the participating volunteers. The centers can hardly gather the minimum number of patients required to legitimize their research results before the Department of Health, whose administration has to approve the drug, which in turn has to be in drugstores before Christmas. Some centers operate with whomever they have or come across. Your job is to monitor this process carefully. But when some of your diligent examinations find a violation and disqualify a patient—which happens," Scott sighed, "well, quite often—sometimes a whole clinical site falls through the cracks. Here, for example, last month, you've rejected," Scott quickly consulted the folder on his desk, "three, four, five . . . eight patients. Two of them will drag two centers down with them and these two clinics will have to drop out of the study. And what this actually boils down to," Scott waves the folder in the air, "is a couple of mistakes on the part of the personnel collecting the participants' data."

"One of the girls jumped from the twenty-seventh floor a week after that. If I had left her in study and she had done what she did while taking our drugs, the media would have destroyed us!"

"That's why we're grateful, Zack! That's why you are an invaluable associate."

"Thanks."

"Having said this, though, if we carry on this way—if everybody is as detail-oriented as you are—it'll be hard for us." Scott slams the report back on the desk and furrows his brow—that's how he illustrates deep concern. *"It'll be hard."* He shakes his head. *"It will be really hard for us."*

"So, I shouldn't dig into the details so much?"

"No, no, I never even thought of saying something like that." Scott throws his arms in the air. *"Be as detailed as you want."*

"But not too much?"

"I haven't said that."

"So I should be detailed. Because my first responsibility is the well-being of our patients. But I should also make sure we have results."

"Exactly!" Scott exclaims and claps his hands. *"It's all about results. And the well-being of the patients."*

•

At the last second, I see the brake lights of the truck ahead of me. I hear his loud horn and sharply swerve to the left to pass. But there, the shining lights of the oncoming vehicles blind me as I manage to hit the brakes and get back in my lane. I take a deep breath, rub my eyes and try to calm down. I realize that I was inches away from an accident and I offer one more *thank you* prayer to the one above. And just then I realize what I had seen in the split-second before avoiding the crash. I saw two glowing red spots in the bushes to the left of the highway—perhaps a vehicle's brake lights? I pull over on the shoulder and shift into reverse. I drive backward for quite a while until I see the sharp tire marks on the asphalt and the tail-lights in the dark green shrubbery. In the twilight, the back of the pick-up truck would have been invisible if it weren't for the red brake lights. Perhaps the truck driver in front of me had also seen them and had hit his brakes, nearly killing me. I jump out of my car and cross the highway. I stop in the middle for a second to let a car pass. The back of the pick-up is hanging in the air. The wheels are still turning.

Just then, I see a woman slowly step out of the shadowy bushes next to the side of the pick-up. She sways back and forth. Cars zoom between her and me. I lift up my camera, open the aperture to two, and take a few shots. In the dusky bluish twilight, only her silhouette—cut horizontally by long white lines, the headlights of passing automobiles—will be visible. Damn, I grabbed the Nikon, and even used it completely instinctively. I hang it around my neck. The woman across from me keeps rocking back and forth as if mourning someone.

"Hey!" I yell. She starts walking toward me. "No!" I scream frightened. "No!" I gesture for her to stay where she is. I make eye contact. "Stay there!" Two cars pass, one between me and her, and one behind me. I see the headlights of several more cars, which are too close for me to cross the two lanes that separate us. She seems not to notice the speeding automobiles. It's strange that they also seem to ignore us. For a moment, all this seems unreal—this unknown twilight, this unknown swaying woman, the road between us. "Don't move!" I shout. "Don't move!" She stares at me with bleary, uncomprehending eyes until I manage to cross over to her side. "Is there anybody in there?" I point at her vehicle. "Is there any one else with you?" She shakes her head. "No? No? Thank God. OK. OK." I wonder what to do, I don't know what to do, goddammit. "Are you OK?" She keeps shaking her head. "No? You are not OK? Are you hurt?" A tall, white pick-up truck with absurdly big tires and round lights on top of the cabin slows down and blows its horn. Laughter, booing, a beer bottle shatters a few yards from where we are. Somebody screams "assho-o-o-o-ole" as it disappears toward Albuquerque. "Are you hurt? Does it hurt anywhere?" Then, she lifts up her arm and makes a horizontal gesture in front of her throat. "You can't talk?" Her eyes, I notice now, are filled with tears, but not a single one falls. "What's your name?" She repeats the gesture. Maybe she has something in her throat and cannot speak. Maybe it's the shock. She makes the same gesture again and, only then, a tear rolls down her cheek. She opens her mouth and struggles to utter something. I reach for her arm. Finally, she manages to squeeze out a few words:

"I wanna . . ." A huge semi is approaching. I see how she measures the distance with the corner of her eye, pushes me aside abruptly, and attempts to jump in front of it. I manage to grab her waist and press her to my body until the danger passes. She doesn't resist. Her whole body reeks of alcohol. "I wanna . . ."

"Not here," I say. "Not like this."

Half an hour later, the failed suicide and I sit in the 66 DINER—a classic joint, as if teleported from the forties—and quietly sip coffee. She tries to concentrate on the menu as I check out the black and white photos on the walls.

The 66 DINER—the lights, the juke box, the Budweiser signs, the maroon seats, the chrome, the tables, the ketchup, the salt shaker, the pepper shaker, the middle-aged waitress with the coffee pot . . . Americana, Americana, Americana . . .

The 66 DINER, I learn from the photos, burned down in 1995, but, fortunately for everybody, three years later—under new ownership—it was completely restored to its former glory.

I don't know her name. I don't want to know it. We are waiting for some Joey guy, whom she called from the pay phone by the restrooms. Joey who will come pick her up so I can go on my way. She doesn't have any relatives. She doesn't have any friends. She doesn't know what happened. She has no memory of what took place. Oh, yeah, she wanted to . . . and again the gesture towards her throat, but it didn't work, obviously. She wanted—Bam! Bam!— and that's it. But, in life, I guess, if you are out of luck, you are out of luck and that's that. An even bigger loser will show up and ruin the whole thing, trying to save your life. Why in the world did I have to show up there?

"Some more coffee, hon?" The waitress asks her.

"We are ready to order," I say.

"No, we are not," the woman says.

"Yes, we are."

"I'm not."

"I have to go."

"Then go. Joey is coming to pick me up, I told you. Go."

"I will as soon as Joey shows up," I say. "The lady here would like to order something to eat."

"A half-pound burger with cheddar cheese, please, and fries. Rare. Add bacon on it. Lots of it."

I order spicy Buffalo wings.

"And what can I get you to drink?"

"Octoberfest draft, please," I say.

"I want a Bud." The waitress looks at me, I shake my head "no", and she fill up her coffee cup.

"One little beer," the woman begs.

I shake my head.

"Just one?"

"When your Joey comes, do whatever you want."

"I want to die."

"I got that."

"So?"

"I can't help you."

"Why?"

"Because I don't like helping people."

"What's your name?"

"My name is Zack."

"Zack, I don't want to live."

"That makes two of us."

"Really?"

"Really."

"I've got an idea."

"Yeah?"

"Let's die together."

"No, thanks."

"Why?"

"I don't want to die with other people."

"OK then, you die by yourself. I'll watch."

"I don't feel like dying in Albuquerque."

"Where do you want to die?"

"Where I was born."

"Why?"

"That's what lions do."

"How do you know what lions do?"

"*Animal Planet.*"

"So you're a lion?"

"I am a lion."

"Then why are you such a sad lion?"

"My lioness left me."

"Where is she?"

"Gone."

"Big deal. You'll find another lioness. Can you order me just one beer, Zack?"

"No."

•

Two hundred and ninety-seven.

That is the annual average number of sunny days where we live. Yet, I can't remember a gloomier year than the last one. I wandered aimlessly through airports and hotels, read tabloids, watched CNN, ate Toblerones, followed the stock exchange, and dressed like a widower.

Why had I been so sad, I wonder, now, when Stella was healthy, sound, and at home? So what if she had a little crush on some artist. Maybe it was temporary, maybe it wasn't anything serious, maybe she simply needed a break from me. It wasn't the end of the world. Maybe in I-won't-mention-his-name she found something that I didn't have. But what was it? His passion for his work, his belief in his own importance, his successes, his confidence that the world would know his name and work, his megalomania? How arrogant do you have to be, for God's sake, to paint canvases as big as Niagara Falls? What's so goddamn important to express that you have to use canvases that large?

Or perhaps those were the sizes of the holes in your soul, Artist, which you try to conceal with buckets of paint?

I learned everything that was out there about Bernard Foucault. I even dug into the crown of his family tree, trying to find an explanation. His father, an entrepreneur, had supported his only son through his undergraduate years in Lyons, then as a graduate student in Paris, and later in America. His father was still available if needed. But now, he wasn't needed. Bernard Foucault was on his way to becoming one of the most successful artists of the new century. Nothing in his biography suggested, even in the slightest, Stella's mysterious withdrawal from me.

•

An hour later, still no Joey. But she won't stop whining that she's bored. She's sobering up now, and asks me where I'm going.

"New York."

"Can I come with you?"

"No way."

"Why not?"

"You wanted to die, didn't you?"

"Exactly. I will die of boredom riding with you."

"Boredom? You have no idea who you're dealing with here," I snap. "I'm funny."

"You're boring."

"I am hilarious."

"Boring."

"No, I'm not."

"You are, too."

"No."

"Yes, yes, yes, yes, you are boring!"

"Shh, be quiet." I put a finger to her lips. On the TV above the bar, I see the San Diego suburbs in flames.

"You're boring!" Pictures of buildings and trees on fire. "Buy me a beer. Only one beer, please." The Santa Ana winds, human nature, the original human anti-nature, fire, Prometheus, knowledge, the greed, the madness, the self-destruction, deeply coded in our DNA . . . "I want beer. And I don't have any money."

"Where's your money?"

"In my wallet. You took my wallet."

"Excuse me?"

"My wallet's missing, my ID is missing. HAS ANYONE SEEN MY WALLET!?"

"Be quiet!"

"Buy me a beer then!"

"I won't!

"Buy me a beer or I'll scream." The wild fires keep creeping west toward the ocean. The governor has declared a state of emergency. The president has declared a state of emergency. "Hey!" She yells. "What are you watching over there?"

"It's burning." I say.

"What's burning?"

"California's burning."

"What do you care about California? We're in fuckin' New Mexico!"

"The fire's very close to where I live," I say. "My neighborhood's next."

"You have a neighborhood?"

"No, I have a house."

"Hey, motherfucker, you have a house and you don't wanna buy me a beer? Why can't you buy me a beer? Why don't you buy me a house, too? I want a house, I want kids, I want to die, where's my wallet? Why did you take my ID? Where am I? Why did you kidnap me, who the hell are you? WHO ARE YOU?! Please don't hurt me, please don't hurt me, I want to go home, please take me home . . ."

A few heads from the neighboring tables turn in our direction. I take her by the arm. She pulls it back abruptly.

"DON'T TOUCH ME! DON'T YOU DARE TOUCH ME! I DON'T KNOW YOU! HELP!" She starts scratching the place on her arm where I touched her as if there are insects crawling underneath. "WHO ARE YOU? I DON'T KNOW YOU! LEAVE ME ALONE!" I get up quickly and make an attempt to call the waitress, but a man in a flannel shirt and a Red Sox cap blocks my way, fixing his belt.

"Is there a problem, pal?" He asks.

"No." I attempt to go around him.

"What about the girl?" The flannel shirt blocks my way.

"What about her?" Only now I notice that the woman I saw rocking back and forth next to the pick-up truck's red tail-lights alongside the freeway is actually a girl no older than nineteen.

"I think the girl is upset." The flannel shirt lifts a plastic cup to his mouth and spits tobacco in it.

"Leave him alone, Randall." I hear the waitress.

"I don't know this girl," I say.

"Then why is she upset?" He turns his baseball cap backward and advances on me.

"I haven't upset anybody," I say.

"You're making me upset."

188

"Hey, hey . . ." I flip out. "I found this kid by the highway. She's been in a car crash. We're waiting for her friend Joey to arrive . . ." All of a sudden, a jug of coffee smashes over the baseball cap and splashes me with hot brown liquid.

"You dumb redneck, leave my man Zack alone!" The girl jumps between the flannel shirt and me, holding the handle of the coffee pot. Two more flannel shirts jump up from the tables around us, grab her and twist her arms behind her back. The flannel shirt with the baseball cap, with a painfully twisted face and a hand over his left eye, makes his way toward the bathroom.

"Fuck! You bitch, you fucking bitch!" Coffee is dripping from his yellow mustache.

"Randall, don't think about it, or I'm calling the police." The waitress yells in panic. A youngster in jeans, a brown leather jacket, and long blond hair enters.

"Joey. Joey!" The girl waves her hand. "Over here."

I leave money on the table and rush out. Getting into my car, it crosses my mind that *66 Diner* sounds like a title of a short student film, shot on 16 mm and shown to an audience of about thirteen people, relatives and friends, on a cold rainy afternoon.

•

I make just one more stop in New Mexico. In a small parking lot in front of a liquor store, a plump Native American bangs on a ritual drum, his eyes squinting, and his right ear lowered to the leather, humming gutturally. Another Indian, dressed in a Navajo poncho, slowly dances, shifting the weight of his heavy body from one white Puma sneaker to the other. A few more fellows are watching the dance indifferently, sipping from brown paper bags.

I walk into the liquor store and buy water, chips, and a bottle of bourbon.

I drive toward Texas on the desolate night highway. The white line of the road hits the hood ornament of my car at 140 miles per hour.

I love American roads at night. The prairie outside is dark and cold. The American West. Ever since I can remember, I've wanted to be a part of this. But why? Is it possible that I had simply been charmed by the idea of the West, the West of absolute, raw freedom? I grew up with my grandparents' fairy tales, with innumerable stories of our own national heroes—my mom read me to sleep every night.

The American West, however, was the myth I discovered on my own in books and, later, in films. The myth that included all other myths. In *my* American West, there was a place for everybody—for Old Firehand and Winnetou,[1] Levsky[2] and Jesse James, for the Apaches and Benkovsky's Flying Squad,[3] for Sitting Bull, Ivanko,[4] King Arthur, Botev,[5] Richard the Lionhearted, and Budyonny[6] . . . In my American West there was room for all of these horsemen. In my American West, they were all Sons of the

---

1   Fictional Native American heroes of several novels written by Karl May.

2   Vasil Levsky (1837–1873), a Bulgarian revolutionary and national hero, key in organizing resistance to the Ottoman authorities, who eventually captured and executed him.

3   Georgi Benkovsky (1843–1876) was a Bulgarian revolutionary who led a cavalry band in an uprising against the Ottomans.

4   Murderer of Tsar Ivan Asen I, ruler of the Second Bulgarian Empire, in 1196.

5   Hristo Botev (1848–1876), a Bulgarian poet and revolutionary killed while leading an uprising against the Ottomans.

6   Semyon Mikhailovich Budyonny (April 25 [O.S. April 13] 1883–October 26, 1973) was a Soviet cavalryman, military commander, politician, and a close ally of Soviet leader Joseph Stalin. He is also famous for creating a new horse breed, the Budyonny horse, still kept in large numbers in Russia.

Great Bear.[7] As a child, I often fantasized that the hordes of Khan Asparuh[8] were closely related to the Iroquois.

I remember when our history teacher took us on a field trip to the archaeological museum where we were shown the restored head of a Thracian chieftain, I was ecstatic. It was the face of an American Indian. So that means the Thracians and the Indians . . . and since Bulgarians are part Slav, part Thracian . . . so I, too, am maybe related to . . . I fell asleep tangled in my own infantile hypotheses.

I now realize that *my* American West was not a geographical place, but a sacred territory in my dreams. Perhaps everybody has their own Wild West. From a very young age, I knew with certainty that one day I would live in mine. I'd caress the yellow prairie grass and the wind would kiss my face. When did I lose all that? How did I manage to desecrate *my* West by replacing it with the plastic version of what I've been living in for the last few years of my life?

I press the gas pedal harder.

California, of course. The end came with California. That blonde bitch—silicon breasts, whitened teeth, fitness-firmed buttocks, pink tank top, frozen smile, and empty blue eyes—California. The bitch I couldn't afford but still wanted, infatuated with *the idea* that I was with her, in her, that even for a little while I shared her with rock stars, movie stars, TV stars, porn stars, photo stars, kid stars, I shared her with millionaires, billionaires, multibillionaires, and bums. I don't want to think about California right now.

---

7 *The Sons of the Great Bear* was an East German "Red Western" film from 1966, very popular in the Eastern Bloc.

8 Khan Asparuh was a ruler of a Bulgar tribe in the second half of the 7th century and is credited with the establishment of the First Bulgarian Empire in 680/681.

Suddenly, something underneath me rumbles, startling me. I must have dozed of for a second. The car has veered onto the gravel of the shoulder. I get a tighter grip on the steering wheel, shake my head energetically, and swerve back into my lane. Later, I stop to stretch my legs. I inhale the prairie. The cool air wakes me up. Far away from populated areas that fill the night sky with light pollution, the stars are much bigger and closer.

I step in front of the headlights and gather a few dry twigs from the prairie bushes. To the side of the road, in the dirt, I clear a little space, make a square out of the sticks, and perform the ritual I learned from my grandma. I *close up the little devil.* That's it—I close up the devil. Whatever I have lost, will be found. I have to find Stella, I whisper, I have to find her. I lift my eyes up and look at Orion—our favorite constellation—for a long moment. I remember a poem Stella wrote:

> Clear night.
> Shivers with cold
> The belt of Orion.[1]

I think she wrote that looking at the stars from the ugly, glassed-in balcony of our apartment, that last freezing winter we spent in Bulgaria. I bend over the magic square and change the spell—let me find myself. God, let me find myself!

•

Stella sold her first painting. An architect from Los Angeles bought it. In a deeply sincere thank you letter, which she gave me to read, he clearly articulated his first impulse upon setting his eyes on the painting. He

---

1   Haiku by Silvia Valentino.

described the excitement of looking at it, and how he discovered new and different layers and images each time he looked at it, and how it touched him in a very special way. With the money from the painting, Stella moved to a larger studio. The architect bought three smaller pieces from the same series. Around that time, Stella started working on installations and video projects. She came home less and less often.

•

I keep driving until I reach the exit to the first town. I follow the sign towards a motel named The First Motel in Texas. In the parking lot, I see several trucks and a Harley Davidson whose shiny chrome reflects the yellow lights installed above the ground-floor rooms. The building is shaped like an upside-down L, the parking lot is gravel caked with dirt. In front of the motel, there is an installation made out of a pile of rocks and cactuses, covered with dry grass. A dozen wooden poles stick wickedly out of it, and old, crooked cowboy boots are fixed on each of them. Texas. The small bungalow that serves as reception lights up, and an old man in a large cowboy hat, white shirt, and suspenders slowly opens the door. I respect his silence. That is why, without saying a word, just like in a silent movie, I count off the dollar bills, hand them to him, wait for my change, take the key to my room from his bony hand, nod, and leave. I unload the bag of marijuana and drag it over to the bed. I take out the bourbon, step out of the room, sit on the doorstep, drink a few sips, and let the stars slowly find their places in the night sky. I close my eyes and lean my head back. A bed squeaks in the room next to mine. I take another sip, and then another. I need to stretch my legs after the long drive—plus, I need to check this place out.

The lamp sheds its light on only half of the parking lot. I cross the bright half and, the moment I step into the dark one, I can hear how the gravel under my boots starts crunching more loudly. I take a swig from the bottle, then set off down a small alley into the dark void. The void is actually a little street lined by several wooden hovels with screen doors; I can hear loud snoring coming from one of them. I lift the bottle and keep walking in the dark, trying to be quiet. Suddenly, somewhere ahead of me, a dog starts barking furiously; I jump, try to calm down, and, choking, turn and rush back towards the motel. I manage to down a third of the bottle before I reach my room. I want to drink myself to sleep. I find the door, go in, lean against the wall and, without switching on the lights, start taking off my pants. I grope in the dark until I find the bed and flop down in it:

"A-a-a-a-a-a-ah!"	"A-a-a-a-a-a-a-a-a-ah!"
"He-e-e-e-l-p!"	"What the fuck! Who are you!"
"H-e-e-e-e-elp!"	"What the hell . . . !"
"A-a-a-a-a-a-a-a-a-a-ah!"	"A-a-a-a-a-a-a-a-a-ah!"

I jump, sober, and scared to death, death, death. The lights go on and I see a man in white boxers with a tattoo of a woman and a snake on his six-pound biceps. He's got a gun in his hand, his hairy, blond chest is heaving up and down. His face—the expression of an ancient, angry ritual mask. I throw my hand in the air.

"No-o-o-o!"

"What the fuck you doing here, motherfucker?!" His eyelid twitches.

"I'm going to bed," I mumble and almost piss my pants.

"Are you a homo?" I manage not to piss my pants.

"No."

"The fuck you doing in my bed, then?"

"I thought . . ." The man goes to the door, opens it, and peeks outside.

"You alone?"

"Yes."

"Take your shit, and get the fuck outta here . . . Wait, what is that?" He points at the bottle.

"Bourbon," I mutter.

"You scared the living crap out of me, man!" His anger begins to mellow.

"So did you," I say.

He rubs his eyes. "Let me see your key!" I show it to him. "You're next door, buddy."

"Could you please put that away?" I ask, eyeing the gun. The man suddenly bursts out laughing, grabs his belly, and just laughs. He laughs as only people on the wrong side of the law do—people with limited occasions for a laugh, so when they do laugh, they roar like Niagara Falls. I join in from time to time only to fuel new outbursts. From some of the other rooms somebody yells angrily: "Shut u-u-u-u-u-p!" My man lifts the gun to his mouth and yells back: "Fuck o-o-o-o-o-o-ff."

I slip my pants back on, find two plastic cups by the sink, pour some bourbon, and make a toast.

"Cheers."

"Cheers." We drink.

"I'm Doug." The man leaves the gun on the nightstand and stretches out his large hand.

"Zack." I say. "Pleased to meet you."

"We almost fucked even before introducing ourselves." Laughter again. We finish the bottle and part ways. I find my room, crawl over to the bed, sprawl over the blanket with all my clothes on, and die.

•

H-m-m-m-m-m-m-m-m-m. I wake up. H-m-m-m-m-m-m-m-m-m. I'm not sure whether this is the blood in my ears or the noise of the arteries of America—the eternally busy highways. I sit up in bed and rub my eyes. The door is wide open. I jump to my feet to check if the bag is here. Relax—it's here. Not only did I leave the door unlocked, I didn't even close it. I step out. The Harley is gone. My midnight friend has ridden off south. Had I dreamt him up? I walk over to the reception bungalow. Just then I notice the large buffalo skull with huge horns hung over the door. I also see the sign LAST MOTEL IN TEXAS. What the heck is wrong with me? Last night, it was the *first* motel, now it's the last? Clearly, I wasn't quite OK. Maybe because I was coming from the *enchanted land*. I cross the parking lot. Through the screen door, I see the cowboy hat, white shirt, and suspenders—the man is sitting on a wooden chair, watching a small TV. I ask where the closest coffee shop is.

"Nowhere." He answers.

"What's the name of this . . . town, whatever it is?" Behind me, a truck grunts loudly and comes to a halt in the dust.

"This is a border town," the motel man says. His chair squeaks as he slowly gets up and approaches the screen door. His face is marked with scars from who knows what. "This is the border between Texas and New Mexico."

I return the key and leave. I notice that the east side of the sign reads LAST MOTEL IN TEXAS and the west—FIRST MOTEL IN TEXAS. Welcome to Texas!

I drive slowly past the few houses I had walked by last night. In the daylight they seem even more ghostly and forsaken. Beat up pick-up trucks, backyards covered with weeds and dry grass, horse skulls on the fences, clothes lines, peeling mail boxes unopened for years, rusty nets used as fences with dry snake skins hanging on them. The only traces of life are the invisible barking dogs. Down the road, I stop to take a few pictures of an abandoned gas station with black holes instead of windows and doors. I walk up to the next dead building, which happens to be a post office. I take a close up shot of a rusty sign with an inscription reading: GLENRIO, TEXAS, 1938. A long time ago, letters arrived here, telegrams, sad and happy messages were sent and received, the telegraph had been clicking, phone numbers had been dialed, newspapers had arrived, brochures, WANTED DEAD OR ALIVE.

A little further down the dirt road, on the other side of the street, I find another small building, which happens to be another post office. This time, however, the sign on the door says: GLENRIO, NEW MEXICO, 1938. Aha. I think I'm beginning to picture the drama of this little Berlin. Situated on the border between two states, Glenrio was torn between the *charm* of New Mexico and the *prosperity* of Texas. And while the legendary Route 66—America's Main Street—had passed through it, the little town had managed to juggle the passions and animosities. But later, after the freeway was built a little north of here, the town started dying away. Glenrio (Texas or New Mexico), little by little, lost its *important* geopolitical status and gave in to the mercy of the prairie, which slowly gathered it back into its dry bosom.

Further down, at a fork in the road, sits an abandoned white diner with a hitching post out front. On its door, a heavy lock and a CLOSED sign hang on a thick chain. On the window sill, salt and pepper shakers, oil and vinegar bottles, and porcelain vases with no flowers are lined up on top of old newspapers. In the corner is a rusty steam iron with a gaping mouth, squatted by spiders.

I walk about fifty yards further until I reach an old water tower, tilted to one side and tied with barbed wire. Around it, a few elm trees have thrust their thin bodies up into the air. I scare a little gray rabbit, who scurries away with ears pressed back and white tail bobbing up and down like a tennis ball. One black-and-white roll of film later, I get back into the car, find the exit to I-40, and merge with the fast caravan of vehicles heading east.

•

Stella sold a few more paintings at prices she'd thought up while I helped her pack and transport them. What is a painting worth? she used to joke. If you keep the receipts for the materials you've bought, you have your answer. How much does a painting cost, really?

Around Christmas the proposal arrived—an entrepreneur from Florida had seen her pieces in the architect's home and thought they would be perfect for a small boutique hotel he was just finishing. He wanted to purchase seventy-eight medium-sized pieces in the same style. The money he offered was excellent. Stella politely declined.

After that, Stella spent time getting familiar with the Los Angeles art scene. She went to gallery openings, met artists, sculptors, and curators, and looked for galleries where she could exhibit her work. She participated in a few group shows before she found a gallery in Santa Monica that would represent her. The gallery owner, Jane Goldstein, was a fifty-year-old platinum blonde lesbian, with lead-gray eyes and dry Californian crow's feet. She knew everyone who was anyone in that business. No one knew how exactly she picked her artists, but when a friend of ours learned that Stella was among Jane's chosen ones, he rolled his eyes, flipped his pink scarf with his soft wrist, and winked at her: "If your work is in Jane's gallery, girlfriend, be ready to say goodbye to anonymity." He was right. A few months later, there was a opening in Jane's calendar, so Stella had the dates for her first solo show.

•

—do you sometimes think that everything is meaningless, zack?
—i don't think in paradoxes
—what's a paradox?
—a statement that seems logical but contradicts itself
—where's the paradox in *everything is meaningless?*
—you see . . . the statement *everything is meaningless* is part of everything. hence, it is also meaningless. which means that everything *is not* meaningless. a paradox
—this won't be in the picture, right?
—no, baby
—then why are you pointing the camera at it?
—relax, it's not in focus

•

I stop at a gas station, fill up, and check the tires. I look at the map and calculate that from here to Columbus, Ohio, is about twelve hundred miles. If I keep an average speed of sixty miles per hour, it will take me about twenty hours to get there. I am not sure that this stretch of road has more than twenty espresso machines total. And how many of them are in decent shape is a different story. That's why I fill up my stomach with thin, gas station coffee, buy a dozen doughnuts, and take off. I'll stop only for gas and for short breaks. I'll try to drive the whole distance in one fell swoop.

•

Jane had managed to sell half of Stella's paintings before opening night. I didn't want to miss this occasion, which was extremely important for Stella. I organized my schedule so that the day of the opening, I'd be in L.A., inspecting a site. I made a hotel reservation (at ICONIQ's expense, of course) so we could spend the night there.

The cab stopped in front of the gallery. I paid the driver, stepped out of the car, and while I was tucking my wallet in my blazer pocket, just a second before slamming the door, my glance slid over the yellow top of the car and landed on the woman behind the gallery window, whose face burst into inaudible laughter at that very moment. Her mouth—a perfect O. *Her eyes—wide open. Her eyebrows—racing to meet her high forehead. She was wearing a black dress, fitted tightly over her beautiful breasts and revealing her bare shoulders. Her hair was pulled back neatly, and the curve of her graceful neck was sliced by a necklace I'd chosen for her. Behind her were the paintings I recognized. She was a copy of the woman I knew better than myself, she was the girl I had met in a café by the sea, she was my other half, whom I planned to grow old with.*

There, on that boulevard, one hand in my inside pocket and another resting on the cab door, the world froze and went mute in a kind of reverse déjà vu, *in which I saw Stella for the first time.*

I slammed the door, the sidewalks came to life, the street filled with the sounds of car horns and music, and she was laughing at the punch line of a joke the moment I entered the gallery.

I have never seen an artist more beautiful than Stella. For god's sake, she was not an artist who tried to look like an artist.

That night, I saw her paintings the way they should be seen—as she had always seen them. They were in the order she intended and lit with the appropriate lighting. I never suspected the impact.

·

There are a very limited number of things more boring than driving on I-40 in Texas. Two hundred miles later, I discover one of them—driving on I-40 in Oklahoma.

I've heard that the Aborigines have many words for *sand.* I know that the Eskimos have about twenty different terms for *snow.* I try to think of how many words the Americans have for *road:*

Toll road

Run   *Avenue*

Interstate

Boulevard

Path

Track

Trail

Road

Parkway

Expressway

Freeway

Lane

Street

Pathway

Highway

Drive

Artery   *Route*

Public Road

I decide to look for an analogue in my own language. The only thing I can think of are the words pointing out who is who in the family tree:

dyado i baba

vuina   *bate*

chicho   *kaleiko*   *chinka*

kaka   *balduza*   *maminka*

vuicho   *svat*   *svatia*

strinka   *krustnik*   *zulva*

svekurva   *svekur*

badjanak   *eturva*

kuma

shurei

tushta

tust

kum

kaincho

I keep driving northeast on I-44. A little past Oklahoma City, the heaviest skies I have ever seen gather above the prairies. I stop. A sky like this will either drive you insane or leave you cold How did the first settlers endure it? I stretch my limbs and body and lean on the steel guard rail. I spend a long time there, listening to the wind. I start moving my head slightly—if it's half-turned to the left, I hear the wind one way, if it's turned to the right—another. I even try to compose a little melody. Strange, there are so many ways to have fun with the wind just by turning your head left and right like an idiot.

I keep driving east.

Around Tulsa, a few fat raindrops hit the windshield. It hadn't rained in California for months, so now I feel excited. I open the window and breathe in the storm-charged air. All of a sudden, the truck I'm following disappears into a giant waterfall. I barely manage to close the window before I'm deluged. Tons of water splash over the car. It's like being in a carwash tunnel times ten. I slow down abruptly and keep driving, even though I know the sensible thing to do is just stop and wait for the flood to pass. The wipers race full speed with no effect whatsoever. I've never been in such downpour before. I slow down even more. In about twenty minutes the rain subsides a bit and I step on the gas again.

A house appears before my eyes without warning. I hit the brakes and the house disappears. I rub my eyes, grip the steering wheel, and accelerate a little. I see little red flags, then a sign reading OVERSIZED LOAD as I catch up with the house again. It has windows, red curtains, a roof, and a chimney. It looks like a house that has been lived in, not some newly built pre-fab home. It is tied to the back of a truck that is driving extremely slowly. If you can balance a whole house on a truck, I wonder, how hard is it to balance a life in one house? If Stella and I couldn't do it, such balance is probably impossible. Or it's only temporary. How long will the house stay on this truck? It can't stay there forever. Balance, if

I have to be loyal to my employers at ICONIQ, is pharmaceutically reversible. They claim that balance is a question of chemistry, and so is imbalance. They say microscopic pheromones, hormones, and still undiscovered chemical compounds rule our behaviors. Being unhappy is an imbalance. Being happy is an imbalance. The balance is probably simply *to be*.

I crawl behind the house at five miles per hour for a long time before I manage to pass it. I take out the camera and shoot the sky through the windshield, through the wipers, through the sunroof. Somehow, the windshield recalls the format of 35mm film, in which, out of habit, I wait for Stella to appear.

I photograph an Oklahoma washed by the rain and turning gray with the coming winter. At some point, the rain almost completely abates and I find myself in a drier, brighter space. The sky looks higher now, too.

I speed up as I cross the Missouri border. Around Springfield, I see herds of buffalo. The weak, sour gallons of gas station coffee do not wake me much, but they do make me urinate every other hour. The night catches up with me a little short of St. Louis, Missouri (which locals pronounce *Muh-zur-ah*). I decide to grab a bite to eat, so I find a roadside restaurant.

In the parking lot in front of it, a row of semis rumble, their engines working 24/7 to maintain both a comfortable temperature in the rig and the size of the hole in the ozone layer. I go inside the place, take a seat and, order a bacon cheeseburger and a Coke. Like it or not, I need to use the toilet, almost as urgently as before the Ramona incident. The design of the American public toilet is the embodiment of discomfort. Its door is cut low at the bottom, so one's legs are visible to the knees, and also on top, so there are no secrets about what one is doing in there. The American public restroom should not encourage suspicious behavior. This seat is cold and unclean, which is why I experiment with stepping on it and squatting over the opening. Very unpleasant. A second later, with loud belching and nose blowing, two of the drivers come in. One of them barges into the stall to my left and drops down his pants hurriedly; his metal belt-buckle clanks on the tiles. The other one, obviously thinking that my stall is vacant because my feet are invisible, tries the door, which I have thoughtfully locked. Since I did not indicate my presence at the very beginning, I hold my breath and try to remain awkwardly incognito while the following conversation, accompanied by loud plops, takes place:

". . . and she?"

        ". . . she's like, leave me alone"

". . . leave her alone?"

        ". . . she wants me to leave her alone"

". . . and so you?"

        ". . . and so I'm like, oh, really?!
        She goes, yeah, really."

"A man comes home,
he wants to fuck, right?
What's the big deal."

        "Yeah, what's the big deal!"

"Leave her alone, huh?"

What kind of screwed up world is this, I wonder, if men want one thing and women want another? The conversation continues on a less existential topic, then carries on with endless ass wiping, hand washing, coughing, spitting, huffing, and puffing. I wait for them to leave and also exit. Half of the distance to Columbus is behind me. Before me is a night that I must stay awake through.

I enter Indianapolis early in the morning, fill up my tank, and ask for the closest Starbucks. I find it, order a triple espresso, buy a newspaper, and go outside. It's chilly. A thick army-surplus parka with a homeless man in it is sitting in one of the chairs. His bearded face is covered in big pimples, his hair is disheveled. On the ground next to his muddy boots rests a full black trash bag. I nod and take a seat. He nods back. We are the only ones at the outside tables. On the front page of the paper, there is a map of Southern California stamped with huge fiery letters reading RAG-ING INFERNO. The wild fires are indicated with little fire symbols in different shades of red (depending on their intensity)—they start at the mountains and crawl down toward the ocean. No one really knows how many of the fires are accidental, how many are the work of arsonists and psychopaths, and how many are simply attempts by ordinary citizens to replace their old houses with new ones using insurance pay-outs. The worst part, I learn from the report, is that the Santa Ana winds are still blowing full speed and are unstoppable.

Despite scientists' warnings that California would be wiped out by either a mega-tsunami or an earthquake, she is on her way to going down in flames.

I lift my head from the paper and look inside the coffee shop. On the other side of the window, at a small round table, sits a lean, blonde girl in a white shirt and jeans. She is bent over a notebook, writing, occasionally tossing a strand of her hair back, and checking something in the open text book in front of her. In the glass between us, the reflection of the homeless man over-laps with the empty seat next to the girl inside. Semi-transparent, the homeless man finishes up his coffee, leans back comfortably, crosses his legs, and extends a greasy sleeve over the back of the seat as if throwing his arm around the girl.

She doesn't mind.

He pulls out a Zippo from his torn breast pocket and lights a cigarette.

She sips from her cup without lifting her head from the book.

He blows a cloud of smoke, drops his head back, and scratches his knee.

She fixes her bra strap and keeps writing in her notebook.

There they are—another impossible couple. I take out the Nikon, place it carefully on the table, and take a few shots. A minute later, the girl finishes her coffee, closes the notebook and the textbook, puts them into a leather messenger bag, leans toward her reflection in the glass, adjusts her barrette, slides lipstick over her lips, and smacks them a few times to soften the effect. Then she tosses the bag over her shoulder and walks out. Only the semi-transparent homeless man, who grinds the cigarette butt on the sidewalk with his muddy, untied shoe, remains in the window glass.

·

Stella's first solo exhibition was a success. There were reviews, articles, a radio show, a few seconds of TV time, a paragraph in Art Globe *magazine. There was also a producer who wanted her to be the art director for a music video. There was talk about including her work in a catalog about contemporary American art. The thing about Stella's paintings, however, was that they seemed as if they were created by different people. Massive squares in rusty browns, which Stella achieved through mixing oils and graphite powder with fine metal particles that she borrowed from the metal shop next door to her studio, had attracted Jane Goldstein to her work. These were non-representational works, save for some atavistic slashes, lines, strokes, and circles. While she was working on them, she would come home as black as a coal-miner and would cough over the sink, spitting out graphite. I convinced her to wear a mask—there was no point in ruining her lungs.*

The militaristic brown texture of her next painting cracked, however, and a piece of the blue California sky shined through. In the following few works, the sky gradually pushed the graphite toward the periphery of the canvas. This series ended abruptly with a white, thickly layered rectangle in oils. After that came two nine-foot squares in black and white, which some saw as an aerial view of burned forests, while others likened to bird feathers. Totems in dark green and dark red followed. Then a series of self portraits—almost black paintings —suggesting female bodies or depicting female torsos in dark rectangles.

In the beginning, Jane Goldstein almost cut her out of the circle of artists she promoted, but, gradually, she became accustomed to Stella's randomness and eccentricity.

At times, Stella's interest in painting would cease, and she would spend days reading Anna Karenina, *writing in her journals, or doodling in the margins. I'd find her miniature proto-projects scratched onto the back of bills, car insurance forms, or the calendar next to the phone, scribbled down while she was talking to somebody. Sometimes she would spend days searching for the meaning of a single word, like* identity, *for example. She would dig out everything that could define it—passports, drivers licenses, all sorts of diplomas, marriage licenses, birth certificates, credit cards, library cards, and just about every form of identification—and would arrange all these in a certain order that made sense to her.*

Other times, she would concentrate her entire attention on a single number. Or a symbol. Or a letter. During these periods, she didn't go to her studio and we spent more time together. Then the appetite for work would take over again, and she'd disappear into her creations.

The labels describing her work varied from neo-abstract expressionism, through late postmodern minimalism, to meditative realism. Those -isms, of course, had nothing to do with her.

After summer break, Stella quit her job and dedicated all of her time and energy to painting.

The curator of S gallery in L.A. invited her to join a project with two video artists. For it, she created an installation made of 274 white sheets—the idea came from a dream of clothes hung on a line to dry. The curator of the Museum of Contemporary Art in Seattle included her in an exhibition with her series entitled On Kinkade, *which consisted of twelve paintings rendered over Thomas Kinkade reproductions, which Stella had salvaged from a dumpster behind an office building. She kept their melodramatic titles*–The End of a Perfect Day, Home Is Where the Heart Is, The Light of Calmness, Last Autumn Morning *and then covered them with a thick layer of charcoal and paint.*

More and more circled dates started to appear in her calendar.

Things were happening for her. "If something has to happen, it will," she'd say. "If it doesn't, then it wasn't supposed to."

Then came the job offer from the Los Angeles Art Institute. Before she accepted, however, she asked for two weeks to think things over. She bought a plane ticket to New York with an open return.

Her last year with me was a year of things-come-true. The biggest thing, however, was yet to come.

•

I enter Columbus at dusk. I park in the familiar driveway, get out of the car, and am just about to ring the doorbell as Ken opens the door and hugs me.

"Zack!" He pulls away a little, then hugs me again. "Come on in. How was the drive? Here, here . . . I'm sorry about the mess, but I had to call a plumber to fix the pipe that broke off behind that thing." I don't see any mess except one old cabinet that's been slightly moved. In Ken's world, perhaps, this is a major event. "Let me close the door, so the cats stay out." I sit down just as I used to—on one of the bar stools. "Do you have any luggage?" he asks as he opens the refrigerator.

"I have a bag in the trunk of my car. I'll get it in a minute." I stretch my shoulders, stiff from the long drive.

"How about a beer first?" He lifts a brow.

"Oh, you're drinking these days?" I'm surprised.

"Only on special occasions. And only beer." A couple of glasses appear on the bar. Two green bottles go bottoms up.

"I'm flattered." We raise our glasses for a toast. There are very few things, I do believe, better than the first sip of good beer. I close my eyes to stretch the moment as long as I can.

"So, tell me, what's going on with you?" Ken smiles.

I have no idea where to start or end my story. "You go first. How are you?"

"OK. I'm OK." Ken looks at the edge of the counter for a moment.

"How are things with Linda?" I finish what's left in my glass.

"Fine." Ken gets up and brings two more beers. "She's the best thing that ever happened to me, Zack."

"Then why don't you live together already?" I ask the question that is likely on everybody's mind. "What are you waiting for?" Since Stella left, I've obviously forgotten some of my manners. Ken tops us off again. We look at each other over the foam in our glasses. He sighs and tears his eyes away. I drink.

"We almost did."

"So?"

"I fucked up."

"What do you mean, you fucked up?" I take a look around. It's been a while since I've been here. God, everything looks so . . . bachelory. I bet that nothing has changed since Ken bought the place. It has been left untouched for years and is poorly lit. I feel the urge to jump off my stool and pull down the old curtains, peel off the appalling wallpaper, cut the ugly sofas to pieces, and knock out most of the walls.

"She was going to move in with me here, right? So, before she . . . well, the night before that . . ." Ken stops and swallows hard. "I got really drunk the night before." He looks at me with the blue eyes of an alcoholic. "I drank till I got shit-faced. Alone.

Here. And I felt so lonely—I almost went out of my mind. And I couldn't stand another second without her. So I decided to convince her to move in earlier." He pauses. "Can you imagine? I get drunk alone, here, at this very counter. So, I'm talking to my cats and one of them—that one, the black one, she is *the devil*, I swear—makes me go and bring home my fiancée. I swear. The black one made me do it." I glance at the cat on the other side of the glass door. The animal opens its mouth, meowing soundlessly, throwing green looks at us. It really is demonic. I figure that if I had to spend months and years in this brown, gloomy house, I, too, would start listening to what cats had to say to me. "So, I get in my car and drive to her apartment in the middle of the night. I ring the doorbell. She answers the door—who knows what she was thinking. I stagger, reach out and try to kiss her and take her home with me, but I lose my balance and land on the floor, facedown. You get the picture?" I nod. "Months passed before we revived the relationship. I don't think it's the same, you know. The trust is not there anymore somehow, but on the whole . . ."

"Listen, man!" I clear my throat, imitating deep thought. I know one thing about Ken for sure. In his head, Stella—whom he's never seen—and I are the perfect couple. Everybody thought that. Until two weeks ago. At this moment, though, Ken doesn't know that we are not the perfect couple. Hell, he doesn't even know that we are not a couple at all. The only thing that's left of *us* is me, whatever is left of me. But at this moment, Ken doesn't know any of that. He still believes in me, in us. "You have no reason, whatsoever, to be ashamed of what you've done." I cut directly to the point. "You shouldn't think too much." Now, I have to continue with a personal example. "For example, at Stella's birthday party—the first one we celebrated together—I got so drunk that I shat myself!" I take a sip of my beer. "I mean, literally. Don't even ask." Ken bursts out laughing. "That's right. In my pants. It's not funny . . . Well, it *is* funny now, I mean, but it wasn't funny *then*. I shat myself. Right in my pants. So please stop talking about screw ups. You are cool, so if somebody doesn't appreciate you, it's their loss." Several beers later, we're more relaxed and cheerful. We drink ten bottles each, so we need to pee every half-hour. I stop caring about the brown interior, as well as some other things. Here we are—two losers in Ken's brown house, drinking beer, keeping the cats out.

At one point, Ken gets up. "Zack, I'll make us something to eat. I cooked something here." He opens the fridge, takes out some containers, turns on the microwave. I am tired to death from all the driving and loneliness and so exhausted that I don't have the energy to tell him I'm not hungry. I slip down from the bar stool, go to the bathroom (decorated with a dusty plastic flower), urinate for a long time, flush the toilet once before I finish, and flush it once more while I'm zipping up my pants. I go back in the room and recline on the sofa for a while. I find a pillow and hug it.

I wake up to laughter. I wake up after the most beautiful experience I've had in a long, long time. A warm spring day. Stella and I are walking slowly, shoulder to shoulder, in the shadow of young, green, blossoming trees, on a road that climbs upward. Stella slows down from time to time to admire the acacias. Further up, we pass some apple trees with large pink and white blossoms. She pauses at one of them, reaches up, picks a handful of petals, and puts them in her mouth, squinting with pleasure as she chews them. Then, she opens her eyes, comes closer, puts her hands on my shoulders, and smiles. She looks me firmly in the eyes, and says: *"Do you think we are finally free?"*

My spontaneous answer is, *"Of course,"* but I don't remember saying it. Then we both laugh. We laugh loudly. We laugh purely and deeply like innocent, innocent children. Her laughter wakes me up, but when I open my eyes, I hear only mine.

.

It was one of the few nights we spent together during that last year. We sat in the patio chairs, wrapped in blankets. We lit a candle, sipped wine, and gazed at the dark canyon before us. The frogs were croaking. Suddenly, the phone rang in that particular way it does when someone from far away is calling. The neighbor's cat was on my lap, so Stella picked up. She stood quietly for a long moment, then said, "But, of course. Thank you!" She replaced the receiver, topped off her glass, and asked me if I wanted more. "No," I said. "I don't." She came back, sat in her chair, hugged her knees, narrowed her eyes, lifted her head up toward her favorite Orion, and started rocking back and forth. I swear I saw a tear roll down her cheek, but she quickly wiped it away with her shoulder. Or maybe I just imagined it. I watched her face for a while—lit by constellations, softened by the trembling candlelight. For the first time in a long time I felt the urge to get my camera and photograph her. I suppressed the impulse.

"I've been invited to the Berlin Biennale next year, in October."

"What!?" I shouted. The frogs grew quiet. I lifted my glass to toast her but it was empty, there was nothing in the bottle either. Stella smiled, leaned over, and poured some of her wine in my glass. We toasted. We drank. Then she gently held my face with both her hands and kissed my lips. She kissed me like she never had before. Again. And again. She kissed me wetly and warmly, she kissed me long and deep, she kissed me as if one of us was dying.

The truth was that what remained of me in that patio chair was a papier-mâché mask, growing cold.

•

Pennsylvania. Lancaster County.

Autumn has settled in here long ago. Old woodlands sunk in misty clouds. Silence. The dark gray line of wet asphalt draws a stretched out *S* and disappears up ahead in the fog, which is growing thicker with every second. Atop a little knoll stands a bunch of tall, dark shrubs, like widows resting by the road. I pull over. I load a new roll of film in the camera, walk through the thick, wet grass, take a few pictures, then notice the wooden poles tied with barbed wire, open the aperture to focus only on what I need, and get closer. I let the wire come down from the top left corner of the frame and lead the eye toward the focus, which I choose to place down in the right third. The shutter clicks. I stride further into the moist meadow until I see the ruins of an abandoned barn. A bottomed-out roof, protruding beams and poles, shattered wooden planks, and rusty tin sheets are buried in weeds and obstinate shrubbery. And, as if the years of solitude and harsh climate were not enough, a wild walnut tree growing through the middle ruptures its insides spring after spring. How abandoned could an abandoned barn be! Couldn't somebody simply tear it down?

My grandfather, Stefan Nichts' shop looked somewhat like this the last time I saw it. Stefan Nichts was not my real grandfather. He was one of my grandmother's brothers. He had been an artist and a master carriage-maker before World War Two—a quite wealthy man who had traveled and lived in Venice and Germany. Then, the communists came, appropriated everything he owned, and tossed him in a labor camp. After some years, he was released, went to the countryside, scraped some money together, and opened a shop in his village. Not for horse-drawn carriages, but for handmade donkey carts. He became a cartwright. I remember how people would come from all over to order and buy carts from him. I liked to hover around him in his dim workshop, handing him tools, listening to his stories (he had lots), fanning the fire with the bellows, and watching him work. I remember how, sometimes, in his dusty little windows, never touched by a woman's hand and covered in thick cobwebs and mummified flies, a beam of sunlight would squeeze in, and countless tiny specks of dust would dance in it.

Grandpa Stefan Nichts would weld the carts in his shop and then drag their naked torsos out under the thick shadow of the walnut tree to dress them in warm, vibrant colors. I sometimes think that he got into crafting carts just so he had something to paint without his townsfolk taking him for a complete loon. Not that they took him for *normal* anyhow. When he was young, Grandpa Stefan had had an affair with a Greek woman who, malicious rumor has it, sucked his brains dry before leaving him. After her, he never married or had any children. Every day, he would drink bitter Turkish coffee that he boiled in a beat-up, ancient coffee pot, smoke filterless cigarettes, and cough. Every evening he'd go down to the pub, where he'd get drunk on *menta* (mint schnapps) and curse the communists. He would threaten to hang himself, wave his fist in the air, and yell, *Nichts! Nichts! No!* That's why they called him Nichts. In my memory, he looks like the late Ezra Pound—messy haired and stubbly—in that 1971 Henri Cartier-Bresson portrait. Grandpa Stefan Nichts spent the last winter of his life sick, broken, and bedridden under the window in his lonely bachelor pad.

The last time I went to see him, I was a senior in high school. I hitchhiked from the city to the village. It was foggy and dreary. I rode in an old Soviet car, a tractor, and a truck and arrived in the village just before dark on a donkey cart. First, I peeked into his abandoned shop. It had been looted and torn apart. There were no windows, hinges or doors, half of the roof was missing. Wild walnut trees grew everywhere. I went out, crossed the weeded yard, climbed the run-down steps, and opened the door to his room. I swear I saw a fat rat clumsily jump down from his pillow, where somebody had left a piece of hard bread, and slide under the kitchen cupboard. Grandpa Nichts was trembling, freezing under the army blanket, soaked in his own urine, his head turned toward the ugly tapestry hanging by his bed. I had brought freshly ground coffee. I boiled it in his grotesque coffee pot. The scent of coffee chased the stench from the room for a moment. I managed to lift the old man's pillow a bit, propping it up with two dusty wool coats. I found some cups, rinsed them with cold water, and took a few sips of coffee. He also wet his parched lips with the black liquid, but only to stain them a little. His once shiny and expressive eyes were now soaked in the foggy light of that departing winter day.

I promised him that I'd come see him again and asked if he wanted anything from the city. "Nichts," the old man said, slipped down in bed, turned his unshaven face toward the tapestry, and closed his eyes.

I get in the car, turn on the lights, and drive.

Why can't I remember what exactly we talked about? Why didn't I spend more time with that fascinating old man? What more important things did I have to do?

Suddenly, in front of me appears a black, rectangular, coffin-shaped four-wheel buggy pulled by a black horse. I drive behind it, slowly taking a few pictures with my right hand. If it weren't for the red reflective triangle affixed to it, this mysterious monochrome vision would have horrified me.

Lancaster, Pennsylvania.

This is Amish country. The Amish people, I know, have lived around here for centuries as if time doesn't exist. They plow the land with horses and don't use electricity, telephones, or cars. The Amish don't believe in civilization, government, progress, art, music, secular love, taxes, 401ks, war, colorful attire, secondary education, or terrorism. The Amish believe in the Bible and its sufficiency, non-violence, equality and brotherhood, and the healing power of religion. The Amish believe in Jesus Christ as only Jesus Christ would believe in another Son of God. The Amish call themselves "plain people," and Lancaster County is their territory. I take a little detour through Bird-in-Hand, Intercourse, and

Paradise. These are all Amish towns. I can't help but think about the vulgar connotations of their names.

I park in the center of Intercourse and step into a small, wooden cabin-store, illuminated by a gas lamp. The clerk is an elderly woman dressed like a servant out of a Vermeer painting. I also see two blond boys with typical Amish haircuts, wearing black pants, suspenders, and white cotton shirts. There is a red-faced old man with a beard but no mustache. All Amish men grow beards after they get married. Only beards, no mustaches. To them, the mustache symbolizes aggressive masculinity, conflict, and war. Intercourse, Pennsylvania. What if I ask the woman behind the counter for condoms? However, the silent humbleness of these people strangely tames my demons. I wonder if I should spend the night here. Intercourse. How righteous do you have to be, I wonder, to live in a town whose name meant "communion" two hundred years ago, and now is just the proper term for "fucking"? I exchange a few words with the old guy. I buy bread and milk, then get into my car, and figure out how to catch I-78 for New York. In a few hours, if the fog clears, I'll arrive where this story has to end.

•

The morning Stella left, OPEC suspended most of its drilling projects, a train in southwest Germany crashed, killing forty-eight; in Kabul a suicide bomber took thirty-seven lives and injured 120; China approved sanctions on Iran; Pope Benedict XIV visited Turkey; seven American soldiers were killed by friendly fire in Fallujah; the problem with Kosovo's status remained unresolved; and the Phoenix Space Mission was looking for a place to land on Mars . . .

•

In Pennsylvania—and during most of my drive as a whole—it just drizzles, but in New Jersey, it really rains, in Newark it pours, and in New York City, it's a deluge. I slide into the tunnel to Manhattan and drive in the left lane, with only a few cars ahead of me. The camera is loaded with color film now; the aperture is set at 2.8, the speed at 3 seconds. I open the window, holding the steering wheel with my left hand and pressing the shutter with my right. I know that the chrome throat of the tunnel will stay light gray, I know how the brake lights of the vehicles ahead of me will look—like curly red lines in the middle of the picture—the fluorescent lights under the roof will leave two diagonal white streaks that will converge in the middle to form a Y in the center of the rectangular frame. I know how this photograph will look, so why do I take it? Why do I keep taking pictures? Because I can or in spite of that? Why in the world do we do the things we do?

I step on the gas and accelerate. I want to get out of this tunnel. I want to cross to the other side. I've wanted to go to the other side for a long time now, damn it. For such a long time I've dreamed about going beyond and finding Stella and hugging her and taking her face in my hands and squeezing it like a rubber toy, and kissing her the way only I can—hurting her lips with my crooked eyetooth. I've dreamed of messing up her hair, digging my face into the small of her neck, sniffing the skin behind her ears like a dog—like the dog I really am. *Shoo, doggy.* She'd pretend to chase me, *Shoo! Go away, bad dog,* and she'd laugh, and I'd push her down into the snow, and we'd roll around in it. She hates when I whitewash her, *shoo, doggy! shoo!* Stella hates the cold, *shoo, doggy,* but I do it anyway because I don't know what else to do with my love. I don't know what else to do. I don't know how not to hurt her, when I now enter Manhattan through the merciless chrome throat of the Holland Tunnel.

Manhattan.

I am nearing the end of my journey. I can feel it. That buzzing in my head is stronger than ever. Buzzing in my head. Buzzing in the speakers is a sign that the system has not been grounded properly.

A little after midnight, I ring Danny's doorbell.

"I'm coming," the intercom crackles. Danny opens the door wearing a robe and white tube socks bunched up at his ankles and sagging in front, a couple of sizes too big. The loose socks with the dirty heels lead me up a flight of squeaky, wooden stairs. No woman should ever have to see a man in such socks, it's disgusting. On the second floor, one of the apartments has no door—it's just missing. The smell of marijuana, loud Indian disco music, and the voices of about fifty shouting people come from the inside. "We can join them later, if you want." We climb up to his apartment. It's the size of my garage in California. Loud Miles Davis blares from the speakers. "I'll turn it down. I just can't stand that shit they play down there. I don't even know how they listen to it."

A red paper lantern decorated with dragons from a Chinese restaurant has somehow been attached to the naked light bulb. The walls are painted yellow. Every inch is filled with books, movie posters, CDs, vinyl, tapes, paintings in different stages of development, photographs, newspaper cut-outs, and magazines. In the corner, there's an amplifier and a guitar. Half of the wall is dedicated to small digital tapes labeled in Danny's beautiful handwriting. "You'll sleep here and I'll sleep over there on that mattress." I sit down. "What do you want to drink?" I lie down on the mattress, spread my arms, and look at the red dragons around the light bulb.

·

I had gotten up earlier than she did and was sipping coffee from a big yellow mug. The telephone rang. I turned down the TV and picked up. Jane. We exchanged words about Stella's invitation to the Biennial. Stella appeared on the stairs, rubbing her eyes sleepily, wearing black cat slippers and a worn-out Fruit of the Loom shirt of mine covered in holes from countless washes.

Jane, Jane, how lucky was I supposed to be if Stella was getting out of the same bed I had slept in just moments ago?

Jane understood Stella, and Stella understood Jane. They talked about the theme of the Biennial—Author-Time—about Stella's choice of medium, about the other participants—Kate Mason, Sarah Morris, Lou Meyer, Julian Hope, Malcolm Sype, Mary Heilman (unquestionably the star of the Biennial), Jim Dein, Robert Fox, Pyotr Oblonski (the new Russian prodigy), Bernard Foucault (who already lived in New York), Yasuma Morimura, and many others whom I hadn't heard of. Stella would be one of the newest names there. I sat on the sofa with that stupid yellow cup in my hand. Between the muted CNN screen and me, the black cat slippers paced back and forth. Above them were the long, beautiful legs, covered with eternal blue bruises, the torn T-shirt which hardly covered her slowly freezing nakedness, the hand that scratched the knee, the other hand that held the receiver of the old black telephone.

•

I wake up in the morning from car alarms. Danny's not here. I take a quick shower. As I go to open the refrigerator, I notice the tiny magnet calendar on the dirty door—today is Halloween. Danny comes in, carrying donuts and a newspaper.

"Good morning. Big fires in that California of yours, brother. Are they anywhere near your house?"

"Yep."

"That's not good."

"Nope."

"One would expect tsunamis."

"If you're meant to hang yourself, you won't get hit by a car."

"True." Danny takes out a gallon jug of orange juice and pours what's left of it into two glasses. "Now tell me everything. Last night you fell asleep like a baby."

"I haven't slept like that in weeks."

"That's why I let you."

"Thank you."

"What's with this grass now? Where did you get it?"

"It's a long story. You go first. Are you still working with Hito-san?"

"From time to time."

"How's he doing?"

"Well, so, so. It's not like before." We munch on donuts.

"Why?"

"Those tricks he did by hand in a darkroom twenty years ago can now be done with Photoshop in a couple of hours. A whole bunch of his clients left."

"Why?"

"Cheaper photographers."

"But it's *Hito* we're talking about here, man. He's a fucking legend. He's world famous . . ."

"Famous-shmamous. They don't care. Should we have coffee here or do you want some fresh air?"

"Let's go out."

Starbucks. Danny is buying.

"How's the job at Christie's?" I ask him.

"Still wrapping."

"It's the Bulgarian trademark. Christo[1] started it."

"Somebody's got to do it." Danny shrugs and stirs his coffee.

"I guess. And what do you do exactly?"

"I handle things people have bought at the auction. The auctions are on Sundays, right? So we pack whatever's been sold and transport it to the new owner. Every single day, I go to work knowing that today, maybe I'll pack another Picasso or Clemente, a Rubens, a Michelangelo, or an Etruscan mask . . . that kind of thing. I've wrapped . . . well, everything you can imagine, man—paintings, sculptures, photographs. The installations are the hardest, of course."

"Sounds exciting."

"Whatever." Danny takes a sip of his coffee and stares at the rim of the table. "But sometimes I . . . cry. Tears start falling from my eyes, just like that, I don't even know why."

"You've got to lay off the drugs, pal."

"No drugs, bro. Forget the drugs. There's no drug like art, man. No other high like that. If I'm lucky enough to come across something real my hands start trembling, my whole body shakes, tears roll down my cheeks, I don't even think about smoking, shooting up, drinking, popping pills, fucking . . . I'm telling you, man. Theres no high like that, nothing even comes close! Everything just stops. Seriously."

"So do you always handle . . . such artifacts?"

"Not that often, actually. There aren't that many out there, man. They're . . . it's like . . . it's pure energy, bro. Energy. Life." Danny is getting worked up. "That's what makes a painting different from an identical copy. The life in it. I mean—*life*. A piece of life is built into it. And it just recently dawned on me what it's all about: life. That's

---

1 The Bulgarian-born artist Christo Yavashev, famous for wrapping large objects such as the Reichstag and the Pont Neuf.

what every true collector wants—to buy a piece of someone else's *life*. Do you really think somebody cares about what you paint, what style, or how good you are? No one spends millions of dollars on craftsmanship. They only write million-dollar checks for *life!*"

"Life, huh?"

"Fuck yeah."

"Life."

"That's what they buy, the vampires. I'm telling you . . . pieces of *life*. If it's there, the price doesn't matter."

"Danny boy . . . I'm gonna get myself another coffee. Do you want one?" I leave him alone for a minute. I get back. His knee has not stopped bouncing up and down. He's all nerves, shaking the table, spilling coffee. "You're so passionate about art, man. You're on fire."

"I know, right? It comes with the territory, I guess, ha ha. I bubble-wrap masterpieces. How many people in the world have touched as much art as I have? And I mean *touched*."

"No kidding."

"I've been blessed."

"Good for you. And how about money? You OK in that department?"

"I'm hurting, man. I'll never be able to buy a car or a place to live. I won't be able to get married if I keep going like this."

"There must be a way."

"Easy for you to say." I stare at my coffee and decide not to go there.

"What are your plans?" I ask.

"I just want to save up some money and continue my education."

"The one you have isn't enough?"

"Christie's offer these classes. They take about a year and a half. For art specialists, appraisers, consultants, and such. You can work in galleries, museums, etc. . . . But it's a lot of money."

"How much?"

"About fifty grand."

"That's a lot."

"Yeah, it is. If I'm good, though—and I'm good enough to know I'm good—I will end up making decent money. And I'll be surrounded by art all the time, I'll be a broker, a consultant, I'll be in the process . . . so to speak. I'll start collecting on my own, too." Danny downs his coffee and groans. "So that's why I'm doing the Cartoon Network."

"The Cartoon Network? I didn't know you were into animation." Danny laughs. "That's what we call the network, dude. The enterprise I sell dope for—the Cartoon Network."

I get up. "Let's go check out the art galleries."

"I have a couple of things to take care of, so how about we meet in Chelsea? Let's say at . . ." Danny looks at his watch. "How about . . . well, I can see you in about three hours. Let's meet at this Italian place on West 26th." He writes down the name and the address on a napkin. "I'll get the key to Hito's studio and we'll leave the bag there until my man calls."

•

I went out in the yard with my yellow cup. I felt her approaching. She put her hand on my shoulder. The Santa Ana winds had desiccated the canyon beyond recognition. It was quiet. I remember the powerful impulse to caress her fingers, to turn around and bury my head in her breasts, still warm from the bed. But I swallowed it.

"Can I ask you something?" I say without turning to her.

"Since when are you asking permission to ask me anything?"

"It's about . . . Bernard that night?"

"What!?" Her hand jerks away. "What night?"

"In Paris. In front of . . . the hotel."

"Oh, that one!? The night you got drunk, acted like an idiot and ran up to our room, and we stayed a little longer downstairs?"

"Yes."

"We talked."

"About what?"

"About pigments."

•

Downtown New York. It is ridiculous to wander around the wet sidewalk of Fifth Avenue with my hands in my pockets, amidst all these people. Most of them are just like me—ridiculous—but some are not.

Some have, I imagine, absurdly huge bank accounts.

Others, I see, are outrageously poor.

And there is another group—the clearly insane.

Yes, it's ridiculous for me to think that I belong here. It's ridiculous to assume that I could be as happy as that couple in Central Park, or as miserable as that loner in the subway, or as carefree as the dog over there in the fat lap of the lady getting into the cab.

What am I doing here?

The streets are empty this time of day in Chelsea. I check out a few galleries, each exhibit is more boring than the previous one. I pop into a small gallery with an Armenian name. I stand before one painting—a black and white painting of that famous photograph from the seventies in which one Vietnamese man is shooting another in the head. The street behind them is empty, there are two clouds in the sky; the short-haired man with an outstretched scrawny hand holding a small pistol is General Nguyen Ngoc Loan. The other one, who's going to be dead in a second, has longer hair, a flannel shirt, and his hands tied behind his back. His face is distorted in one last convulsion captured on film. He has no name. I grew up with that photograph. It was printed in a thick book of communist propaganda entitled *Soldiers of the Quiet Front*, which I often flipped through with a kind of juvenile voyeurism, each time expecting to see a different ending. But no, *deus ex machina* never showed up. The captured Vietnamese fighter crumples to the ground, his head blown up. His executioner, along with his family, immigrated to New Jersey, where he opened a pizza parlor and lived until July 15, 1998. He died at sixty-seven.

I stand for a long time in front of the painting depicting a photograph depicting a murder. Nowadays, every artist is expected to come up with a new gimmick to make a breakthrough in this Art Armageddon saturated with new gimmicks. The gimmick in this painting is that it was made with human hair. The Chinese artist pedantically portrays shocking images like this one, as well as iconic portraits of Marilyn Monroe, Elvis, Coca-Cola, Mona Lisa, and Madonna, with the living tissue of human hair collected from the floors of Beijing barber shops. You have to be very close to the piece to notice the medium he uses.

I leave.

.

—can i at least draw while you're taking these pictures?

—no

—please

—can you just be an object for a moment?

—no

—be patient for just a few more minutes. we're almost done

.

The Italian restaurant.

Danny is here. The only free table is in the corner, close to the bathrooms and overlooking the kitchen where dark Mexicans knead mounds of dough. A fat man in a white shirt with raven-black hair parted in the middle and a thick, gold chain around his neck writes something down. He looks like a Sicilian. He looks like the owner. The waitress has a French accent.

A girl with short, blonde, messy hair in a tank top and back-pack enters, yells *ciao* in raspy voice, and whispers something to the owner. His eyes open wide, his jaw drops, and his belly starts shaking with noiseless laughter. She says something else to him, he lifts his notebook from the table and tries to smack her butt with it, shouts *bast-a-a-a*, and keeps on laughing. The Mexicans in the kitchen throw small pieces of dough at the girl as she drops her backpack and goes over to the other side of the bar. I realize she is the bartender who is just starting her shift. She rummages through her backpack, starts taking out journals, books, a Walk-man, pulls out a CD labeled with permanent marker, puts it in the stereo, and points the remote toward the small TV, which comes to life, but with no sound. The comfort of the place makes me feel like I've been here before.

"Danny, have we been here before?"

"No."

"Are you sure?"

"Yes."

"But what if we *have* and now we are simply watching the tape backwards?"

"I don't understand."

"What if, let's say, the way we see our life is fundamentally wrong? What if we live in reverse? What if we all simply live according to—I've got a working term here—*the principle of back-ward time*?"

"Zack," Danny leans back in his chair. "There's too much caffeine in your system!"

"No, hear me out."

"It's too early for this. What do you wanna drink?" He motions to the server.

"Uh. dirty martini, thanks. I mean, what if we are returning..."

"Are you going Nietzsche on me now? The *eternal* return?"

"No, no eternal returns. There's nothing eternal here. I'm talking about . . . Do you sometimes get the feeling that your life has been predetermined? Not by someone else, but by you. For example, you meet somebody new, but you have that I've-known-you-my-whole-life vibe going. Or, the feeling that you've actually known all along something you just learned? Thank you, mmmm, nice martini. Excellent. Can I have a few more olives, please? What was I saying? Oh, yes. We teach a child from a very young age that life goes in a certain direction, and everything begins with birth and ends with death. Right? We send the kid to school where everybody reads books and watches movies in a particular way and spends their lives like that, this kid will think, no . . . he or she will *know* that that is the natural order of things, that is the truth. Right? But, what if we're just wound backward?" I rest my elbows on the table. "You know, Danny, my father was essentially a loser. An alcoholic, a weak man who couldn't do a single thing right. If he had to hammer in a nail, he'd bend the nail *and* hurt his fingers. And still not manage to pound it in. So, on one of my birthdays—maybe my fifth one—my grandparents gave me a present, this little model battleship kit. A little battleship with a little electric motor that spins the little propellers that move it forward in the water. There's one tiny detail, though—the ship has to be assembled from scratch. After a lot of putting it off, my father agreed to help me assemble the battleship. He pulled out a bunch of tools from the trunk of the car, we spilled everything on the floor and started gluing, building, fitting the pieces together. After a while, I can't remember how long, we managed to put the boat together somehow and it looked just fine. So I took a tub, filled it with water, put the boat in, pushed the button to start the motor, and the boat started going backwards."

"Backwards?"

"Yes."

"Why backwards?"

"Well, my dad had obviously installed the motor backwards, or hooked it up funny, I don't remember. But the battleship sailed backward."

"So, did he fix it?"

"Nope. He said—'Well, no biggie, you can still play with it the way it is, can't you?'" I smile and take a sip from my glass.

"And what's the moral of the story, Zack? That some loser—sorry—deity has put in our motors backwards?" Danny flags down the server. "One more martini, please!"

"Zack. Who would benefit from turning our lives upside-down?"

"I have no idea."

"Man, you need help." He says.

"Cause and effect, bro—you reverse their order, you rule the world." Danny sighs and keeps shaking his head. I bet he thinks I'm insane. "Jesus Christ. Look what happens with Jesus! The dude knew how everything would end. Moreover, Danny, he chose how everything would end. In the *principle of backward time*, every choice you make now is already . . . You already *lived* the choices you are about to make now. Get it?" A waitress passes by our table, I gesture to her to bring another round, and glimpse toward the TV above the bar. At that moment, I see our neighborhood in flames, I see fire trucks turning onto our street and firefighters putting out the fire at the neighbor's house. Danny has his back to the TV. There is our house, whatever is left of it. A female reporter wearing a respirator interviews a neighbor whom

I've only greeted twice, and this neighbor now points at the pile of burnt rubble atop the canyon and looks upset. There lie the ashes of all the photos I've taken, all the negatives I've left for later, dozens of notebooks filled with notes, projects, fragments, and dreams. There are the ashes of letters and postcards, the books we read, the movies we cried over, the music we loved, the bed we kept warm.

I wonder how people faint at such sights. I can't. The news continues with preparations for the New York Halloween parade. Danny orders vegetarian lasagna. I order ravioli with mushrooms.

•

We leave the restaurant and walk toward the car. It has just started to rain again. Where I had parked though, is now a dry rectangle. They've towed my car? In New York City? I run to the intersection, peek around the corner, come back, run to the other corner, looking around—nothing.

"Where did you park?" Danny still hasn't grasped what's going on.

"Here. Right here! Here. Here. Here!" Danny rolls his eyes, takes a deep breath, and bites his lip. He scratches his eyebrow, pointing at the sign on the fence. It reads that the parking spaces are for residents of that building only and all violators will be towed at the owner's expense. For more information, call this 1-800-whatever-seven-digit number. Danny takes out his cell phone and dials. Half turning his back to me, he talks to someone, then takes a pen out of his pocket, looks around, picks up a smashed cigarette pack from the ground, writes something on it, and hangs up.

"It's there."

"Where?"

"There."

"How much?"

"Two hundred and eighty dollars."

"They'll eat two hundred and eighty fucking dicks, fucking motherfuckers." I'm furious. A cab passes, I try to flag it down but it doesn't stop. I see another one behind it and almost jump on the hood.

A Pakistani with a turban.

Danny and I get in the back. Danny knocks on the plexiglass divider and shows him the cigarette box with the address. The Pakistani rolls his eyes like a madman and starts waving his hands, screaming.

"No cigarettes. No smoking." Danny calms him down, points to the address written on the pack, and the Pakistani starts driving somewhere. We pass through dark, desolate places. It's raining harder now. The red brake lights of the vehicles in front of us dwindle. We pass through grim housing projects and arrive at something that looks like a prison with a gate, prickling with barbed wire, fences, and an aluminum roof. We pull up and I pay the cabbie. We go into a trailer with barred windows. Behind a plastic divider sits an obese Arab in a white *Radio Love 93.1* T-shirt, eating barbecued wings out of a plastic box, his fat face smeared with Tabasco sauce. He notices us and starts wiping himself with a pile of napkins. And he wipes, and wipes, and wipes, and wipes, and wipes without giving a shit about the number of trees felled in the Amazon just so he can wipe the orange Tabasco sauce off his unshaven, greasy face. All the jungles on the planet would not be enough for you to wipe the grease off your muzzle, freak!

"What do you want?"

"Our car, what else?"

"The Mercedes with the broken trunk?"

"Excuse me, you opened the trunk?"

"The trunk opened by itself. Your car had been rear-ended,

the trunk opened by itself. We are not responsible if the car has been rear-ended." The room spins.

"What was in the trunk?" I ask.

"A spare tire."

"What else?"

"An emergency kit." You will need an emergency kit now, you fucking pig-face! I shove my head through the small window and try grabbing the fat freak by the throat. He swings back surprisingly quickly, the chair flying out from under him. Half-eaten chicken wings, Tabasco sauce, celery, napkins, and dressing fly up in the air on the other side of the plastic divider and land on the dirty linoleum. My head is inside, behind the fiberglass. I want to squeeze my shoulders in like a rat, to crawl inside, knock the Monstrosity to the floor, grab the fire extinguisher from the wall, and bash his head with it, just like in that horrifying French movie, to release the world from his weight (Five hundred pounds? Six hundred?). I'm sure the world would be a better place, a far better place, if this pile of meat dies, rots, and turns into soil, fertile soil in some cemetery, upon which green grass will grow, clean morning dew will fall, the sun will shine, and harmless bugs will crawl. Swine-man, however, is in the corner of his little office, a safe distance from me. Centrifugal forces have pushed out the jelly around his neck. Grunts and snorts come out of his mouth as a walkie-talkie appears in his hairy hand, decorated with a heavy golden chain.

"I'm calling the police!" Wheezing.

"There was a bag in the trunk of the car,"

Wheezing. "That's not my problem." Wheezing.

"It will be your problem in a second."

"Are you threatening me, huh? Are you threatening me? I'm calling the police!" Danny pulls me by my legs into *our* half of the office.

"I need my car."

"It's two hundred and eighty dollars."

"Pay him," He says. "And let's get out of here!"

"Danny," I whisper. "These fuckers took the bag of marijuana."

"All the better," says Danny, "Now you won't have to deal with it. Just pay them what they want and let's go!"

"Danny, are you kidding me!? I expect fifty grand from that pot and you want me to leave it here in this pigsty? I crossed the whole continent, rain soaked me, fire burned me, frost frosted me . . ."

Danny whispers even more quietly. "These fucks . . . you can't reason with them. There's nothing you can do."

"They've just brought the car here, the bag is around here somewhere. It's here, you understand?" The fatso looks at me, looks at Danny, swallows, and snorts. He lifts the walkie-talkie to his mouth and says something in his language.

"Hey," I yell. "Hey!" I gesture for him to get closer to the fiber-glass. "How much?" I rub my fingers together rigorously. "How much?" He's quiet. "Hey, listen. I'll leave you the car. I'm giving you the car, man, give me the bag that was inside." The swine-man pulls out a calculator the size of a notebook from the pocket of his sweatshirt, digs his chin into his fat neck and starts calculating. "I'm leaving you the car, hey, hey . . . What are you calculating? I'm leaving you the car!" Fatfuck lifts his head and says:

"You leave the car plus thirty grand."

"What!? You fat Arab swine!"

"I'm Persian."

"Well, go back to your fucking Persia that's not even on the fucking map, you fat fuck. There's no Persia on the map, there is *Iran*, but no Persia! And there's an *ayatollah* ruling Iran, but soon there will be neither an *Ayatollah* nor an *Iran*, nor a *Persia*, because there are even more radical fucks than all of you dirty Arabs, right here in this country."

"I'm not an Arab."

"You are too, dirty Arab! I'm leaving you a Mercedes, a sports model. I paid over thirty grand for it two years ago."

"Those Kompressors lose value quick."

"You're nuts!"

"Yeah, I'm nuts? And you aren't—keeping drugs in a car trunk that opens by itself!"

"Fuck you!" I try to calm down a little.

"I'm calling the police." He grunts.

"Listen," I say. "I don't have any money. I just don't. I have about three, four hundred cash. I'll pay my fine for parking in a tow zone and that's it." At the door, on our side of the office, two Arabs with gaunt faces, blue Adidas jackets, gold chains, and white sneakers show up.

"Hey, get the Mercedes here, 'cause I'm in a hurry." I yell. They are all silent. "C'mon, bring the car. The bag, too . . . I'll share some of it, no problem, we'll make a deal, ok? I'll give you a deal. I'm leaving you a Mercedes, it's a Mercedes, boys."

"Ten grand each."

"Are you nuts?"

"Ten grand each."

"But I don't have thirty grand, people! I'm not a drug dealer!"

"Then you don't need no drugs."

"I don't. Here's 280 dollars, no, here's three hundred, keep the change and the keys, we're leaving, I have work to do . . ." Fatso picks up the walkie-talkie.

"I'm calling the police." It's pouring outside. I look at the amber light of the single street lamp out there, the barb wire. Winter's in the air, I can feel it. Why don't I just give up? Why do I have to agonize in this world that doesn't really need me? Why do I keep entertaining the gods with the twists and turns of my self-inflicted fiasco?

"Hey, wait!" Danny says. "We can find twenty grand. Twenty and not a penny more."

"What are you doing, man?" I pull on his sleeve.

"Twenty cash and that's it." He shakes my hand off. "Who's gonna drive me to my place?" The three Arabs/Persians exchange glances and mumble something. Pig Man nods to one of the blue Adidas boys and he zips up his jacket. A key chain with a BMW emblem and a small soccer ball jingles in his hand. He and Danny leave. I'm left with the other two Arabs. I pull up a chair by the greasy back, sit in it, and curse them with dirty looks for the next hour or so.

•

Danny works as an assistant to one of the most famous names in New York fashion photography, Hito. Hito (Yasuhito Kabayashi) immigrated to America from Japan in early sixties. He was eighteen at the time and worked in the Osaka subway as a train-pusher, shoving in passengers during the morning and evening rush hours and closing the doors of the train car. One day—Hito told Danny—he saw two men getting off the train. They looked different from the people whom he usually pushed and spoke a strange, but beautiful, language. Hito followed them. He kept following them all day long, wherever they went—to restaurants, office buildings, and shops—trying to understand who they were, what they were saying. He was fascinated. From the reception desk of the hotel they were staying in, he learned that they were American businessmen. Ten months later Yasuhito Kabayashi arrived in New York to study at the Institute of Photography. Three years later, he became an assistant to the great Avedon. Later, he started shooting for *Vogue, Harper's Bazaar,* and other fashion magazines. In the seventies, he opened his own studio in Manhattan; in the eighties, he did the ad campaigns for Gucci, Rolex, Dolce & Gabbana, Lincoln, Hugo Boss, and others. On top of this, he did gallery shows. His images are famous for their unbelievable detail, which he achieves with a large format camera on 8x10 negatives, specially ordered from NASA. He's also known for the mathematical accuracy of his work. When he shoots in black and white, he uses extremely low-grain film, which Kodak makes especially for him. When he shoots in color, he does it in saturated, electric, bright colors on Fuji negatives, again special ordered. In Hito's frame, everything is in focus, from the green nail polish of the female model in the foreground, to the delicate scales of the black molinesia in the fish tank somewhere in the background. In his photo sessions, Hito uses tons of light and countless make-up artists, designers, and art directors. Hito's trick is that he manipulates things in a mind-blowing way in his lab, creating his own new, surrealistic world. Hito captures reality with militaristic mercilessness, then plays with its elements and rearranges them the way he likes. Hito has several assistants. One of them is Danny. He helps in the lab, primarily. And he has a key to it.

•

"Thank you, brother!" I say as I unload my things from the car. "Thank you." I want to believe that I would have done the same for him.

"You would have done the same for me," Danny sniffles. "I'm getting a cold or something. You'll pay me back tomorrow when we sell this. Let me carry the bag, you take your shit and let's get the fuck outta here." The Arab-Persians bring two large trash bags. I put my stuff in the first one and the grass in the other. Pig Man is now outside, on the steps under the amber lamp, smoking a cigarette. He looks at us with a peaceful smile, as if seeing some relatives from another city to the door. I take my camera and point it at him. I know that it's too dark for a good picture, but I take it anyway. He places the cigarette in his mouth, laughs through it, grabs his crotch through the fabric of his sweat pants, and shakes it vigorously. I'll bet he hasn't seen his penis in years.

•

The cab pulls up in front of a tall, red brick building. Danny points to a building on the other side of the street.

"Do you remember Bernard Foucault, the French guy I introduced you to several years ago?"

"How could I forget *him*?! The Artist?"

"Yeah. He moved here with his partner a few months ago. They rent the top two floors on that building on the corner."

"Is she . . ." The knot in my stomach, again that damn knot in my stomach. "Is she an artist, too?"

Danny starts laughing. "Are you for real?"

"Why?"

"She? Really?"

"Yeah. Is she . . ."

"*She* is a six-foot-seven dude. A sculptor. With a mustache and a beard this long."

"No. Are you . . . ? So you're saying that . . . Bernard is . . ." I start breathing harder.

"You didn't know?! You couldn't tell? The guy was so . . . Zack, Zack, Zack . . ."

His paintings run through my head now. The first one I saw—those enormous monochromatic canvases with male bodies, reclining male bodies, naked male bodies, naked but deprived of sexuality. Actually, that's what repelled me in his work—the total lack of sensitivity and eroticism. Perhaps in trying to conceal his own homosexuality, the Artist had preferred to deny sexuality all together. Why did he have to hide his queerness, God damn it? His patient smile, with which he welcomed my furious attacks on *high art*, runs through my mind, his kiss goodbye, his wet lips, which I naively took for a French farewell, the card he put in the palm of my hand, and my fingers, which he tenderly closed over his name.

How did I miss all that?

On one of the doorbells, there is a sign reading BUTTERFLY ENTERPRISES—Hito's lab. The name comes from one of his passions, Danny told me. Hito likes to photograph butterflies in the act of mating. In the thirty-five years of his photographic career, he has amassed a rich collection of mating butterflies. Black and white and color photographs, captured during his countless travels all over the world, carefully cataloged and dated with all the necessary technical information.

We drag the large bag to the elevator and go up to the top floor, which belongs to Hito entirely. Danny turns the lights on in one of the rooms in the lab, quickly shows me where he works and what he does, we hide the bag in a storage place that no one uses, and Danny pushes me towards the front door. The next two days nobody will be working here, it's absolutely safe. Now let's go.

"Danny." I say. "I want to stay here."

"What?"

"I want to spend the night here. Please. Leave me here for the night. Show me the chemicals and the paper and give me just one night here. Only one. Please!" I pull out my negatives, turn on one of the light tables, lay them on it, find a magnifier, and bend over them. I have never, ever been in a lab like this. And this is everything I used to dream about. The perfect working conditions. Why did I come to America, why did I move to California?

"Hey!" Danny exclaims. "What's this?"

"Some stuff."

"You didn't tell me you've been taking pictures."

"I forgot."

"When did you take them?"

"Over the last couple of days."

"What are you going to do here?"

"Make a mess."

"Make sure it's not a big one."

"I can't promise."

"Zack?"

"Yes."

"Everything will be OK, brother."

"You think?" Danny leaves the keys, shows me where the chemicals are, and we say good night. I am alone. One of the faucets in this enormous lab is not completely closed and is dripping. I don't know why, but this sound makes me feel indescribably alive. I get to work.

•

Stella hated the hassles of departures and arrivals. She had packed her luggage two days earlier; she was dressed and ready to go. Now we just sipped coffee.

"You have some gray hair," she said suddenly, while trimming the stems of a dozen freesias she had just picked from the garden.

"Thank you," I said half-sarcastically and got up to refill my cup. I wasn't offended, but her remark sounded almost like reproach.

"Don't mention it." She ignored my tone. "I like you this way."

"What way?" I secretly glanced at her.

"This way." She smiled as if there was someone else in the room besides the two of us, with whom she was communicating silently.

"You like me this way, with . . . gray hair?" Opening the refrigerator door to grab the milk, I managed to steal another glimpse of her under my arm.

"The gray has nothing to do with whether I like you or not. We should be over the gray already, shouldn't we?" She arranged the freesias in the small vase with fresh water.

"I'm still not over it." I said. "Do you want more coffee?"

"No, thank you. But could you bring the sugar, please?" I went to the sofa and sat next to her. She put three spoonfuls of sugar in the vase. "They'll last longer this way."

"Can I drive you to the airport?" I knew what the answer would be, but offered anyway.

"I don't want you to."

"It's on my way to work."

"Please," she said firmly.

"I'll miss you," I say after a pause. I knew I shouldn't have said it, but I did.

"You need to be alone. You need to decide what to do with your life." And with that, she ended the conversation, got up, and tapped the tip of my nose with her index finger as if turning something on. She smiled that smile of hers again, wrapped the long, blue, sequined scarf around her neck, and tossed her favorite black bag with the little skulls over her shoulder.

Then the cab arrived. The driver was chewing gum and smelled like aftershave. While he was fitting one of her suitcases in the trunk, one of his shoes came untied. He bent over to tie it and I loaded the second suitcase. It wasn't heavy.

Then we kissed and she slammed the door on the end of her blue scarf. I went to knock on the window, but then stopped as a warm feeling came over me. I smiled, watching the car pull away, with the blue scarf with its tiny sequins waving good-bye, like in a melodrama.

•

—what happened, zack? it was supposed to be short. i'm cold, and hungry
—just stay like this, this is the last shot
—how many times have i heard you say that!
—last one

239

—zack?

—yes

—i have something very important to tell you . . .

—can you wait 'til after this shot?

.

Buzzing, buzzing, buzzing. Ring. Ringing. Doorbell. I lift my head up. I had fallen asleep sitting in a chair, with my head buried between a tray of Dektol developer and a tray of Ilford fixing solution.

Ringing, buzzing, ringing. I get up, stretch my numb body, my head hurts from the chemical fumes, the messed-up doorbell half-buzzes, half-rings. I find the button and push it. I hear the elevator, I open the door. Danny seems pale. Upset.

"Hey, where's the fire?" I try to joke. He doesn't answer. He comes inside. He fusses about, looks very upset, more upset than ever, he can hardly stay in one place.

"We've got go." He stops in front of one of the photos I've left to dry.

"Danny," I say. "I'm starving."

"What have you done?" Danny's eyes start moving from picture to picture, the whole space is now filled with images—from 5-by-7s to gigantic 36-by-50-inch enlargements as big as the posters in a teenager's room—the desolate places, the highways, Melody, empty streets, mailboxes, faces, diners, people, desert, trailers, raindrops on the windshield, skies, woods, barns, buildings, people, faces, people . . . Danny looks at them carefully, touching the drying paper with the back of his hand. "You took all these? With what?"

"Is it that bad?"

"It's as if you were taking photos for the last time!" Danny squints, standing in front of the sheets of paper curled by the dry air.

"As if for the first time or for the last?" The truth is that I got ecstatic last night when I discovered the huge quantities of Lumina—my favorite fiber-based photo paper that's been out of production since the end of the nineties. Obviously, Hito had supplied himself with this high-quality paper, made of nothing but natural ingredients. You can pull the best medium values out of it, the most vibrant nuances of gray. I notice, however, that Danny is very, very upset.

He suddenly grabs me by the wrists and tries to look into my eyes. "I know everything."

That said about medium values, the shades of gray and life, I'm thinking about the iconic images of stars—Marilyn Monroe, Che Guevara, Levsky, Elvis. "You know everything?" The truth about stars is that they don't need medium values. The best way to create a star is to get rid of the medium values, to increase the contrast and to reduce the face to its characteristic eyes, lips, hair, mustache. To dark and light.

"Everything. I know everything." Danny is worrying me, he's digging his nails into my wrists, his knuckles are white.

"Chill, man. Of course you know everything. We all know everything we need to know." Danny tries to say something. I guess he's trying to tell me something important. All of a sudden he bursts into tears like a baby. He lets go of my wrists and embraces me.

"I know everything about . . . Stella. About you and Stella."

"What do you know about Stella?" I say and feel the knot.

"I know. I'm sorry, Zack. I'm sorry, I'm so sorry about Stella." Suddenly, Danny hits me on the chest, and then again and again on the chest. "But why didn't you tell me? Why the hell didn't you tell me?

"What did you need to know?"

"Why didn't you tell me that she's gone?! She's gone? She's . . ."

"Dead?"

"Dead."

"You didn't ask. But now that you mention it—yes, it's true, Stella has been dead to me since . . . uh . . . for almost two weeks."

"She's not dead to you, stupid! She's not dead only to you! Stella is dead, dead, dead, dead, dead! To you, to me, to herself, to everybody. She's dead, gone!" Danny is crying. "Wake up!" Danny is trying to stop crying. "I called friends in California. I called Tony. He told me how it happened." Danny grabs my shoulders. "Stella died in a car accident on her way to the airport! Stella died in an accident, Zack! Stella is dead. She died there, on the freeway. Tony said you went crazy, you turned off your phone, and you wouldn't talk to anybody. Not a single one of your friends could reach you. I found out that you'd disappeared. They told me about the fire, about your house. You need help, brother. You need help . . ." The cell phone in Danny's pocket rings. "You need . . ." He sniffles, rubs his eyes. "Let's go. We have to . . . We'll come back later. We have to go, we have to . . ." His cell keeps ringing. "We have to get the bag, to take it to . . ." Danny is confused, the cell phone is ringing. Danny is more confused than me. His Adam's apple jumps up and down. Danny reaches into his pocket, pulls out a Nokia, takes a deep breath, and wipes his eyes on his sleeve. "Yes. When? But, Boss, it's too . . ." Danny looks at his watch. "What? No, I'm OK. I just got a cold, a flu, that's all. Yes. I got it. We'll be there."

•

Taxi cab.

It's getting dark.

It's Halloween.

I didn't know.

I knew that Halloween was coming but I didn't know that today was Halloween.

Today *is* Halloween.

People in masks all over the streets.

We have to wear masks, too.

I tug on Danny's sleeve.

"We have to wear masks, Danny."

Danny gives me *that* look. The look I couldn't stand in California when Stella . . . after Stella, which was the reason I ran away and came here. Nobody is supposed to look at me like that.

I open the cab door. Not that I want to jump out while it's moving, but I simply can't stay in a car where people look at me with *that look*.

The taxi driver gets mad and kicks us out somewhere around 36th and Lexington. Why?

All around us there are people in costumes—nurses, vampires, witches, bitches, Neanderthals, cowboys, Darth Vaders, Gene Simonses, angels, devils, Grim Reapers, maids, Batmans . . . It's getting cold.

A traffic light with a red figure reads: DON'T WALK.

We walk, then stop.

On the other side, a guy dressed as a huge yellow telephone is handing out fliers.

In a puddle on the asphalt I see the star of Empire Sate Building trembling. I've never been in the Empire State Building. Stella used to call it Vampire State Building. Stella liked playing with names. I want to go into the Empire State Building. I have to go up the Empire State Building before they destroy it, too. I tell Danny that I just saw the Empire State Building in a puddle. He isn't paying attention to what I'm saying.

"I want us to go up in the Empire State Building!"

"No."

"OK then. Hey everybody-y-y-y-y-y-y-y-y-y, this big bag here is full of marijuana-a-a-a-a-a-a-a-a-a!!!" I start yelling. Danny turns to me and gives me a look as if I'm insane.

"Pe-e-e-e-e-e-e-e-ople! Here." I point to the bag over my friend's shoulder. "This is gandja-a-a-a-a-a-a-a-a-a-a-a-a-a."

Danny puts his hand over my mouth. Not that anyone's paying attention to us, but still, he shuts me up.

We get in line at the entrance to the Empire State Building.

•

There had been a fatal accident on the freeway and traffic had stopped. After that, they probably drove too fast to get to the airport on time. At Laurel Avenue and Cass Street, a floral-shop van made a left turn on red. The cab driver hit the brakes, honked his horn, managed to avoid a collision, spun ninety degrees, and came to a stop. Stella's body, with no seat belt on, hit the divider behind the front seat from the momentum. The Yellow Cab had stopped sideways in the middle of the road. Passersby and people witnessing the accident sighed with relief—thank God, nothing had happened. The driver turned to see if Stella was all right. She gave him an OK sign, smiled, and put her seat belt on. She pulled out her cell phone. Then a black semi doing sixty miles an hour and carrying a platform with layers of totaled cars hit the side she was on. The intersection cameras captured the moment when the taxi driver flew out of the car as in a Chagall painting. He got away with two fractured ribs. They managed to pull out Stella's severed body half an hour later, only after cutting the car.

•

Twenty minutes later, we are atop the Empire State Building. Tall, impassable nets have been installed to prevent suicides from doing their job. The wind is very strong, but there are still visitors. Boats are sailing on the Hudson River. The city, from this height, looks like a poster of a city. Suddenly, out of the dark, a black pigeon flutters and lands on the net next to me. I look into its eyes. I can't be sure, but I think the pigeon looks me in the eye as well. A cell phone rings. Danny takes off his gloves and digs out his cell from the depths of his parka. He turns aside and talks, shouting over the wind. I understand that it is getting late. I realize that we are late already. Danny sneaks a peek at me, then turns his back, says something else into the phone, and hangs up. I help him put the bag over his shoulder and we leave. We needed to hurry. We would go to this place, we'd leave the bag, it would be over in a minute, and everything would be OK. I would stay in New York until I pulled myself together.

The numbers in the elevator melt down to one and the doors glide open. We are in the spacious lobby. We get out on Fifth Avenue.

People, people, people, people, masks, masks, masks, masks, costumes, costumes, costumes, Halloween, Halloween, Halloween . . . Blue, green, red, yellow balloons float over Fifth Avenue. In the distance, amidst skyscrapers, a piece of building with the letters 666 on it pierces the light-polluted sky above Manhattan. In front of Rockefeller center, a fat vendor woman with green glasses is selling something. She has a live iguana on her head, actually there are two live iguanas balanced on her head, fucking. A toy store with horribly bright colors and countless Mickey Mouses, Bambies, Donald Ducks, Simbas, Tarzans, Sleeping Beauties, dwarfs, King Kongs, Pocahontases, penguins . . . GOTHAM.

The end is near, my friends, the end is near.

Danny is holding my hand and we are threading our way through crowds of people in masks, masks, masks on this last Halloween night, which doesn't matter to me in the slightest, which doesn't matter to me at all. Broadway—*Cats, Rent, Chicago, Mamma Mia, Les Miserables, Mary Poppins*—musicals, musicals, musicals . . .

The wail of ambulances; the rising underground steam; a Buddhist masseuse; a horrifying mime, painted in white; a guitarist wearing a bandana; a clown; a man-statue; a saxophone player; the lights of Manhattan in and out of focus.

We turn onto a side street. I stumble over the cardboard boxes of a homeless man, he curses, lights a flashlight, stares at me viciously, and spits at me. I understand, I'd spit if I were him, too.

We go down a few steps. We ring a doorbell. A six-foot-something black man, dressed as a Russian butler in a Gogol play, opens the door. We go down a narrow red corridor which turns into a narrower, dark-red corridor. We climb a few steps and enter something like a bar with normal-looking people who are drinking. No one is wearing costumes, of course. Costumes are for the idiots outside. This here is a hideout from the street masquerade.

We sit down. The black butler turns to leave, but I pull him by the sleeve. I want to drink. The man gives me a look. Then, with a hand like pliers, he frees his jacket from my grip and pushes me back into my seat. Through a smile, he hisses that someone will take our order while he is relieving us of our baggage. I hold tight to the bag. I don't let it go. I've dragged it across the whole fucking continent; I can't just give it to some black Russian butler, I just can't. Not without a fight. The black man grins at my friend. Danny shakes his head apologetically and whispers in my ear not to worry. This man will take the stash to the *Boss*. I clutch the bag even more tightly. I press my cheek to it—we have a past together, you big old bag. We have a history, you and I.

Danny rests his arm on my shoulder—I don't have to make a fool of myself. I sniffle, force a smile, and leave the bag in the black hands of the butler.

A waitress comes—a beautiful girl with short, platinum blond hair, bright red lips, perky breasts, and slender thighs—what would we like while we wait?

Danny wants a cappuccino.

I want a martini. A dirty martini with three olives. I actually want two dirty martinis.

The girl smiles and leaves. I want to embrace her and sleep with her. I want to kiss her, kiss her, and caress her, and fill her up with myself. I want to sink and dissolve in this beautiful girl with her short platinum hair, expressive red lips, perky breasts, and slender thighs. This girl who will kiss me, will kiss me, will kiss me with tobacco kisses and will fall asleep on my chest, listening to my mad, barbarian heart.

I look around and lean back. In the booth behind me, a gentleman in a short, striped blazer with short hennaed hair and a small earring leans across the table toward a young girl, smiles, lifts a bottle of champagne from an ice bucket, tops off her flute, and then refills his own. I hear him start in, "Love is . . ." and jerk away as if stung. I feel sick to my stomach and cover my ears so I don't hear what follows. Any sentence that begins with "Love is" does not deserve to be heard out.

The two martinis arrive. I finish the first while the girl is transporting the second from the tray to the table. I drink the second one before the cappuccino reaches Danny. I smile broadly and charmingly. I can smile very charmingly when I want to. The girl answers with a smile. I love smiling strangers and waitresses. I love stranger-waitresses, pretty stranger-waitresses. Love is a stranger-waitress. Two more martinis have been ordered and things are already looking up. Danny tries to tell me something. I stop him with a finger. No one can tell me things now. I, I, I want to tell things to Danny. To people, to mankind. I hear the soundtrack of an un-started film in my head. It's beautiful in my head. The stranger-waitress with the perky breasts and slender thighs is beautiful, too. I drink two more martinis before going to the bathroom.

The tiles are white and beautiful. I like white tiles, no matter what they say. I love white porcelain tiles—they've suffered so much abuse from mankind. White porcelain should be placed on a pedestal, a pedestal made of gold. Gold? Forget gold, my dear mankind. What has gold endured?! What has gold endured besides a few eccentricities of kings, tsars, and khans—a tray for the head of John the Baptist, the skull of Nikephoros Logothetes,[1] and so on. But now porcelain . . . porcelain takes the everyday abuse of millions—pissing, shitting, puking, ejaculating . . . I need to pee so badly, yet I can't start. I feel stiff, as if someone has kicked me in the ass. My neck is limp. I look up at the ceiling trying to think about something other than porcelain, I'm sick of it already. What can I think about besides Stella?

All of a sudden in the stainless steel flush handle in front of me, two mutants appear in black blazers, black shades, and heads that distort depending which direction I move. I start shaking it even before I manage to pee. I watch them exchange glances.

I zip up my pants, turn around, pass between them, heading out—and almost make it.

"Tsk, tsk, tsk, who didn't wash their hands?" I hear one of them say, while reaching for the door handle.

"I didn't touch anything dirty."

"We all have to wash our hands after using the bathroom."

"Oh, OK. I gotta write that down."

"Come back here and wash your hands!"

I look around demonstratively. Where's the hidden camera, you faggots? I decide to fight to the death—the key word here is *death*—with two dumbfucks in shades who think they can give me private lessons in hygiene.

"Before you do anything stupid, you better wash up, because you'll have to shake hands with the Boss and he's kind of squeamish."

•

---

1 Byzantine emperor from 802–811, killed in battle by the Bulgarian Khan Krum, who supposedly made a drinking cup of his skull.

The mutants and I pass through the bar. Danny gestures that he'll wait for me here. They usher me through a corridor toward an elevator located in a cold storage space. We get into the elevator. One of them pushes the top button and we rise up high into the New York night. The doors slide open and we find ourselves in a loft with at least a 260 degree view of Manhattan, literally a multimillion-dollar view. A view of everything that deserves to be viewed. The loft is minimalistically furnished and warmly lit. The fireplace is burning. Among the many pieces of art, I see some which I would love to own if I could afford them. Then the mutants step back. I am alone and so vulnerable now. I have the feeling that the building is swaying and am not sure if it's from the strong winds outside or the martinis in my head.

"It's the wind." I hear a low, soft voice and then I see where it's coming from. The Boss is sitting in a small, dark-brown leather love-seat with his back to me. He is looking outside. I see his reflection in the window—a normal, middle-aged man with gray hair, a glass in his hand. In front of him, on the table, is a crystal, unlabeled bottle. A decanter, rather, full of—guessing by the color—scotch, single malt. "Single malt?" I nod.

The Boss smiles and suddenly his reflection turns its back in me. He pours some scotch into the empty glass.

"Do you want ice?"

"No, thank you."

"Macallan, special order, aged twenty-four years in cherry barrels. Who in their right mind would dilute it with ice made of tap water filtered in New Jersey?" The Boss raises his glass in a toast. I take a sip. If I have to compare the liquid to something, it is ambrosia. Not that I have ever had ambrosia, I just think it should taste like this.

"You'll be richer in a few minutes." he says.

"It's about time," I say.

"My associates are testing the quality of the stuff at the moment." I don't know what to say, that's why I drink whatever is in my glass at once. The Boss pours me some more. I drink it up, too, and blurt out: "Happy Halloween!"

The Boss smiles slightly and stares out into the darkness. The door opens and, who knows why, a wheelchair rolls in with a bandaged soldier, or perhaps someone dressed up as the Invisible Man.

"Nice costume!" I exclaim. "Very impressive." The person in the wheelchair looks at me for a long moment without moving. "Very authentic, very. Bravo." The Invisible Man doesn't shift his eyes from me, but doesn't say a word, either. Then he looks at Victor Boss and nods. I shrug and turn toward the Hudson River, where at least I see ships sailing.

"I heard about your misfortune," Boss says. I'm quiet. I don't know which misfortune exactly he's talking about. "I want to tell you so many things, but I'm not sure whether they'd be enough." Most likely not, I think to myself. The Boss lifts his glass, whirls it gently, squints with one eye, and looks through the liquid as if aiming at something out there in the dark. "Once upon a time I also had a girl like yours. We were young, innocent, the world was different, I loved her, she kissed me. We were happy. I was so . . . sure about everything then. I had a job like everybody else, I paid my taxes and we made ends meet somehow. We went to the movies, ate apples, woke up in each other's arms, laughed under the sheets—and for a very long time it seemed like this was enough for both of us. The words 'success' and 'failure' were like . . . words from a foreign dictionary—I didn't care about them. And so, I crawled through life doing twenty-five miles per hour. I watched the speed limits, I was careful crossing the street, I picked up the mail, I came home with groceries. And without realizing how and why, I started getting smaller. I was getting small, smaller, very small, very, very small. Big love makes men small." The Boss gets up, glass in hand, and goes over to the window. Only now do I notice that it's quiet in the apartment, very quiet. "Then one day something happened. The world turned upside down. I don't know why, but it happened." The Boss snaps his fingers. "Like that. One day . . . one November day, like today, I came home and found the house empty. They saw my girl at the subway station—we lived in Brooklyn then—with a winter coat and a suitcase. She left me for someone, I later learned, who knew both the taste of success," the Boss takes a sip from his glass, "and the smell of failure." He rubs his eyes with his thumb and index finger. "I cried then. I cried, and cried, and cried, and cried a lot. I lost weight from crying. My clothes hung from my body, I drilled holes in my belt, I was weak. I had no strength to climb the steps to my apartment, I had turned to *nothing*. She had not simply gone; she had been . . . amputated from me." He finishes what is left in his glass. "And that is how I learned what failure is, Zack." After a short pause in which the loft seems to sway even more in the wind, the Boss continues. "Time went by. A long time went by. One evening, it finally dawned on me that she would never come back, so I started throwing away the things that reminded me of her—clothes, pictures, books, records, everything. And I came across a vase that she had bought at a flea market. She kept flowers in it. A pretty, brown vase, made of clay." With a gesture, he traces the silhouette of a vase resembling a female figure. "I held that vase in my hands and didn't have the heart to throw it away. I started caressing it, kissing it, whispering to it, and I started crying again. What should I do with it now? And then . . ." The Boss turns his back to me and steps closer to the window, his words steaming up the window glass. "I filled the vase with warm water. I pulled my cock out, stuck it into the narrow throat of the vase and started . . ." The Boss swallows hard, "to . . . make love to it. I fucked that vase, fucked its warm throat and cried. Fucked it and cried, fucked it until I came. I liked it. I felt like a pervert, of course, but I liked it. I did it again the next day, and then the next, and the day after, and after that. I fucked that vase until one day it broke. I can say that I broke that vase . . . from loving it." He turns toward me again. "But I didn't need it any more. I knew I could replace it with a new one. Clay and warm liquid—that's all." The Boss gazes at his shoes for a moment before continuing. "And something changed in me then. My eyesight seemed to get sharper, I started hearing better, the air around me filled with scents. I stopped being afraid of the dark, the cold, diseases, emotions, enemies, and failures. I was not afraid of anything. My strength started coming back, little by little." The Boss closes his eyes for a moment and part of him seems to leave the room. "And one day I saw myself as I wanted to be. And I turned into what I am now. And you know what? It was far easier than I expected." The Boss goes to a shelf, opens a small glass humidor, and picks out a medium-sized cigar. "But I learned something in those years. When we fail, we—men—always find a way to cope with it. We manage. Nature has seen to this. It has programmed us to survive our biggest failures. We have been nurtured with the milk of failure, it's in our DNA." He gestures toward the humidor. "Here, pick one. But, think now, Zack, think about how we men cope with *success*. How we manage the idea of *success*." I accept the invitation and choose a seven-and-a-half-inch-long Cohiba. He cuts it, hands it back to me and pulls out a lighter. "Success," the Boss massages the cigar between his fingers before lighting it, "comes, they say, with lots of hard work, perseverance, education, experience, skills . . . blah-blah-blah-blah-blah-blah-blah. That's what they say. So you tell yourself—oh, *success-shmucksess*. Fuck *that*." The end of his cigar comes to life with the flame. "Why bother? Fuck it. You might succeed and you might not, and most likely you won't. Do you know anyone who's succeeded in anything meaningful? Anything you find remotely meaningful?" I shrug. I light up, draw in the smoke. My mouth goes numb with the unexpectedly strong taste. It's my first time smoking a cigar. "That's what I thought." The Boss keeps the flame burning at the tip of his lighter. "And you tell yourself, I'd better quit fantasizing. I'd better get busy training for the inevitable fiasco." The flame disappears. "No one prepares us to expect success or tells us how to welcome it, how to deal with it. So if it actually comes, often, despite ourselves, it catches us off-guard. We don't know what it is. We have been primed to deal with failure. That's why we do the same things we do if we fail—we drink as if there's no tomorrow, we eat until our stomachs burst, we smoke cigars, fuck like animals, we go nuts!" The Boss refills his glass with scotch, mine, too. "The truth is," he takes a sip and glances down, toward the busy streets of the city, "we choose our own failures." I take another drag. This time, part of the smoke finds its way to my lungs. "Because we know, deep down we always know that we can cope with them." I start coughing. The Boss watches me motionlessly, patiently waiting for my cough attack to pass, then draws away from the window, coming closer to me. He waves away the smoke from his cigar and stares into my pupils. I bet he can't see anything there. I don't know where his monologue is going, but it starts wearing me down. "The grass you brought in today is moldy." I stop coughing, but my ears are ringing like after a slap in the face. "It hasn't been stored properly, it got wet, it's got mold everywhere, maybe from the lemon peels, I have no clue whose idea that was. It's a mess." From the coughing, my eyes start filling with tears and everything begins spinning. "The cannabis is fucked. It's good for pretty much nothing." I quickly wipe the moisture from under my eyelids with a sleeve. Suddenly my attention is distracted by a dozen female buttocks in different shapes and sizes, tastefully lit with small spot lights. They are made of bronze and arranged on a special shelf by the dark bookcase.

"Very nice." My voice rasps. The Boss lifts an eyebrow.

"Excuse me!?"

I point at the installation of beautiful female asses. "*Kalepa ta kala.*"

"Pardon?"

"Simple is beautiful. An ancient Greek saying. Or . . . beautiful is simple. I don't remember how it goes."

"Oh, that?" the Boss grins. "Those are casts of some of the women whom . . ." he shrugs, "whom I've had the privilege of knowing . . . up close."

"I see." Now, I feel embarrassed to keep looking in that direction, which takes me back to the marijuana problem, to the problem with Danny's money, to the problem with Stella, the problem with the burned-down house, with the forever-gone past, the problem with me, the problem with all these problems. A door opens, somebody brings the bag.

The Boss opens it, goes over to the fireplace, pulls out a fistful of marijuana, rubs it between his fingers, squints, and smells it. Then he throws it into the fire.

"Like I said, it's no good." He takes another fistful, and another, and another—they all end up in the flames. I have no idea how this night will continue, but I want it to end right here and now. I wonder if there's a way for these windows to open. I look up at the night sky where the *deus ex machina* will not be arriving from. Where are the *planes* now, when I need them? "Cannabis, cannabis," the Boss keeps throwing fistful after fistful in the fire. "why does mankind have problems with you of all things?" This is a trick; a desperate thought crosses my mind suddenly. It's a dumb trick. A set up. They must have switched the bags. It's impossible that I damaged the stuff—it's not like Jack London's one thousand dozen eggs. The smell of burning marijuana fills the loft. At this moment I turn my attention to the Invisible Man, or rather the Mummy Man in the wheelchair.

"Hey," I say. "How you doing there, Mummy Man?" I grin. Sometimes I laugh at my own stupid jokes. No one else in the loft reacts to my joke, though. "For the first time," I go on. "I'm seeing a mummy in a wheelchair. Clever."

"This is Billy," says the Boss. "I wanted to properly introduce you, but I got carried away. Anyhow. You've actually seen each other before."

"No way, we've seen each other before!" I continue grinning even more stupidly, *george-bush* stupidly. "Isn't that the Invisible Man?" I'm funny when I want to be funny. Damn it, I'm hilarious.

"Billy is my son. He saw you in Mexico."

"In Mexico?" My mouth goes dry.

"Tijuana. When you showed up, two Mexicans were kicking him." The Boss takes a remote, points it, and a few screens light up on one of the bookshelves. Danny, shaking the table with his nervous knee, can be seen, looking around. Then the Boss rewinds the tape to a moment in which I down a martini and grin at the waitress. I'm unshaven, I've got a black eye, a small-town policeman hairdo, and my nose is big and crooked. "About a month ago, I sent Billy and one of my associates to take care of some business down in Tijuana. The Mexicans, however, had a different plan—they decided to kidnap them and hold them for ransom. We're talking about money, of course, a big chunk of money. One night, my boys managed to take care of the guards and snuck out with one of the vans, in which there was a bag of grass. The Mexicans, though, caught up with them before they reached the border. They shot my other guy dead. They crushed Billy's legs and arms and beat him senseless. And then you showed up." The Boss refills our glasses. "Billy's alive now." He shakes ashes from his cigar. "I flew to the West Coast, of course, and took care of things. While I was at the hospital with Billy, I asked around. One of my partners in Santa Monica, Chris, mentioned that someone . . ." the Boss emphasizes the next few words with his intense eyes, "someone with a black eye and a thick accent was inquiring about selling a large bag of marijuana without getting caught." Pause. "Then Danny asked me if I wanted to buy a bag of Mexican grass, and I put two and two together and said, yes, of course." He gently kicks the bag. "I don't actually need this. But come to think of it, it's mine, in any case." The Boss places his cigar in the ashtray, opens a small safe, takes out one, two, three, four, five stacks of money and extends his hand. I don't reach out, he holds them for a while, then shrugs and piles them up next to the scotch decanter. "I wanted to see you, Zack. I just wanted to see your face and what were you made of. Here's fifty thousand." He takes a pen out and writes something on a yellow piece of paper. "Here's the phone number of one of my associates. Call if you need anything. Anything." I slowly walk to the coffee table, touch the money, pile the stacks on top of each other, pour some more whiskey into my glass, and drink up. I walk to Billy's wheelchair, put my arm on his shoulder, look for his eyes through the bandages, and nod. I think he nods, too. Then I squat down and touch my forehead to his bandaged head. I close my eyes and, for a moment, we stay like this. I hear the cold wind outside, the crackling of the fire in the fireplace, and the labored breathing of the man next to me. I open my eyes, get up, go back to the table, put the stacks one by one in the pockets of my jacket, and finish up whatever is left in my glass. The city lights outside sway back and forth.

The Boss comes closer and extends his hand. I understand that our meeting has come to an end. I shake his hand. Hardly able to keep my balance, touching the edges of the furniture I pass by, I head toward the elevator. I reach for the door.

"Zack." I stop. "To the left, Zack." I hear the Boss' low voice. "The elevator is to the left. That's my bedroom. You have no business in there."

•

Danny is staring at a squeezed out bag of green tea at the bottom of his empty cup. I pat him on the shoulder from behind, he's startled, and gets up.

"What happened?" I take two stacks of money and hand it to him. He tucks them under his belt, grabs my elbow, starts pushing me toward the exit.

"Wait!" I yell. "Stop!" I look around for the waitress with the platinum hair. "Wait!" A few heads turn. I scan the place until I see her. Then I lose her again. Danny is holding me up. I find her again. I feel like my legs are challenged by the weight of my body, my physical body, I mean. The girl appears again. I smile and try to say *good night*. That's all I wanted to say in the first place. I want to say good night to someone, what's the big deal? I stutter a few words and drop to my knees. The black butler grabs me under the arms and drags me by some red walls and more red walls and hauls me up some stairs.

Before they shove me into the cab, I start to sing. I sit behind the driver. On the fiberglass divider between us is an ID card with a mustachioed photo and a name. I try pronouncing the name but stumble on some Ukrainian clump of consonants, then vomit endlessly and painfully before I pass out.

•

—what difference does it make which direction we live our lives,
zack?
—you build your theories and talk about *backwards time* as if
there is *a straightforward* one
—we live in *some kind* of time, don't we?
—where is time in your photographs? what time are the negatives
of the film you just finished in? and aren't you the one who will
arrange them the way you want to? you're done shooting, right. i
need to get dressed—could you pass me that T-shirt? thanks

—in real life . . .

—and in *real* life you try to exchange one kind of linearity with another. you propose that we look at life from the end to the beginning instead of the other way around, from right to left instead of the way we are used to, you switch *after* and *before* around, you look for a direction in an infinite 18% gray. when actually the one and only sure thing is the *now*, which is the beginning and the end, the before and after, *18% gray* and 100% *now*, and nothing else

•

I lie down on the hard mattress for a long time and stare at the ceiling until the room comes into focus. I'm in Danny's apartment in Brooklyn. Fucking Brooklyn, I don't want to be in no fucking Brooklyn right now. I jump up, the room gets fuzzy, I lean on the table, stars sting my eyes, my head is going to explode. I go into the kitchen, look for coffee, find coffee in the cabinet over the sink, and turn on the coffee machine. I open the window and inhale the cold November air. I slam the window shut again. I find a cup, pour myself coffee. It smells promising. I return to the room where I woke up.

I bend over to fix the bed up a little, but the effort sends a new surge of pain to my brain. I have to be still. I lean on the wall in front of the bookcase filled with digital video tapes with one hand and hold the cup of steaming coffee in my other hand:

. . . *first recordings 1999, may, manhattan, june 16, project 1999, june 1999, brighton beach, atlantic city, december 2000, las vegas, july 2000, the strip, los angeles december 2000, manhattan new year's eve 2000, Y2K celebration, full moon 2001, october, sozopol, winter 2001, snow over dunes, swans, the black sea, varna, winter 2001, 2001 chelsea, galleries, jazz van der holden . . .*

life in Sony video digital zoom lens, diameter 37 mm,
life in *Precision CCD* chip, recorded on *FUJI* super 8 film
life digitally translated into 0 and 1, 0 and 1, 0 and 1, 0 and 1,
0 and 1, 0 and 1 . . .

. . . *dave matthews band concert in central park, alex's party, birthday party 2002, jeffrey's play, opening night, grandma in the garden, summer 2002, gypsies, caravan in the woods, 2002, interviews, bulgaria 2002, silvia's paintings, pouring rain, new jersey, amsterdam, den haag, amsterdam, my sister in disney land, eva in coronado, zack and stella, new york, penn station, departure* . . .

My heart starts pounding. I finish the coffee and go looking for something to kill this headache—aspirin, Advil, Tylenol, anything will do. Where's Danny now when I need help, really need help. I can't find any pills. I find half a gallon of milk in the fridge and drink, drink, drink . . . I go back to the tapes, pull out *zack and stella, new york, Penn Station, departure* . . .

I remember that day. What I had forgotten was that Danny was taping.

I find cables, plug the camera into the TV, and play the tape.

I sit on the floor, hug my knees, and try to calm my breathing.

FADE IN:

Close up on an old record player thrown onto the side walk. The camera pulls back, points to a ONE WAY sign and the dome of a church. We are somewhere in Greenwich Village. Then I see myself and Stella. Her hair is long and light brown. She is wearing a brown suede blazer with a belt hanging at the back, light-blue jeans and high-heeled black shoes with hippie soles. Over her shoulder is her black leather bag with the little white skulls. The wall we walk by is covered in graffiti and the camera turns to see it.

In a moment, we see Stella and Danny, which means I have taken the camera now. A flock of pigeons fly in the blue sky, the camera follows them, then pans down to a chocolate-brown Manhattan, passes through the naked tree crowns with fluttering plastic bags on the branches, goes back to the street, and finds Stella again, who is walking away.

"Stella-a-a!" My voice booms near the camera microphone. We pass the fence of a school yard, the voices of kids playing basketball fill the air. Stella doesn't turn back, she keeps walking.

"Stella-a-a-a!" I hear my voice again, the camera stops, she keeps walking. From the entrance of a building she passes a little girl steps out, carrying a rag doll in her hand. A little girl with thick brown hair and big beautiful eyes, who from this distance could pass for her daughter, for our daughter.

Stella smiles, stops, and turns around, looking at the little girl. The camera zooms in on the girl, who furrows her brow and moves her lips, perhaps scolding the doll, then the camera jumps and cuts to Stella's face, which . . .

Suddenly, something knocks the camera aside, Stella disappears, trees and buildings turn a cartwheel, the blue sky revolves, and Manhattan stands on its head. Before the unblinking eye of the camera, lying on the sidewalk, the wind blows a few pieces of paper.

"Oops, sorry." A child's voice comes from somewhere, and then the camera is up off the sidewalk. I see myself and a ten-year-old boy walking away with a basketball in his hand. I see Stella laughing and waving her hand.

FADE OUT.

Wide angle on Manhattan late afternoon, almost evening. Central Park—the lake, lilies, reflected clouds.

Medium shot of Stella and me, holding hands, walking away from the camera.

Close up on Stella, who throws her hair back.

Close up on a crane in the lake, a beautiful crane, emanating calmness.

CUT TO:

Street merchants have come out on the sidewalks with the falling of evening, Police sirens are heard more often. The neon nightlights take over Manhattan. Stella walks down Fifth Avenue, which looks exactly the way it should, since Stella is walking down it.

Suddenly, I hear a key in the key hole, the apartment door opens, and Danny walks in. I say good morning, take a sip of coffee without diverting my eyes from Stella, who walks down the busy sidewalk of the most beautiful city in the world.

"Zack, we need to talk," Danny says.

The camera is now on one side of the street and Stella and I are at the other. We pass a black guy in Adidas sweat pants and a white hoodie, selling bootlegged CDs on the sidewalk. I stop to take a look at his collection, Stella keeps walking. Danny's camera follows her. Vehicles, yellow cabs, bums, bicycle riders pass between the camera and Stella.

"Zack . . . did you hear me? I have something to tell you."

The camera zooms in on a saxophone player with a gray beard and yellow hat, who is playing a slow and breathy jazz tune. The sax case is wide open with some dollar bills and change in it.

"Hito called this morning."

Stella tosses the leather bag with the skulls over her other shoulder, striding forward alone, while I slow down to put a dollar in the sax case.

"Hito went to the lab and found your photographs, all of your photographs."

The camera follows me as I make my way through the crowd to catch up with Stella.

"So check this out. Hito was like"—Danny mimics a Japanese accent—"'Who took this pictures? They look like ol' pictures. I use to take this kind of picture back when I was young. I like the shadows and people, see?'" Danny laughs. "He wants to use a whole series of your images for a new ad campaign for Benzin, New York!"

Close up of my face in profile.

"Zack, I can't imagine what you are feeling at this moment, but . . . goddamn it, turn off that video. I want you to listen to me."

Wide shot—Madison Square Garden—evening.

"You have a chance! A real chance! The ad campaign is . . . You know what I'm talking about, man. Benzin, New York . . . Your stuff will be in magazines, on fucking billboards, you'll be all over. If Hito liked your work . . . and he loved it . . . Everything fits, dude. Your photos are unbelievably strong and true. What you captured on that trip, man—faces, roads, buildings, nature—everything is raw and real. You've captured America as if you were seeing it for the first time, as if you didn't know how to take photographs. You've captured her the way she no longer is—real. And at the same time, everything is . . . somehow calculated, everything fits. You have . . . I'm struggling to find the word . . . synchronicity, yes. You've achieved synchronicity. Believe me, you've succeeded. You have!"

Penn Station. Stella goes down the stairs. I catch up with her, pull on her bag like a thief, she is startled, lifts her hand instinctively, sees me, relaxes, kisses me on the ear, takes my hand, places it over her shoulder, cuddles me, and we continue walking through the crowd, embracing and walking down more stairs. The camera loses us for a while, then finds us again. It zooms in on us, drops us, then we are in focus again.

"Hito wants to meet with you this afternoon. We have to go to the lab. I think I know what he is going to offer you, Zack. Pull yourself together. You have to pull yourself together, man. This is important. You start in New York. You start up so high. You start your life over. You'll work with Benzin, you bastard. This is a one-in-a-million chance. Life goes on, Zack."

The camera runs through ads and posters on the walls of the station. It's nice that they have classical music playing as a background, a violin and orchestra. Classical music should play in every train station and every airport, damn it. Every departure needs a soundtrack.

There's a poster advertising an Italian movie entitled *Life Is Beautiful*.

Our train arrives. Stella gets in first.

"Zack, do you hear me!?" Danny blocks my view. *"Do you hear me?"*

It's hard to ignore his presence now. And I should not ignore Danny. Danny is a friend. I get up, pain pulsates in my head, life is beautiful. I press the left arrow on the remote and rewind a little. There it is—*Life Is Beautiful*. I push pause. The frame *Life Is Beautiful* freezes on the screen in one trembling digital pause.

"I can hear you, Danny, my friend! Hito, Benzin, photography, advertisement, success, dreams, success. Life is beautiful, Danny."

"Excuse me?" Danny doesn't understand what's going on. Danny doesn't understand that life is beautiful.

"Where is my money, Danny? Bring the money. And do you have something for a headache?" Danny goes to the kitchen. I hear cabinet doors slamming and water running; Danny comes back with my three stacks of bills, two pills in one hand, and a glass of water in the other. I chew the bitter aspirins, caress my money, push pause again, and the film starts.

I get on the train after Stella. On the upper step, before I go in, I turn around and gesture to the camera to come closer. The camera jumps to Stella, who waves goodbye, then returns to me. I impatiently gesture to Danny, who is holding the camera, to come closer. He does.

Do I need help?

"Nichts," I say and shove the three stacks in his hands.

He panics and pushes them back at me. Am I out of my mind?

Nichts! No. I don't touch the money.

Danny tries to hand it back.

I don't care.

He refuses to take the money.

I laugh.

He thrusts the stacks back in my lap.

I tell him that if he doesn't take it, I'll throw it on the rails.

What rails?

The rails.

The rails?!

The rails, Danny. The rails.

Danny throws his arms in the air and almost starts crying. Zack, there are no rails in here.

It's falling, Danny, it's falling, the money's falling, I'm dropping it, it's falling onto the rails.

Danny shakes his head, he doesn't understand.

I reach out and am about to drop the money between the train and the rails. It's falling, Danny.

He takes a deep breath, reaches out, and takes the money. But I can't accept it, he says.

You will.

Zack, this is a hell of a lot of money!

Take it, go to school, and make art for the rest of your life. Life is beautiful, Danny.

I push my friend aside. I have to go. There, I'm already on the train. Thank God it's almost empty. I hear a whistle. We take off. I look around for Stella, I see her sitting by the window. I pull a bottle of water from my backpack, sit next to her, and embrace her winter-phobic shoulders. She smiles, drinks, and rests her head on my chest.

We watch the world outside through our reflections.

THE END

Acknowledgements from the Author

My sincerest thanks to:

- my wonderful translator Angela Rodel, with whom I share the love of music, words and–amazingly–a birthday. Is it because we are astro-related, or is it just that you can read my thoughts in both languages?

- my weekly coffee-and-almond-croissant literary "circle"–Arthur Salm and Jennifer de Poyen, talented writers, the sharpest editors, and above all, my best friends. I owe you both so much.

- Elizabeth Kostova, a great writer and a gentle cultural diplomat with her own literary embassy, the Elizabeth Kostova Foundation, as well as the wonderful people running it.

- Svetlyo Zhelev, my awesome Bulgarian publisher and friend; also everybody from Ciela Publishing–*Nazdrave!*

- Maya Sloan–the talented, gifted, and funny as hell "Burn Sister" of mine.

- Mariana Juliette–a powerful generator of genuine positivity, a true friend without borders–please accept my deepest gratitude.

- my many thousands of Bulgarian fans–*Blagodaria!*

- my film producers–Boris, Viktor, and Georgi–you saw the movie between the lines.

- Chad W. Post and Nathan Furl for saving the day one particular Wednesday afternoon, just before Happy Hour.

- Open Letter Books for giving me this opportunity.

- Kaija Straumanis.

- my Bulgarian editor and dearest friend, Pepa Georgieva–I don't know if I would have ever written this book if it hadn't been for you. Your merciless editing helped me tremendously.

- thank you, Sara, for being a kind, extremely intelligent and funny kid, AND for being my beautiful daughter. I love you "from the depths of the sea, to the heights of the sky," remember?

And finally, thank you, Silvia–for everything. Always.

p.s.

I grew up in a country whose language is spoken by fewer than nine million people. Most of the literature that shaped me as a reader and an individual, and later as a writer, was in translation, mostly English works in Bulgarian.

This translation of *18% Gray* from Bulgarian to English is, in a way, my chance to give back what's been borrowed, a raindrop returning to the ocean it came from.

Zachary Karabashliev is a Bulgarian-born novelist and playwright, now living and writing in the U.S. His debut novel—*18% Gray*—is a bestselling title, winner of the VIK prize Novel of the Year, and one of the 100 most-loved books of all time by Bulgarians in the BBC campaign "The Big Read." He is also the author of the short story collections *A Brief History of the Airplane* and *Symmetry*, as well as the awarded stage plays *Recoil* and *Sunday Evening*. He also wrote the screenplay for the film adaptation of *18% Gray*.

Angela Rodel is the translator of *The Apocalypse Comes at 6 P.M.* by Georgi Gospodinov, *Party Headquarters* by Gerogi Tenev, and *Thrown into Nature* by Milen Ruskov. She was awarded a 2010 PEN Translation Fund Grant for her translation of several stories from Tenev's *Holy Light*.